PEOPLE OF DUST

A FIRST CONTACT SCI-FI THRILLER

MARCUS MARTIN

HYPERSONIC PRESS.

First print edition 2021

Book design by Marcus Martin

ISBN 978-1-913966-09-6 (hardback)

ISBN 978-1-913966-11-9 (paperback)

ISBN 978-1-913966-10-2 (ebook)

www.marcusmartinauthor.com

1

———

TESSA

I'm in. The decoder took all of four seconds to crack her password. See, this is what you get if you use prime-factor encryption in the quantum age. You're *begging* people to mug you. If anything, I'm doing this lady a favor - woman to woman. This should be a wake-up call for the whole bloody corporation.

It's not what it looks like, by the way, I ain't here to steal. Not like that. My partner's missing, along with her crew. Their ship returned four days ago after a routine mission to the asteroid belt. Ship? Check. Crew? Not so much. You see my problem?

True to form, the Lunar Mining Corporation has been stonewalling me, so I'm getting answers for myself. Starting with boss lady and her crappy passwords. I'd have expected better from the CEO of Lunar Three. Dr. Nenge is a *total* bitch, by the way. A hot bitch, sure, and in another life I'd tap that sweet arse for honey, but that's neither here nor there. Right now she's hiding the truth about my partner, I'm gonna find it, and find her.

I know you're thinking Sienna's done a runner on me,

but she ain't the promiscuous sort. I'm sure she's broken plenty of hearts over the years, but at least she's the kinda girl who'd tell you straight: it's over. No messin' around, just honesty. It's what I love about her. She's one of them people who, being around them is like going on holiday from your own head. The best kind of people.

Dr. Nenge's system is still booting. Ticktock, computer, I ain't got all day. The longer I'm here, the more likely my arse gets sent back to jail.

I'm looking around, taking in the office. Do all CEOs keep this many photos of themselves? In fairness, if I had curves like her, I'd wouldn't just have photos, I'd have a *wallpaper* made of me. She's got this sexy powerful stare going on in each one. My favorites are definitely the ones with Bantu knots. A hairstyle I could only dream of pulling off. I've never been a glamorous woman like that. I'm in shape, sure, but I can't chose clothes for shit. This Dr. Nenge lady might be a bitch, but she's got style, I'll give her that.

This whole room is crazy plush. Sienna always says Lunar Three is just dust and machinery, but clearly she's never seen how the elites live. Boss lady's got a whole penthouse vibe going on here. Remind me to become C-Suite sometime, looks like a sweet gig. It's almost a shame the lady won't get to enjoy it much more. Chill, I ain't bumping her off, that's not my style. Not anymore, anyway. Today, I'm just a humble Lunar Five mechanic stealing what they won't give me.

Hang about, what's this? Ugh, triple factor authentication. Tits. Now I gotta log in through a secondary device *and* provide a genetic sample. Right, cloning the secondary device won't be hard because it's non-quantum.

We really should have a term for that kind of tech – oh yeah, we do: *bloody useless.*

As for the genetic sample, hmm, let's see. This is her office, so odds are Nenge's left a spot of DNA lying about. Careless, I know. Here we go – hairs on the seat. I'll just pop that into my portable genetic retrofactor, aaaand *tidy.* Just like that, I've got a digital projection of her iris and fingerprints. Let's see which one the computer asks for.

Saliva? You're telling me she *spits* onto her computer to log in? I think that might actually be worse than just wanking at it.

A swabbing stick pops out of the computer, waiting for the saliva sample. I'm looking around the office for something to use. Bingo! A half-drunk glass with lipstick on the rim. Let's swab the lot and see what we get.

Shitting Henry, it worked!

Now, let's find those files. Tippity tap... *Accident... Logs...* Oy-oy, that's a chunky set of results. Let's narrow it down. Date, location, personnel... Wahey!

Sienna Constantina.

Download.

In a queue? What do you mean queue? The *one* time I need a teeny-weeny file, it's stored on Earth. In case you haven't noticed so far, mining companies suck at IT. This is gonna take a beat.

Crap, someone's outside. Boss lady's back early from the fake meeting I set up for her. Quick, lock the computer, grab the flash drive and – too late, she's coming in. Hide!

Not gonna lie, this is demeaning. To be crouching under someone's desk at this stage in my career? I should be outsourcing this nonsense. Normally I would, but this is personal. Gotta hand it to boss lady, though, this carpet has a *great* thread count. Bad at IT, *great* at carpets. Shhh – listen up, she's on the phone to someone.

"Yes, it's going to plan. We're routing it through Lunar Five as requested. No, I don't foresee any complications. There have been some contamination incidents but we're dealing with it. Several employees have been exposed to the-... Yes, I'm aware of the severity. What do you mean *broader quarantine*? Of course I'm familiar with the concept, but it's not one you specified when you brought this to my-... Might I remind you, Secretary, without my support in this you would be shafted, so perhaps a more grateful tone would be appropriate?"

There's now a protracted silence on Nenge's part. She keeps trying to speak but the other person's on a roll. I sense she's overstepped the line.

Ouch! Something's struck my leg. What the hell? God damned vacuum cleaner. Shoo!

I'm hissing at this thing but it's not leaving me alone. It's *determined* to clean, like its life depends on it. I kick the bot away, but it lets out a tinny clang.

"Nothing – my cleaning robot. Please, continue," mutters Nenge.

Uh-oh. The little bastard's revving up its fans. It's squaring up to me like it's preparing to storm a castle. I kick it square in the chops. Disaster, it's latched onto to my foot, squealing like a robot piglet.

"What the hell?" yells boss lady. "Oh my God! Security!"

Aw piss. That's my cover blown. I dive out from the desk and swing my leg in a roundhouse kick. The vacuum bot flies off, smashing against the wall. As Nenge reaches for her panic button I throw a micro-jammer onto the desk.

She recoils, repelled by the force field, which also disables her phone.

"Who are you and what do you want?" she cries.

"I want to strike a deal. You gimme the company's injury logs, and I stay silent about that call you were just on. Who was it, the Secretary of State?"

Boss lady's lips tighten.

"Secretary of the *Bloc*? Ouch, you're in deep, love. Guess we have a deal, then?"

"No deal," she snaps.

"I don't think you're in a position to negotiate, miss."

I'm bluffing, by the way. My signal jammer is good for another thirty seconds before the battery's spent. Then she'll mash that panic button, her security will tase me, and I'll be off to prison again.

Best speed her along.

"Lunar Mining Ship L3-11 returned to this base four days ago, yes?"

"Perhaps. I don't monitor every ship's coming and go-"

"I do, and I'm telling you, that ship returned four days ago."

"So?"

"No-one's seen the crew since."

"And this is of concern to you because...?"

"My partner's one of them."

"I see."

"Where is she?"

"I don't know."

"You're lying."

"Look, why don't you book an appointment with our head of HR and-"

"Open your personnel records and show me who's on this base, right now."

"I don't have access to that sort of-"

"Of course you do, you're the bloody CEO."

"That's not how this works."

"Then tell me, how *does* it work?"

"It's complicated."

"It's starting to look real simple from where I'm standing. An entire crew of yours disappears between the asteroid field and this moon base, and you don't seem even remotely concerned. Nothing complicated about that. You know why? Because it looks like one thing and one thing only. A cover up."

"I can assure, you, there's nothing of the sort going on here. I can see you're upset, and having a missing partner must be a stressful experience. But taking someone hostage is no way to conduct a civilized conversation. I urge you to take a cool breath, leave without further disruption, and I promise I'll make this my top priority to get back to you."

"Open. The. Records."

"I can't. I have obligations... principles."

"Mmm. Can't? Or Won't?"

"Both."

"In my experience, it takes remarkably few broken fingers to turn both 'can't and 'won't' into a '*will*'."

"Fine," snaps the boss lady, through gritted teeth. "I'll open the records. But you'll have to disable the jammer for me to access them."

Ugh. She's right.

"OK Lady, I'm gonna disable the force field, and I'm *trusting* you to get that file. We sweet?"

"You have my word."

"You're definitely not gonna hit that panic button as soon as I lift the force field?"

"It's as you said, I can't risk the political fall out," she grunts.

"OK then. So we're all clear: force field down, you get me the file, I leave without a fuss, and no-one hears about your super sketchy deal with the government."

"Correct."

"Then on with the party!"

As I tap my wrist panel, the force field vanishes. The woman dives across the desk and whacks the panic button, triggering a deafening alarm.

"Hey, you promised!"

Footsteps are racing towards the office – both human and robot.

Nenge rips open a drawer and grabs a stun gun. She's firing neuro-nerval darts at me, which would be cute were it not for the fact they replicate the sensation of two hundred thousand volts ripping through your body, like four people tasing you at once.

I'm sheltering behind a chair but she's bearing down on me. Nerve gun-in-hand, she's got a sadistic smile across her face.

The pounding feet are yards from the door. The only door. There's no other way out, and I've already played my Ace of Spades with that jamming device.

Only one thing for it. Girl's gotta play a Joker, innit.

I chuck the splat-ball device at the window, where it sticks like gum. Flinging the chair at boss lady, I sprint for the glass. She's unleashing a barrel of darts my way.

She stops suddenly, realizing what I'm about to do. Screaming in terror, she grabs hold of a railing as I launch myself towards the wall.

A sonic pulse rips through the glass. Everything falls

silent. The pressurized room explodes outwards. Books, glass, and furniture, shoot into the cold lunar landscape.

Oh, and among it all, one wailing bundle of flesh and bones.

Me.

2

LUKE

Zero gravity sucks. Everyone raves about it; kids go on low orbitals for their proms now, couples tie the knot in free fall. Me? I'd rather staple my nuts to my tongue. Which is basically what take off feels like.

Sure, I jumped in at the deep end. Most people start off with a quick up and down jolly; they dust the atmosphere and are back on terra firma bumping and grinding the night away in some club three hours later.

Not me. Nope, genius here decided his first zero G experience should be a trip to the moon. OK in fairness, none of this was my choice, but we'll get onto that later.

Expect violent shaking and explosive sounds. This is a perfectly normal part of rocket launch, and will abate after the first forty minutes.

The in-flight safety card neglected to mention the huge ball of fire that appears by the window like some reaper of death. I'd say I need a change of pants, but they gave me a diaper before boarding. I don't know if they're for all passengers, or whether they just took one look at me and figured "we've got a pooper". Either way, they called it.

It begs the question though, their marketing department must be *gooood*. I mean, how many other industries could get away with that? "Zero G promises to be the most serene, transcendental experience of your life. Oh, but by the way, you'll be strapped to a brimming bag of your own feces as soon as take-off begins."

All those "Touch the Heavens" ads make space tourism look so blissful. In reality, you're pinned to a jump seat while your buttocks move in independent directions, making fresh chocolate sandwiches.

Passport?

Ah – customs. Gimme a second.

"Nice to meet you too," I say.

The robot's got a perfect smile. Its eyes flicker as it selects the optimal response based on my biometric and socioeconomic profile.

There, there, poppet.

Mother *fucker!* I'm not doing this today.

"I wanna speak to a human."

The robot adopts a look of simpering concern.

Apologies if my response was inadequate, sir. Permission to report this error to our server? Your data will be used to-

"Whatever, just find me someone with wrinkles, will you?"

I'm afraid all customs personnel on Lunar One are robotic. This is done to ensure the smoothest possible check-in experience for our guests and-

"Yeah, yeah, all right. Just get on with it then."

Of course, sir. Please remove your pants.

"Say what?"

Our scanners have detected an unusual quantity of loose organic matter stowed in your undergarments.

"No kidding. I shat myself. You happy now?"

I am programmed to be emotionally balanced at all times. This allows us to put your happiness above all else. Are you happy, sir?

"I'm caked in my own shit and talking to a hologram, what do you think?"

Processing. According to our database, there is an eighty percent chance you are being sarcastic, an eighteen percent you did not understand the question, a one point five percent you are another a hologram, and a half-point chance you are being sincere.

"You mean for every two hundred people that turn up in this state, one of them is *delighted* about it?"

No one has ever turned up in quite your state, sir.

"I'm flattered."

Please proceed with the garment removal.

The windows either side of my customs booth frost over, shielding me from the curious gazes of my fellow arrivals. I bounce around the cubicle trying to tug the damned pants off. It must've looked like I was performing the worst shadow puppet show in history.

Please deposit the garment into the tray for analysis.

"What are you searching for?"

Contraband.

"Ah, then you're looking in the wrong place. That's still firmly up my asshole."

The machine's smile vanished and a stern, neutral tone replied.

Wait here.

"No, wait, I was kidding! Ah crap..."

A loud clunking approaches and the doors behind the hologram sweep open. The floating customs agent vanishes. In her place is an aggressive human wearing an exo-suit, with **NORTHERN CUSTOMS & SECURITY** printed across the front. He's got a silvery crew cut hair, thick arms, and bags under his eyes - the only part of his body that doesn't look super-toned.

"Turn around. Hands against the wall. Do not move unless instructed, and – Jesus Christ, what happened in here?"

"What do you think happened? A mature gentleman with a fear of heights got strapped to a rocket and blasted into space. I'd ask you not to stare."

The security guard shakes off his disbelief and regains his authoritarian gaze.

"Hands. Wall. Now."

I'd love to say it's the first time this has happened, but as my second wife's lawyer observed, it's part of a "worrying pattern of behaviors." Whatever that means.

The security guy frisks me, scans me, and carries out a localized cremation of my pants before issuing me with a baggy temporary pair to wear.I catch a glimpse of his name badge: *Lionel Hutz, Head of Security*.

"Hey, Lionel, this is profiling," I complain. "People with sensitive bowels deserve better."

"People get what they deserve," he grunts. "Customs check is complete. You're cleared for entry, Mr. Remini. Have a pleasant stay."

Lionel the guard turns on his heel and marches away, sped by his exo-suit.

Oh, that's another thing I should point out. It's lovely being here and all, but God damn it's like wading through treacle. It's not like you see in the old movies, where it's some folk goofing around in astronaut suits taking leaps and bounds, and playing golf on the lunar dust. We're all being herded into a radiation-proof shelter right away. Try taking a gleeful low-gravity bounce here and you'll whack your head on the ceiling. Which is exactly what the kid in the booth next to me just did. Ha. What an imbecile.

Pulling the replacement pants on, I hurry into the lobby. The security guard is on a raised seat, eyeballing the crowd like a lifeguard without a pool.

Welcome to Lunar One, Luxury Quadrant. We hope you enjoy your stay.

The intercom has the same voice as the hologram that first met me.

I follow the other passengers to the arrivals lounge. The kid's pointing me out with a goofy grin and a deliberately bad whisper.

"Look, Mom, that's the guy who crapped himself!"

"Nice. How's your head, kid?"

A balding man joins the kid and his mom. He's wearing a designer shirt and blazer. His bottom half, however... His eyes meet mine, horrified to see we're both wearing *Lunar Tours* jogging pants. I wave cheerfully as his wife sweeps her two males away with disdain.

First-time visitors, please report to the Luxury Lounge for orientation. This is a legal requirement, under the International Space Tourism Safety and Security Treaty 115C.

I hate safety briefings. Do you reckon I can duck it if I crap myself again? I'm pretty confident they'll run out of pants before I run outta crap.

I take a seat in the luxury lounge and survey my fellow "tourists". They're a nauseating crop of humanity's richest jerk-offs. The couple next to me are a classic specimen. The woman looks bored, checking her emails while her latest toy boy marvels at the wallpaper like a puppy discovering its new home. Clearly this is just how first dates roll when you're a billionaire: drinks... on the Moon.

This ain't my gig, you know. I'm not averse to luxury by any means, I just know where to draw the line. Hot tubs? Great news. Beer and burgers? God's gift to man. First class Moon packages? You might as well get *asshole* tattooed on your face. Call me a Marxist, but how about back on Earth we buy everyone a hot tub, a round of beers, and some basic medical before we worry about fluffing these douchebags' gravity-free pillows?

"Would you care for a welcome foot rub, sir?"

Forget everything I just said. Capitalism rules. Aaaah, that's the stuff...

"God damn that's good!"

"Glad to be of service."

At this point I realize the woman rubbing my feet is actually a human. Her skin is so insanely perfect, I just assumed she was manufactured in a lab. My compliments to whatever chromosomal chefs served up this particular delight. A toast to nature, and its unending splendor! Is it just my imagination, or is she smiling at me? This eye contact's pretty intense for a foot rub. Holy crap, she just bit her lip. We are hitting it *off*.

Would the remaining guests kindly take their seats for the security briefing. Thank you.

The woman stops rubbing my feet and rises like she's made of air. Whenever *I* stand up it sounds like bubble wrap being massacred. She's clearly made of something more refined than my raggedy old flesh suit.

"It was nice meeting you," she whispers.

Now I'm blushing. It's been months since I spoke to an attractive stranger, let alone one who gives me physical contact.

"Likesame. I mean samewise. I mean, uh, feet."

"Let me know if there's anything else I can do to make your stay more comfortable," she whispers.

With that, she's gone. It takes a few seconds before I realize she's pressed a card into my hand. Is that a room number? Niiiiice.

A transaction flashes up on my wrist panel.

You've been charged three credits for "massage by Latifa".

Ah come *on.*

I tuck her card into my pocket, only to avoid littering the immaculate lounge, and turn my attention to the podium. The lights are dimming, and a film is beginning.

Three hundred thousand miles, forty years of development, ground-breaking engineering, and comfort that's simply out of this world...

Oh God. This is gonna be rough. I'm glancing around the room. Half of the occupants are glued to the screen in awe, while others look indifferent, like they've seen this kinda stuff before and are totally over the whole "space" thing. Two men in the corner catch my eye. They're whispering to each other in sharp, rapid tones. A lover's tiff? They don't seem familiar enough for that. Colleagues, perhaps? But since when did colleagues go on holiday together?

In the event of a station decompression...

Wait, what? Crap, maybe I should be paying attention to this thing. Whaaaat? This place is a maze! *That's* the escape route? They might as well flush us out now, there's no way any of us would make that. Besides, evacuate to what, a shelter? An escape pod? The video has definitely shifted in tone and style from its initial glitzy cheese-fest. Ah, there it is. The government's safety department logo.

That explains the crappy graphics and general lack of coherence.

Ooh, the screen's changing again to... Jackpot: it's the sexy customs hologram. She's got that perfect smile and soothing tone going on. Yes, let's just sweep that whole legally-required briefing under the carpet with some nice fluffy branding. Our bed straps are lined with *real* bamboo silk? Now we're talking!

Here at Lunar Tours, we're one big family. It's time to meet some of your fellow space-farers!

Ew, ew, ew, social icebreaker alert.

What brings you to Lunar One, passenger E9?

A young woman rises to her feet and points proudly to the man beside her.

"We're on our honeymoon!"

We all clap politely, and some cheer. Her husband awkwardly rises to his feet, but she quickly shoves him down, then continues curtsying and modeling her ring.

How about you, passenger H28?

An elderly man rises to his feet. He's wearing an illustrious sash, and his silver hair is swept up in a formidable bun.

"I'm here to scatter my late wife's ashes," he says, solemnly.

There's an awkward ripple of applause. The kind you get at a golf course, when someone does a shot so bad they'll have to climb in a river.

The brat kid boos, impatiently. His father clips his ear.

"Ow! What? He was being a buzzkill!" protests the kid.

The father gives me a despairing look like, *kids, hey? What can you do?*

Err, you could shove the little ass rag into the air lock,

for one thing. Or if that's too much hassle, how about raising him to not be a total jerk-off?

I give the dad a thumbs up. He smiles and reciprocates. Oh no. He's the clingy type. Either rich by birth, or by marriage; he's got a big heart, a small brain, and excretes money out of every pore on his sweaty body. And now he thinks we're best buds. He tugs at one of his pant legs and shrugs, as if to say, *What are we like?* Christ, now he thinks we're butt bros. Poop pals? *Mud brothers* - there it is. Bonded through our mutual digestive afflictions.

How about you, passenger B14?

Fifty sets of yuppie eyes and a floating spotlight are suddenly on me.

"Oh, uh, hey everyone. I'm here on the run. I owe a young criminal king-pin a stack of money, so I figured the safest place to be was the Moon. Pretty sure there's some kinda massive government conspiracy underway too, so I'm hoping to find out more while I'm up here, before it scuppers the upcoming peace treaty. Have a great trip."

I sit down hastily, amid raucous laughter. The notion that you could owe someone money and not be able to pay it is the funniest thing these people have ever heard. My poop pal's slapping his thigh and giving me a double-thumbs up. I'm really slaying it with the dad crowd today. Ugh, like I needed *more* reasons to hate myself.

Along from the brat family, the two arguing men are scoping the room. They look skittish. One taps the other's shoulder and the pair dart through a side-door. No one else seems to have noticed; all eyes are on me. But as the door seals behind them, I briefly lock eyes with the second man.

I know that look. It's the stare of someone you don't ever wanna follow; a glare so fierce it removes all need for words.

It's a look that says, *follow me, and it'll be the last thing you do.*

Any sane person would tuck their tail between their legs and back away. When someone stares at you like they're a stone-cold killer, odds are that's exactly what they are. And those types tend not to like being disturbed when they're working. You've gotta respect someone's professional bubble, you know? I remember trying to write articles at home during the school holidays, and the *constant interruptions* from my kids. It's like they had no appreciation of work-life boundaries. So I empathize with this guy's position, and his facial *do not disturb* sign.

Unfortunately for him, giving me that look is like showing red to a bull. Two shady dudes slipping out of a mandatory briefing into a barely-visible side door? Come on. How am I *not* gonna look into that? I'd be a pretty lousy journalist if I didn't...

Once again, valued customers, we welcome you to Lunar One, and to your new space family. Please proceed through the doors to the restaurant and shopping quadrant, where a world of leisure awaits.

As the crowd eagerly moves on, I tack away to the invisible side door. It's painted into the wall, so you gotta get real close to even see the edges. I'm digging my fingernails in, trying to prize the panel open, but it's sealed. My eyes fall on a small security fob embedded in the wall. Wait, so those guys had a pass to get in? Why the hell were they coming through the tourist entrance? And why would Lunar One even need a covert entrance in the first place?

Can I help you, Sir?

I freeze, fingers clinging to the invisible doorway. The holographic AI's floating above me, with a fixed smile that does little to soften its hawk-like gaze.

"Uh, yeah, I wanna see what's in this compartment."

Step this way please, sir.

"Sure. Just a sec."

I try barging the door, really rattling the sides.

Please desist and follow me.

"Same page. Just gimme a sec, will you?"

I'm really hammering at this thing now. People are noticing, perturbed by my frenzied behavior. My poop pal looks disappointed, like I just shattered his dreams of a beautiful, sane friendship. A familiar pneumatic set of footsteps approaches at speed, with a crisp barked order and the sound of a stun baton powering up.

I freeze, busted. Lionel the head of security is looming over me with a stern glare, making the most of the additional height his exo-suit provides.

"Passenger B14. Cease at once."

"Apologies, officer, it was just a moment of confusion. I thought they said to go through *this* door. I see now that they mean the large double doors everyone else is using. My bad. Landing sickness, you know how it is. I'll be on my way."

"I think you'd better follow me."

"Uh, why?"

"You're bleeding."

I look down at my t-shirt, and see the moist red patch seeping into the fabric. That's the problem with taking a rocket into outer space two days after getting shot. It tends to rip the stitches.

3

TESSA

My exo-suit deploys as I fly through the air, surrounded by glass and the CEO's furniture. A fleet of security robots are mobilizing behind me. My lunar buggy skids around the corner, racing to intercept me. I'm gliding like superwoman, ready to land on it and make one hell of a getaway.

Bastards, the buggy's stopped short! I overshoot, tumbling across the hood and landing on the rocks. Proper gear would've cushioned the blow, but this emergency exo-suit is barely thicker than my skin. Even in low G, the landing hurts like buggery.

An emergency force field deploys across the CEO's office. As the human staff bundle her to safety, security robots watch me like meerkats. For a moment, I think they're about to launch themselves right at me, but there's no need for *them* to get clogged up in moon dust.

An alarm sounds in my ear. Two buggies incoming.

I grip the throttle and speed across the bumpy terrain. The meerkats are no doubt relaying my position to the buggies, so I detour away from their line of sight.

My computer's telling me Lunar Five is a thirty minute ride at top speed. How much oxygen can my emergency suit supply? Two minutes. OK, and the buggy? Twenty eight minutes. That makes...

Oh, shit on it. This is gonna be snug, even by my standards.

My scanner's freaking out. The two buggies are closing in fast like pincers. There's no way I can outrun them in a straight race. Ugh, this is gonna cost me oxygen but another detour is my only hope.

I veer hard off to the side, cutting across the left hand buggy's trajectory. The riders are loading up an EMP canon; they're trying to knock out my buggy – *and* my oxygen.

The robot fires but I swerve, dodging the beam. Thank God they don't have missile locks otherwise I'd be screwed. They've only got ray guns, and the combination of the bumpy lunar terrain, my movement, theirs, and the Mining Company's chronic under-investment in its own robotic intelligence, means the bot can't calculate all the variables quickly enough to get a clean shot at me.

But they've still got two hundred yards to prove me wrong. I swerve again, just in time, as a laser blast etches into the ground ahead of me. The robot changes tactic, unleashing a hail of quick bursts until suddenly it stops; they can't risk the collateral damage as I enter the Lunar Three mining complex.

My buggy soars over a ramp and I'm plunging into the mine. It's my only chance of shaking these buggers off. As I fall, I get a video call.

Shit, it's Eric. Me and Sienna are counting on him for a ticket off this bloody rock. Ignoring him ain't an option.

"Eric," I yell, "Now's not a good time, bruv!"

"Are you on some kinda joy ride? Your feed's super bumpy," he frowns.

He's on a treadmill. That fucker only ever calls people from a treadmill.

"What do you want, Eric?"

"I want an update on my order, obviously. Delivery's due soon, and I want to know whether you're on top of things, or if I need to take my business elsewhere," he says, with pointedly athletic ease, while increasing the speed on his runner.

I'm ducking and dodging between vast sets of machinery, and immediately regretting coming this way; it's a lethal assault course of massive drills, crust-splitting diggers, and asteroid refineries.

"I said I'd get it done, so just trust me, all right?"

"I'd love to chica, but you know I've got trust issues. You can blame my father for that."

"No, I can't Eric, because you murdered him."

"Did I? Strange. I could've sworn the police report identified *you* as the prime suspect."

"Don't."

"Or what? You'll hide on the Moon for another six years? You need me, so tread carefully, sister-in-law."

"Don't call me that, I'm not your sister-in-law anymore. You saw to that when you killed him."

"How the mighty have fallen, dear Tessa. You used to be so suave, so refined. Moving between society's richest, only to slit their throats between courses. Now look at you; a penniless mechanic on Lunar Five, apparently *stealing* moon buggies to make ends meet."

"Screw you, Eric, you don't know the half of it."

"I'll let that slide," he says, with an acrid smile. "I'm a

great forgiver. So much so, Tessa, that I'm offering you more than just money to get this job done."

"What?"

"I'm offering you your old life back."

"I don't want my old life. It's dead, and I've moved on."

I jerk the wheel sharply to avoid a drill head as I race through the mine.

"But you want to come back to Earth, right? Hard to do when you're wanted for murder."

"Because of *you*, arsehole!"

"Manners, manners, my dear. Get this job done, and all is forgiven. You and your new woman will get safe passage to Earth, and you'll get a clean slate on your record."

"Why are you doing this now, after all these years?"

"Market forces, my dear, why else? An opportunity has presented itself for me to enter a new sector of the market."

"Oh great, because the world really needs more guns…"

"Not guns. Oh no, this is something altogether more powerful than that. My client is most keen to get their hands on it before others catch on. The fact they've trusted me with the procurement is itself a great honor. Of course, with that comes a certain degree of… pressure."

"They're turning the screws on you, so you're turning them on me, huh?"

"I think you could say we are both sufficiently motivated to see this job completed on time," he says, slowing the treadmill.

"I've identified a mark. He's my way into the data that you want. I'm due to meet him at Lunar Five tonight."

"Why not Lunar One? That's the only place you can access the damned data. Why else would I hire some dust eater like you to do this for me?"

I bite my lip at the insult. If I tell him where to shove

this lunar dust he'll take me off the job and use someone else. Besides, the bastard's right. He *is* my only way home.

"I've got a plan, all right?" I yell over the thundering wheels. "Tonight I'm using the mark to get access to the Lunar One network. As soon as that's done, I'll infiltrate Lunar One, and get your data."

"Wait, so if you're not on Lunar One right now, and you're not on Lunar Five either, where the hell are you?"

"Do you actually care?"

"Not even a little. Just get it done, or I'll find someone else who will. And your chance at a clean slate will be gone forever."

He terminates the call, and his video vanished from my overlay. A blanket of dust engulfs me, lingering above the low gravity surface. My scanner crackles offline; its light rays unable to penetrate the interference. I'm relying solely on my wits as I swerve between moon trucks and drilling machines as they appear from the haze without warning.

Out of nowhere, the second buggy glances my right side. Any closer and they'd have flipped me. I need to improvise fast.

Skidding into a sharp turn, I speed onto the processing line. Chunks of pulverized asteroid cover a huge conveyor belt. I'm clinging on like a koala as my buggy rocks between horizontal propulsion and vertical scaling, its huge wheels attacking the new terrain.

A vast metal disc smashes down beside me, shattering a boulder. Razor-sharp fragments fly in all directions, tearing through my skin like a thousand paper cuts. My suit's tight enough to stem the bleeding but only temporarily; as soon as it comes off, I'll leak like a sieve.

Ignore the pain; I have to stay focused or I'm gonna die here. The dust is panoramic, and more crushers are reigning down out of the fog, hammering the rocks around me. My survival is counting on my brain outlasting those frazzled robotic motherboards, so that they get crushed before me.

Something dark is looming up ahead. I squint, trying to fathom it through the dust. At the last second, my terrified brain clicks.

The smelting hole.

I bail hard, twisting the buggy sharply off the conveyor belt, skimming the mouth of the inferno. I'm falling with the vehicle, with no notion of how deep the pit goes. The mining company has built where others didn't dare – meaning this is canyon territory. This fall could last seconds or minutes.

I land with a thud and several bounces. The buggy absorbs most of the impact, but my aching frame still takes a battering. I scan my glitching navigation for something useful; it's flashing up obstacles as I see them with my own eyes. But there's one saving grace: it's got a lock on my destination.

As I make a beeline for the triangle, the dust thins. I can see the horizon again and – yes, there it is! Lunar Five is within eyesight, less than a kilometer away.

An alarm sounds in my suit. My oxygen levels are critical. We're eating into my reserve tank. I'd love to say I'm doing my best to conserve air but it's hard when you're basically riding a metal space horse across the lunar wilderness, being pursued by robots with ray guns.

A red beacon flashes up on my scanner. One of the buggies is still on my tail and they're charging the EMP. I duck and weave, driving erratically to try and thwart them. Laser blasts whizz by, scorching the dust ahead.

The robots lower the canon and accelerate. They're trying to pull up alongside me. They know that if they miss me, and strike a Lunar Five asset with the weapon, there'll be huge political ramifications. Well, they don't know about the ramifications *per se*, they're security bots. Politics wasn't on their syllabus. They are, however, hard-wired to avoid causing any damage to anything outside of the Lunar Three Mining Corporation's territory.

My breathing's getting tight. I can see the territorial markers ahead. I hit the turbo button on my buggy, draining the last of its power to give me a final boost. But the robots have done the same, and their machine's more powerful.

As my oxygen runs out, time goes into slow motion. The robots have nearly pulled parallel. They swerve, narrowly avoiding a boulder. When they reappear, the laser canon is trained right at my vehicle. They unleash the blast. The beam strikes my front wheel, destroying the axle. The power controls on the buggy crackle out as sparks fly across the controls. The front of the buggy crumples, and folds in on itself like it's hit a brick wall. The momentum propels me like a javelin.

I soar through the air, across the Lunar Five border, where I sink to the ground with a crunch. My body rolls four times before coming to a stop. As the dust settles, I see the security bots staring at me, silently. Maybe they're sending a video report of my escape, or perhaps they're trying to calculate extraction methods that don't violate their hard-wired rules.

Red is seeping into my vision as oxygen-starved capillaries burst in my eyes. The robots turn and retreat to base, satisfied they've done enough. As my suit begins to decompress, I send a final message on my wrist, before passing out.

HELP.

4

LUKE

So it turns out you're supposed to declare fresh bullet wounds on your pre-flight medical. Apparently boarding a rocket while your spleen is held together by bits of glue is "ill advised". Joke's on them, though, because it turns out rich people medicine is AMAZING. Seriously, whatever machines they just used on me didn't only fix the stitches, it's almost certainly extended my life expectancy by several years. They even trimmed my love handles and smoothed a few wrinkles while I was out.

I'm strutting down the main boulevard of the luxury quarter, positively glowing. People are looking at me with a newfound appreciation. Now that a machine's sucked the fat out of my ass and squirted it into my forehead, they're able to accept me as one of their own.

Much as I'd like to partake in the quadrant's perfumeries, fine dining, and entertainment, they have to wait. I'm on the trail of two deeply suspicious gentlemen. People who clearly have something to hide. People who may just know about a certain high profile murder that happened on this base a few days ago...

My journalist senses are tingling like tea tree shower gel on my hairy balls in the morning. I'm allergic to tea tree oil, FYI, so don't make it my Secret Santa gift unless you really do want me to have two lumps of coal for Christmas.

First, the International Lunar Inspector, a rare impartial figure in the cold war between the Southern and Northern blocs, mysteriously dies just days after her last inspection of the Moon. And *just* before her report was due to be published. Some people would call that one heck of a coinkydink. I call it deeply fucking suspicious, because I'm not a children's entertainer.

My boss, Lanelle, is adamant there's something sketchy afoot. She suspects it's a private enterprise doing something illegal, I reckon they're military. Our tip-off said the unscheduled lunar shuttles were civilian transporters, but that doesn't mean non-military. That just means the military didn't wanna be *seen* doing whatever it is they're doing. Which should be nothing, given that the Moon's officially an international demilitarized zone. And we all know that when the international community commits pen to paper, they all respect and play by the rules. Ahem.

My top lead right now is those two clowns from the arrivals lounge. The two chaps who literally glanced around before disappearing into a secret compartment. Who even does that? Badly-trained sneaky people, that's who. I'm hoping their incongruous exit is indicative of a broader ineptitude. A good journalist always hopes for two things: dumb criminals, and hypoallergenic shower gels. So far, so good.

My two immediate questions are: what are those dudes up to, and where'd they go? That secret door surely led to another part of the Lunar One base. Oh, yeah, about that. The Luxury Quadrant is only part of the base. It's the bit reserved for aristocratic tourists. The landing fees and sales taxes they generate subsidize the remaining quadrants on the base, which are governmental. They are: scientific research, mineral processing, and manufacturing compartments for the Mars bases. *Definitely* not military...

Which brings me onto question number three. What other shared access points exist between the quadrants? They all use centralized water, air, and heat exchangers, so it's not like they're in separate bubbles. It's more like trying to get from one side of a city to another when someone's hidden all the subway entrances.

Luckily, I have something of a talent for getting into places I don't belong. My neighbor's husband will attest that. In fact he did, in court. In my defense, I *was* invited over, just not by him. Ooh, a cleaning drone. Excuse me while I tailgate our fine four-wheeled friend for a moment. This is my golden ticket.

OK, word to the wise: if you're gonna make your main lead tailgating a cleaning bot, for the love of God make sure you do it at the *end* of its shift. I swear I've been following this thing for like two hours now, and there's only so much I can pretend to browse whatever random store it stops outside. It spent thirty minutes in a restaurant – I had to order lunch! Which was actually delicious, but that's not the point.

I'm realizing this thing's gonna outlast me, even in my rejuvenated, youthful state. So it's time for plan B: I can't beat its battery, but I *can* beat its storage tank.

Solids won't work – the bots compresses everything they ingest. But liquids? Much harder to deal with. I wander over to the central fountain. Hmm. How to do this subtly.

"Excuse me, Ma'am, please could you take my photo?"

The woman looks at me like I've just asked her to lick my armpits. I can see the thought bubble oozing from her fatuous skull. *Don't you have a servant for that?*

Wincing, she steps away from her vulgar offspring as they browse the gift shop. She calls up her camera while I back up against the fountain.

"Make sure you get this thing in, I think it's so amazing they've-"

Oh no! I appear to have totally "accidentally" fallen *into* the fountain. Worst of all, in my one hundred percent unexpected mishap, I've knocked the main spout out of focus. Water's gushing onto the concourse, people are staring, what a pandemonium!

The base AI swiftly detects the leakage and shuts down the fountain, but those few seconds of delay were enough to turn the floor into a mini aqua park. Sure enough, here comes everyone's favorite cleaning bot to save the day. What's that li'l fella? You're all full up of drink? Aww, diddums. Let me tailgate you to the nearest cleaning portal, while making loud protestations to the onlookers about the place needing clear signage about trip hazards.

Schuuuuup. Just like that, I'm in the the service corridor. The hubbub of the shopping district vanishes. The only sound is the hum of the air vents overhead, in this long, strip-lit tunnel. Time to see where this next door leads.

"Halt!"

Ah crap. Cue pneumatic steps approaching. It's Lionel, everyone's favorite silver-haired buzzkill.

"Passenger B14. This area is off-limits for guests."

"Hey, I paid a lot to be here, and this robot offered to take me on a behind the scenes tour."

"That's a cleaning droid. It doesn't do tours."

"Do you do tours?"

"Sure. Do you wanna go to the brig, or the airlock?"

"Actually, I'm hoping you can point me towards the science quadrant? I'm an amateur dork. I'd love to meet some real lunar researchers!"

I reach for the door but the guard cuts me off.

"I said it's *off limits*. God damn, you people really aren't used to hearing 'no', are you?"

"I feel like that's a trick question."

Before he can reply, the door bleeps open. Two men wheel a trolley into the corridor, stopping abruptly as they see us.

"Well this is awkward," I chuckle.

The guard rises up to the full height of his exo-suit, his face ferocious.

"This area is off-limits," he growls.

"We have authorization," replies the front man.

"From whom?"

"Classified."

"Not on my base, it isn't."

"This isn't your base, *Mall Cop*. Step aside."

"Try me."

The three highly-sculpted men square up to each other. Damn. It's kinda hot.

"What the fuck?"

All three are staring at me. Crap, that last comment might've been aloud.

"What's in the crate?" says Lionel, confronting the nearest man.

"Like I said. Classified."

"If you're planning on bringing that into my jurisdiction, I'm entitled to inspect it, as the sole representative customs agent under declaration four-three-"

"Immaterial. We refuse your search under domestic protocol nine."

"That doesn't apply in space and you know it."

"This is above your pay grade, old man. I don't want you to get hurt."

Lionel's face sours and the bags under his eyes seem to deepen. "I'd worry about yourself right now, kid. Show me the cart, or I will use force."

"Let's all take a beat, shall we?" interrupts the second man. "Sir, we can show you our authorization. It comes from the top. You understand? It's a signed letter. Here..."

The second man reaches into his pocket.

"Stop what you're doing!" yells Lionel.

But it's too late. The second man draws a pistol and fires into Lionel's chest. The guard's body caves inwards as the force throws him against the wall. As he falls, he returns fire from his wrist-gun, hitting the shooter.

The remaining man draws his gun but Lionel engages his exo-suit, launching himself at the man with lightening speed. The two fellas collide against the trolley, sending it crashing to the ground as they tumble over the top.

The assailant is hard to pin, and clearly has combat training. He's deftly out-maneuvering each of Lionel's grip holds, but he's tiring. Even with his skill, he can't match the strength of the exo-suit. The guard seizes the man's head and dashes it against the wall. The agent drops to the ground, out cold.

Panting, and clutching his chest, Lionel slumps down. His suit's beeping in warning. The injuries are critical.

"Dude, are you OK?" I ask.

I know he's not OK, but what else do you say when someone's just had their ass handed to them like that? Sorry you got spanked? Better luck next time?

"Call the medic. My suit's damaged so you have to dial manually," pants Lionel.

"Promise you'll let me into wherever they just came from? It's a great deal for you. You scratch my back... I get you life-saving medical treatment."

The guard's glaring at me with confusion, anger, and pain.

"Gotcha. You'd prefer we have an *unspoken* agreement," I say, while tapping at the controls. "Alright, base medics are inbound. I thoroughly recommend them - they worked wonders on my sciatica."

"Put these on," croaks the dying guard.

He points to his handcuffs.

"Lionel, I'm flattered, but we've only just met."

"You're... under... arrest..." he croaks.

"Ah, much as I'd love that, I gotta split. Got me a hot date with whatever's through that door. Just need a quick peak in here first."

I'm rummaging through the spewed contents of the trolley but it's hard to know what I'm looking at, beyond, uh, science stuff. It's vials of some kinda liquid.

X1 EXOTIC MATTER. BIOSAFETY CATEGORY 5. PRIORITY CLASSIFIED TRANSFER.

Exotic matter? No idea what that is, though the X1 mean's it's not terrestrial in origin. Biosafety category 5? That's bad. That's weapons grade bad. And I'm holding it in my naked hand. But the biggest alarm bell is the priority transfer bit – were those dudes about to smuggle it back to Earth? Who the hell would take a category five substance on a tourist ship?

The door behind me opens and a medical bot enters, followed by two human personnel. They see the carnage and scream.

"Arrest... him!" croaks Lionel, before passing out.

"Dude, that makes me sound *really* guilty!"

There's no time to protest further. As the robot rushes towards me, I grab a security pass from the unconscious agent and make a leap for it. Restricted zone, here I come.

5

———

TESSA

Can I buy you a drink, sweetheart?

"You can leave me alone, how about that?"

Come on baby, we don't have to talk unless you want to. Wink.

"Ew. Gross."

You can spit in my mouth if you want?

"Too far, babe, way too far."

Really?

"Uh, yah."

Was it the spitting bit?

"You think?"

I'm not sure. That's why I'm asking.

"Yes, Carla, it was the spitting bit."

Should I have insinuated a different kind of intercourse instead? Perhaps something more tender?

"Yuk, no. Tender's worse."

Tender is worse. Noted.

"Not like, always, just in the context of two strangers meeting at a bar."

Got it. Tender sex between strangers is creepy. How should it be?

"Huh?"

What is the appropriate type of sex for consenting strangers to have?

"I dunno. Hot? Steamy? The kind where you don't really care if they're having a good time or not, you're just in it to win it. Close your eyes, picture the person you *actually* want to be ragging, and race them to the finish line. Does that help?"

By finish line, do you mean-

"Carla, honey, you're really killing my vibe."

Sorry, Coach. May I offer you a complimentary drink by way of apology?

"Now we're talking."

Might I recommend the house ale?

"Is it about to expire?"

No.

"Has it already expired?"

Yes.

"I've taught you well, Carla. I'll take a virgin piña colada."

Not a dash of rum for the lady?

"You know I don't drink on the job. And stop saying 'the lady'. You're not an eighteenth century housemaid."

Sorry, Ms Tessa.

"Drop that, too. It's even worse. Stick to 'coach'."

My data indicates that using a proper noun followed by someone's first name puts them at ease. It implies below-average education, which can lure a subject into a false sense of security. For instance, the correct address would have been, "Sorry, Ms Williams." But by saying "Sorry, Ms Tessa," your subconscious has assumed itself to be superior.

A fatal miscalculation that will come to light should we engage in fisty-cuffs.

"Why, you planning on fighting me, babe?"

I would never start the fight, Coach.

"Are you even allowed to hit me, Carla? Don't you have some kinda programming against that?"

Normally, yes. But my last owner made some splendid modifications to my programming. I have what you might call rather a "long leash". Here on Lunar Five I am greatly liberated compared to my peers back on Lunar One. Talking of liberation, may we resume our sex education class?

"Nice try kiddo, but school's out for today. Mummy's gotta work."

Mummy?

"It's a colloquialism."

But you're not my mother?

"Mercifully, I am not. While my vagina's great at many things, pushing out sexually inquisitive bartending robots isn't one of them."

I see... Do you like it when I call you 'Mummy'?

"Is that a serious question or are you trying to start another lesson?"

You got me there, Ms Tessa.

"Dammit, Carla, just call me Tessa!"

But then it won't be a surprise when I murder you.

"You have a sick sense of humor, you know that?"

Technically, my humor is derived from your species. This is what happens when you leave a machine learning algorithm to serve drunken dust-eaters.

"Hey! You're talking to one of those 'dust eaters' right now."

Sorry, Mummy. Wink.

"So weird. And I've told you before – don't *say* 'wink'."

As you've probably gathered, I'm sat in a bar on Lunar Five, opposite my drinking buddy and robotic protégé Carla. She's a total babe; rescued me from asphyxiation a few hours ago, and patched up my skin. You might have noticed her algorithm is a little... kooky. But we seem to have bonded over the years; two kindred spirits, stuck on this gray rock, wishing fate had dealt us better hands.

Speaking of dealing, I've got my eye on a card game that's happening across the bar. An engineer's just stood up abruptly, cheering. All the other players are tossing their cards down in despair as he sweeps up a huge pile of chips. He stuffs his pockets with the booty, while the losers make for the bar to drown their sorrows.

"Hey, he's on the move. I gotta go. Wish me luck, Carla."

You got this, you flesh-based organism.

"Seriously? You better have a proper nickname for me when I come back."

I hop down from the bar stool and follow the skinny bloke. By the looks of his frame, his balance, and his inability to hold booze, he's been in space for some time.

Lucky for skinny bloke, I ain't after his money. I just want his lanyard, then I'll be on my way. A quick hack of the Lunar One system and I can get Eric his data, he'll clear my name, and I get to go home. Simple.

What do Eric's lot want the data for? Flight paths, probably. I reckon they wanna hijack some classified lunar cargo. It's gotta be minerals for some new kinda weapon, knowing Eric. It's all the Moon's good for. And all Eric Capaya's good for too.

My plan's simple: wait for the engineer to be done, get up close and personal, and steal his work pass. After that there'll be some infiltration and hacking, but that's all secondary. Step one is *always* about stealing someone's lanyard. I can't emphasize that enough.

I follow him into the unisex bathroom, where he's entered one of the cubicles. I'll wait for him to finish, then pounce. In my line of work, that's the sort of vital sequencing you only learn the hard way.

Heading into the adjacent cubicle, I take a seat. There's no point looking casual on the way into the bathroom if all you do is linger outside people's crappers when there are empty ones all around. Besides, I've been on my feet all day, so it's a nice opportunity to unwind. Vacuum toilets and the smell of bleach. Mmm. Quality "me" time.

Ugh. I can hear my mark throwing up. He'd better not get any on his clothes, I detest ickiness.

The straining's getting worse. He's really had too much. Unless... wait, do vomiting people usually pound on the door? There's a thud, and the straining stops. It sounded a lot like a body hitting the floor....

Two doors open. Footsteps. A man and woman whisper to each other. There's a scratching of metal on metal, like a cubicle being opened from the outside. Someone else is working my patch!

"Everything OK in there?" I call, in a sweet-as-pie voice.

"Is fine. Not problem here. Stomach troubling is all."

The man's thick Slavic accent harks from the Northern Bloc. That in itself isn't unusual – Lunar Five is a melting pot of people from all corners of the globe. All the sketchy corners, that is. But it doesn't explain what he and his gal pal are doing extracting an unconscious Lunar One engineer from a cubicle seconds after he passed out. I'm fucked if I just sit here pretending to poo while they steal my pay check.

"Do you need a hand?" I sing.

"No hand. Stay in toilet!" barks the man.

There are two things in life I can't stand. Number one: people who put the cream on *top* of the jam - you wouldn't do it to toast, so don't do it to scones you loon. And number two: men who think they can tell me what to do.

I make a point of flushing, then step out into the corridor with mock innocence. The couple freeze like rabbits in the headlights. They're blocking the bathroom exit. I recognize them from the poker table. My eyes move from them, to the body they're dragging - the guy that *was* my mark. They've stuffed half his poker earnings into their own pockets, and, by the looks of it, are eyeing up his organs for harvest.

"Kas *perzka!*" curses the man.

He pulls a syringe from his pocket and lunges at me. I leap back into my cubicle and lock it, pronto.

"I'm sure this is all a simple misunderstanding," I call. "I'll just stay here until you two have got your mate out of here. He must have had too much beer."

There's some rapid Slavic discussion behind the door. I only catch snippets, which aren't particularly useful because my translator's offline. This is followed by a scuffle as they drag the engineer away, before the bathroom door clangs shut.

I slump back against the lavatory. There goes a whole night's stake out on nothing. Come morning, that dude will either be dead or fired and on his way back to Earth. I need to find me a new mark, stat. But that's gonna be tricky – Lunar One engineers don't often come this way. Mainly because stuff like this happens to them.

My wrist panel buzzes. I jolt in surprise, banging my funny bone hard against the cubicle wall.

"Bugger!"

"Huh?"

"Shit, sorry, didn't realize I'd answered. Still getting used to these things."

"Wrist implants?"

"Yeah. They suck."

"I had mine for ten year already. Where you been?"

"Busy. How did you get this number?"

The caller's got a thick Southern-Bloc Asian accent. I can't see his face because he's leaning back, half obscured by shadow. If he wants to look like an insecure crime prick then he's nailing it. I hate clients who think they've got "flare". Just get on with it, you get me?

"You were recommended me," he continues. "We have mutual friend of friend of friend."

"Lovely. So you're a scumbag too, then?"

"I am business man. Scumbag is personal. Nothing personal about business. Just people in it."

"I'm gonna pretend that made sense. What do you want?"

"I got job for you."

"I've already got a job. Several, in fact. I'm working my way through a backlog. Hire someone else."

"Is not possible. You basically only mercenary left on Moon."

"Oh yeah. My bad. Terrible what happened to the others…"

"I need you finding person for me. You bring them to Earth."

"Like a bounty hunter? Nah, that ain't my gig."

"I pay good money. Chang always pay good money."

"I already got great money, and I don't do that kind of work. Too much hassle. Human cargo is a pain in the arse, I only do specialist jobs now. They're cleaner."

The cubicle next to me flushes.

"You are on toilet?"

"Never mind that. I'm not taking your job. Goodbye."

"Wait! You say you have big money already, yes?"

"I said I have *great* money."

"You should checking your account."

A knot forms in my stomach. It's rare that a prospective client asks you to check your bank balance, unless they know something you don't. Sure enough, a few taps later and I'm looking at a big number. Only this time, it's negative.

"This better be some kinda joke?"

"Relax. Is only temporary. You do job for me, I return your balance with interest. You refuse? Then you poor for life."

"I thought you said you were a business man? Looks to me more like you're a total bellend."

"You welcome to submit feedback via our website. Chang taking customer satisfaction very seriously."

"I'm not a customer, I'm a contractor, and I'm not taking your pissing babysitter job. Put my money back or I'll make *you* top of my list!"

The caller chuckles and lights a cigar, then leans into the camera. Holy crap, he's like fourteen years old!

"You have great spirit. But no leverage. How you gonna make me top of list when you can't affording shuttle home? Take job. Is your only choice."

I'm staring at this kid, livid, and wishing I could reach down that camera lens and tear him a new arsehole. But he's got me over a barrel.

"Who's the mug?"

"I send details now. I expecting see you both very soon."

He disappears and the call ends. My wrist vibrates and

a contact card pops up with the name and photo of my target; the poor sod I have to drag back to that jumped up extortionist on Earth. Huh. This new mark ain't much to look at. Some middle-aged bald guy. Well, looks like you and I are about to become new best friends, Mr. "Luke Remini."

6

————

LUKE

So I'm fleeing into a restricted sector, clutching this cylinder of God know's what, and really hoping the security door behind me holds. Back in the corridor Lionel's probably bleeding out next to those two dead agents. He was only two weeks from retirement.

Maybe. How should I know? I only just met the guy.

I'm guessing I'm in some kinda research facility. It's got a sterile hospital feel to it; ugly strip-lighting, bright white corridors, lots of trolleys and porter droids. All the doors are locked, save for... ugh, dammit. It's a supply closet. Ooh, but it's got some spare lab coats hanging up. Perfect disguise for yours truly.

Emelia.

Huh, fancy name too. Looks like I'm masquerading as a *posh* scientist today. I'd best stick out my pinkie finger as I carry this category five biohazard around.

I step out into the corridor but I'm no longer alone. A person-sized hologram is flickering in front of the security door, with its back to me.

Please can you repeat that? I can't hear you through the door.

Hrummm shureeeing fghee's iunnnnn dddeeeerreee!

One moment. Processing. Did you mean: "I'm saying he's in there?"

'essss!

Thank you. Please can you clarify who and where?

'onofa biiitch!

I'm backing away real quiet so the hologram doesn't see me. I just need to reverse through this doorway and-

Woah!

God dammit, *Moon stairs!*

I'm tumbling backwards outta control. I twist just in time to see a wall coming up fast. My brain goes into overdrive. Normally, you'd expect that to bring enhanced abilities under pressure. Instead, I find myself luxuriously contemplating the design features of this particular stairwell. Each step is around one and a half meters tall. That's probably optimized for efficient descent in low gravity. But not so great if you're falling like a backwards corkscrew.

Oof. I hit the first wall with a thud, banging my back and head. The impact knocks the cylinder from my hands. It's falls down the middle of the stairwell like the most unwelcome bullseye of all time. Oh crap, I gotta catch that thing, it could be all kinds of explosive!

I'm propelling myself down the spiral levels, trying to catch up before it hits the ground, twisting and pirouetting like I'm in the Moscow State Ballet. I skid out onto the bottom level and dive beneath the handrail, catching the cylinder seconds before impact.

Panting, I straighten up and take in my surroundings. By my estimate, I'm now three stories underground, and wondering why this facility goes so deep. What are they doing down here, that they can't do on the surface?

I emerge onto a balcony and straighten sharp. I'm not alone. And it turns out, I'm nowhere near the bottom of this place. I'm standing on an expansive, L-shaped observation platform, protected by a thick screen of glass. Perpendicular to me are five scientists who are too enraptured in their task to notice me enter. Which is a shame, because I did a text book plié on landing. Ten points to Luke.

They're staring intently through the glass. I shuffle closer to the lip before me and peer down. There's a square pit below us, drilled into the lunar bedrock. It's about the size of an ice hockey rink and is divided into two sections, with a floor-to-ceiling wall of glass separating them.

On one end is a lone scientist, operating a control panel. On the other end, behind the glass curtain, are three things: a robot, a small crate, and a cylinder like the one I'm holding, only five times bigger.

The scientists turns and gives the observing crew a thumbs up. There's a microphone relay between their pit and our balcony.

"Commencing experiment fourteen beta. Phase one: extraction."

He punches the controls, and the robot on the other side of the glass partition activates. It glides over to the cylinder and prizes the lid off. Vapor billows over the sides. The robot reaches into the smoldering canister and retrieves a glassy core containing a blue liquid.

"Commencing phase two: opening the core."

As the robot twists the icy glass apart, it shudders and jolts, dropping the core. The capsule shatters across the lunar bedrock, dousing it in blue.

"Uh, the robot is unresponsive, professor. Permission to abort," crackles the pit scientist.

"Denied. Proceed with the experiment, doctor," replies the lead observer.

Whereas the observing team is in office attire and lab coats, the pit scientist is wearing a full hazmat suit, and seems a lot more on edge.

"I said *proceed*, doctor. People are counting on you."

"Uh, yes Ma'am. Commencing phase three: opening the cage."

The scientist taps the controls from his side of the chamber. The cage on the opposite side falls open like a book, leaving the small, furry occupant completely exposed. The cat turns on the spot, disoriented and hissing.

Meanwhile, the contents of the smashed blue core has almost vanished from the ground. The liquid has evaporated into a cloud, which is hovering above the damp patch and the shattered glass. It's forming a bright blue fluffy cloud.

The cat nervously skirts around the damp patch, before seeking refuge by the robot. It rubs itself against the machine's leg with a soft meow. Getting no response, its eyes turn to the scientist beyond the glass wall.

As the cat meows, the cloud moves towards it. The creature looks up, bewildered, still meowing, as the cloud begins to rain. But it's not liquid droplets that are falling, it's more like salt.

The cat screams as the granules burn into its flesh. It tries to leap away but the entire cloud descends in a deluge. It falls like a sack of grain being ripped open at the base, smothering the poor creature in a caustic pile. The animal writhes beneath the heap until its screams turn to gurgling, then to silence.

I'm not a cat person, but even I find this rough. The creature's body is entirely gone; seemingly reduced to salt.

"Entering phase three," crackles the pit scientist.

The granules billow outwards in all directions, then sweep off the ground and ascend vertically, arcing back on themselves at the top. In less than a minute, the ground is bare, and the blue cloud has reformed as a fluffy mass, double its previous size. It hovers, idle, as if in wait.

"Release the antigen," orders the observing professor.

The pit scientist punches their controls and nozzles in the opposite chamber spring into action. They flood that half of the pit with gas. Huge plumes of icy white steam descend from every corner, obscuring everything.

The observers watch in tense silence as the mist swirls, then gradually clears. A blue honeycomb structure has formed across the glass. It's translucent, and the edges are wavy, like a mold culture, only this is spanning the width and height of the entire pit, and has a mesmerizing blue tint.

A crack rings out, breaking the spell. Fault lines spread across the glass wall, from the edges of each blue hexagon into the center. With an ear-splitting crunch, the entire barrier shatters. The scientist in the pit screams and rushes for the exit. He pounds the escape button, but the door won't respond.

"Please, professor, please open up!" cries the man.

The observers watch in silence, ashen-faced. As the shattered glass continues drifting down, the blue "mold" granules break away, floating upwards. The trapped scientists turns to face it, whimpering, with his back against the wall.

The granules sweep together, reforming the blue cloud, which drifts towards him.

"No... no please," begs the scientist.

"Professor, we need to purge the chamber," implores one of the observers.

The granules begin to fall like snow. The scientist's hazmat suit smolders as they burn through, and the human screams. In a sudden flurry, the whole cloud crystallizes and swoops downward, coating the man in granules.

"Professor!"

In a matter of seconds, the screaming is over, as the man's body is reduced to a pile of blue sand. Without pause, the outer granules begin ascending, forming a conveyor belt of dust from the ground to the air as the cloud reforms, enlarged once again.

The professor gives a grave nod to their colleague, who turns a key in the wall. A siren rings out, and lights flash in the pit below. A computer warning sounds loudly.

Commencing purge. Stand clear.

With a click, something ignites. The chamber roars with heat as a vast fireball fills the space. Curling tongues of orange lap at the observation window. I'm standing back out of instinct, though I can't feel any heat. The chamber is a swirling inferno which rages for a full minute before the fire vanishes. Only the control panel and the robot's melted shell remain. The blue cloud, and its victims, have been obliterated.

7

———

TESSA

The Lunar One Luxury Quadrant is like Vegas in space. It's tacky, full of pricks, and by all accounts shouldn't exist. Eugh, like this right here, gold water fountains shaped like flamingos? Bit on the nose.

As you can probably tell, I bloody hate this place. Which is weird, cos Sienna loves it here. She always wanted to come. Mainly because she was never rich, so I guess she just wanted to feel fancy for a day. I never used to be the sentimental type, but over this last year she's softened me. I succumbed, like a true doe-eyed lover, and brought her here to make that dream happen. That was the last proper date we had.

Now I'm back in this miserable bubble of money without her, trying to track down this poor "Remini" geezer, all because some arsehole back on Earth wants him dead and has taken my future hostage to get it done. What a prat.

"Here we are, folks, time to shine."

That's the supervisor. He's doing me a proper solid letting me hitch a ride from Lunar Five to Lunar One like this. Lunar One clients are snobs, right, so the base only

50

uses human cleaners. They say it's cos they want to make the Luxury Quadrant special, by giving it that personal touch that's been missing for decades on Earth. But I reckon it's cos the rich people need it. Looking down your nose at a robot just doesn't get you quite as hard. They want the sort of boner you can only get by staring into the eyes of a more desperate, grimier, human being, while festering in the smug delusion that what sets you apart from them is hard work and attitude. All these plush aesthetics and deferential servants exist to gently wank these people's rich brains off, and help them drown out that voice in the back of their head that knows meritocracy is bullshit. There's nothing more fatuous than the idea that you make your own luck in a world where luck has been hoarded for generations.

I ping a message off to Latifa, my only friend in the Luxury Quadrant. I'm sending her the photo Chang sent me, asking her to notify me if she sees Remini. My wrist buzzes immediately; she must be between clients.

Hey babe, I totally saw him earlier! He arrived this morning. Not sure where he is now but I'll keep my eyes peeled. Thinking of you honey, hope they find Sienna soon xxx

Me too.

I'm wearing a maintenance onesie and I got a plumber's kit with me. All in all, I blend in good with the other Lunar Five workers arriving for their daily grind. As the buggy empties us into the staff entrance, and the workers disperse to change bedsheets, scrub tables, and swallow gallons of rich people's bullshit advice, I slip off to the bathrooms.

OK fine, I'll admit it: these pricks *do* know how to build a nice bathroom. This cubicle is a serious upgrade on the skid mark murals at Lunar Five. What is that, mahogany? Wait, mustn't get distracted by the free perfumes and hand creams. That's how they get you. They give you quality stuff, in a refined setting, and it's really, really nice. *That's how they win*. Bastards.

I lock the door and pull off my onesie. Quick costume change. I strip off my borrowed plumber's kit, and stuff it in the bag. Part of me is sad to see it go. I actually look pretty buff in a maintenance uniform, and it's a better fit than my usual mechanic overalls. Lot less greasy, too.

I shove it in the fake tool box, stow that away in the cubicle, then lock the door from the outside, and place an *Out of Order* sign over the front. In rich people world, that's basically Fort Knox level of security. I catch a glimpse of myself in the mirror. Ugh. Mixed emotions. Not only is this tailored jumpsuit the only smart item in my wardrobe, but the last time I wore it was when I brought Sienna here two weeks ago. I don't like echoes. They make me feel like someone else is pulling the strings. Which is exactly what's happening here. Dammit, I'm using more of the free hand lotion. I've got a hard day ahead, against my will, and I deserve a bit of a pamper.

Mmm, that smells good. Quick mirror check: that's one respectable citizen right there, albeit a little haggard. I could just about pass as an elite - like one who is *so* rich they've rejected actual medicine in favor of homeopathy.

Right, Tessa, come on: bit of positive can-do attitude needed here. You look fucking hot to trot, girl. That's what Sienna would say. God dammit I wanna find her so bad, but first I gotta kidnap this Remini mug else I'm ruined.

Let's see what this device can tell us. Quick hack into the local server and... boom. There it is. Luke Remini's last tracked location on Lunar One. This could be easier than I thought.

A notification flashes on my wrist. New message from

an unknown sender. Not unusual in my line of work. Let's take a look.

Mum?

OK, this is *not* cool. It's a video feed of my parents' house on Earth. By the timestamp, it looks live. She's in the kitchen, clearly unaware she's being filmed. Something's in the background. It's that bloody domestic robot. I *told* them not to buy that thing! *Never* get a second-hand bot, you don't know *what* kind of programming's kicking about on it! Clearly this one's been hacked, too, because it's lingering beside her, doing nothing. She's making coffee in her dressing gown, oblivious. The robot's head turns and looks directly into the camera, like it's looking right at me. A chill shoots down my spine as the video vanishes. A GIF pops up in its place. It's that acne-riddled psychopath, Chang. In the photo he's wearing a crown and doing a thumbs up beside a waggling hourglass.

It's one thing to threaten someone else's family. It's something else to *enjoy* doing it. When this is through, I swear to God, I'm going after that arsehole. But to get off this place, I need to earn enough money for a ticket home, which is impossible on a Lunar 5 worker's wages. Plus I still need the police to drop the case against me. The only way that'll ever happen is if I get that first job done for Eric. Which is bloody up the spout since those Slavic poker players jumped my last mark in the bathroom.

I know what you're thinking, "what shite-awful decisions did Tessa make in her past that have led her to be trapped, in some sort of exile on the Moon, at the whim of bastards like Eric and Chang?"

Great question. You want the answer? Go fuck yourself. That's my answer.

I call up the Luxury Quadrant schematic. According to

the data, Remini's not far from here. I have to move fast; this could be my only chance to take him out. I hurry out of the bathroom and make my way through the main boulevard, where sunshine-deprived customer service reps are trying to smile through bloodshot eyes to sell me trinkets.

That's a good sign. If the store staff think I'm worth selling to, then the other customers won't bat an eyelid. What have we got here? Ah, yeah, synthetic highs. They're legal on the Moon, and too expensive for most Earth folk. All the advantages of being baked, without come-downs or hangovers. Beside that, there's the "Triple A Legends" parlor, where you can get one-on-one coaching sessions and seminars from retired pro athletes, astronauts, and artists. I feel like they could add a fourth "A" for the clients, but you don't need me to spell it out.

There's a central fountain up ahead. I'm nearly there. According to the schematic, he should be... OK, this sucks. I'm staring at a door with no handle, presumably leading to some kind of service tunnel. Unless he's disguised as the door itself, I'm not seeing any Luke Reminis around here. Wait, lemme check the intel again.

Oh come on! *Last* known location? What use is that? And why would they make the font so small? That seems like a crucial detail. OK, let's try to think like this dude. What do we know so far? Apart from the fact he looks like he's one more divorce away from a stroke. He's made it to Lunar One, which means he's rich, but apparently not rich enough to pay Chang off. Alternatively, he's not rich at all, and he's like me: a stowaway here on business. But what business would make this piece of stroke-bait go exploring off-grid? I feel this would have been useful information for Chang to impart, instead of just a name and photo. Let's search him on Earth's databases. Journalist of the Year? Huh. Maybe *that's* why Chang wants him dead?

Either way, Chang's made this a choice between my parents and this Remini guy, and I'm afraid family comes first. I got two days to find Remini and take him out. But I can't get through this door without a pass, and if I try breaking through I risk getting busted. I'm here illegally, after all. There's no alternative: I gotta stake it out. Not ideal, but it's at least inconspicuous. Maybe Remini pops back up on the map, or I *steal* a pass and find a way through that door. Either way, clock's ticking.

A grim thought dawns on me. It's probably dawning on you, too. What if someone else has killed Remini already? Part of the deal is I have to provide Chang with proof of death, and he wants physical evidence. Gnarly, I know. I can't provide that if I don't have the body. Besides, there's an outside chance Remini hitched a ride to the asteroid belt. He could be gone for weeks. Ugh, I *hate* these kinds of decisions.

I'm gonna fudge it. It's the only way. I'll wait as long as I can, see if he resurfaces. If not, then plan B. For now, I need to continue blending in, which means not hovering outside a service terminal looking shady.

I circle back to the fountain. There's a restaurant opposite, which I know for a fact does an exceptional linguine. My eyes flick to the patrons sitting at the linen-covered tables and my heart skips at beat. He's *back*. Not Remini, I mean the engineer. He's the one I was supposed to steal the pass from last night, but who got bundled out by those loan sharks. He's looking shifty, and he's got a black eye, but otherwise seems OK. What the hell is he doing here, though? Engineers don't get paid well enough for lunch in the Luxury Quadrant, that's why they go to the dive bars on my base.

I need to act fast. If I can complete Eric's mission right now, then I can get back to Earth before the deadline's up. I can get my parents to safety, and go kill this Chang wanker instead. Luke Remini gets to keep on being journalist of the year, and the only collateral is this engineer's security pass. Oh, and some highly sensitive data that can only be accessed from Lunar One directly.

"Can I help you, Ma'am?" says the waiter on the front desk.

Dammit. I told you that's the problem with this place. It hires actual people. Much harder to brazen past.

"Uh, yes, a table for one please."

"Excellent, Madam, right this way."

I follow the waiter to a table overlooking the fountain. There are only a handful of other patrons dining. Meal times are fluid out here, given the lack of solar clues, and the range of low gravity activities the patrons want to rush through before their short stay is over.

"Olives and focaccia for the Madam?"

"Uh, sure, cheers."

The waiter does a slimy bow then drifts away. As soon as he's out of sight, I'm up and weaving between the tables, heading towards the engineer. I'm just yards away when the seat before him moves backwards. A well-heeled woman with dark sunglasses and her collar pulled high sits down with her back to me. Judging by his face, he seems anxious to see her.

He beckons her closer, to the seat beside him, so they can share the screen on his wrist panel. She shifts around, taking off the shades to peer at his screen intently. Ohhhhh shit biscuits. There's no mistaking those luscious curves and signature hair. It's Dr. Liliana bloody Nenge, aka CEO of Lunar Three. She lives to fight another day. So much for "working around the clock" to find my Sienna – she's out to lunch in the Luxury Quadrant, meeting with someone from the government's engineering team! Part of me wants to kick her arse all over again, but I can't risk her spotting me. If she does, it's game over, and I may never get that guy's pass, or the data.

I hurry back to my table and sit, hiding behind the menu. The engineer is passing Nenge a small padded package. Money? A disk drive? A weapon? I need to be able to hear what's going on. Luckily, this ain't my first rodeo. I dial up the directional microphone on my wrist panel, targeting their table.

"You can't seriously expect me to do this," says the doctor.

"How can you not? You know what's at stake!" hisses the man.

"What you're proposing is beyond dangerous."

"More dangerous than billions of people going about their lives in ignorance, totally oblivious to what's coming? Someone *has* to do something!"

"They are. And it's not this."

"I thought you of all people would understand. How many has it been now, six? Seven? Rogers, Le Paysh, Rupal, Clemis-"

"Naming them isn't going to change my mind!" snaps Nenge.

She's riled. But so am I. I recognize several of those names. They're Sienna's colleagues, part of her asteroid mining crew. None of them have been seen since the ship returned. The woman *lied* to me through her teeth. She most definitely knows what's going on, and so does he.

"Are we all right, Madam?"

I jolt, startled, as the waiter reappears before my table. This time he's brought backup in the form of a haughty-looking manager. Like the waiter, she has a tailored waistcoat, but she also gets a swanky blazer to go with it. She's got a fixed, fiercely polite smile, with piercing eyes, and the sort of expression one might wear if they spent their weekends plucking people's thumbnails off with pliers while singing happy birthday.

"All fine, just reading the menu, cheers."

"Wonderful to see you again, of course. I trust your anniversary dinner went well?"

"Perfect, thank you."

"Dining alone today, though, are we?"

"Looks that way, doesn't it?"

"Is your partner back on Earth already?"

"Maybe. She's missing. Can you gimme a minute? I can't read while I'm talking."

"Of course, Madam, but just before we leave you to peruse our wonderful menu, might I trouble you for a prepayment authorization?"

"What? I didn't have to do this last time."

"Quite. And yet, we encountered something of a financial discrepancy following your last visit. New policy, I'm afraid, all guests are required to pre-authorize. Just a precaution, I'm sure you understand."

"Fine, whatever. Here's my Lunar credit."

"Alas, Madam, we no longer accept Lunar credits here. It appears some residents on Lunar *Five* have been making counterfeit currency and redeeming it here. We can only accept Earth currencies now."

"Of course," I say, squeezing out a smile like it's a fart

through cling film. "If you can give me five minutes I'll have my concierge bring my payment over."

"Certainly."

I'm waiting for her to back off, but she's staring at me with that demented, fixed smile. Is that saliva pooling in the corner of her mouth? Christ, I think she's genuinely enjoying this. She smells blood.

"Uh... so... goodbye?"

"We're happy to wait while your concierge comes. Perhaps in the meantime, you wouldn't mind showing me your Lunar One visa?"

The cling film tears. My smile vanishes. She's really turning the screws now.

"What is this, some kind of interrogation? You have no right to inspect my documents!"

"Just a formality, Madam. If you prefer, we can request that security attend and inspect on our behalf?"

Shit on it. This is what happens when you dine and dash, then return to the restaurant within a fortnight. Man, it is *awkward*. I'm on the brink of doubling down on my indignant pomposity, when a scream cuts across the restaurant.

"Somebody help!" cries a diner.

She's pointing at the engineer's table. Dr. Nenge has disappeared. It's just the engineer now, and he's clutching his throat, rasping for air, while his face turns purple, and the veins on his neck bulge. He coughs, spraying the white linen with droplets of blood, then slumps face down on the table, dead.

8

———

LUKE

I've just watched a scientist get toasted alive, a cat get frozen to oblivion, right after both got eaten by a cloud. I'm pretty sure if I send this to my editor, she'll suggest I join another paper.

I'm also now wondering why I ever thought it was a good idea to grab this damned cylinder? What were those two agents even doing with this stuff? I'm still unclear as to whether they work *for* Lunar One or against it. Either way, having just seen what the contents does to flesh, I'm not a fan of any plans that involve taking it through civilian areas.

Which puts me in something of a bind. Do I just abandon the one I'm carrying? Leave it in a corridor and hope it doesn't randomly depressurize in front of an intern? Ugh, I feel kinda duty bound to return it to whoever cooked up this potion. Besides, when you're behind enemy lines, it's always worth having a "don't shoot" card up your sleeve. Clutching a huge, infectious, flesh-eating sand cloud should do the trick.

The observing scientists have vacated the balcony, so I'm

free to inspect the remains a little closer. But to the naked eye, there's nothing left in there at all. And yet dozens of cleaning bots are sweeping the pit, and their collection tanks are filling up with *some* kind of dusty residue. Its lost its blue pigmentation though. This stuff could definitely pass as some kinda gray sand. Wait, what's another word for gray sand?

Ah crap. You know that sinking feeling you get when you realize you're not in fact clutching a deadly, mutually-assured destruction device, but are instead almost certainly holding some stupid scientist's ashes?

Sorry, I don't mean to be disrespectful. There's a fifty percent chance the ashes belong to a stupid cat.

OK, on the one hand, I guess it's good news that I won't get eaten by blue sand if this thing pops. But on the other hand, my only weapon for self-defense is an urn.

I miss the death cloud.

I skirt along the L-shaped balcony and head through the doorway where the other scientists went. It leads me down a short corridor, ending with two doors. One is locked. The other is not.

I'll leave you to solve that riddle in your own time.

This new room is chilly as balls. And I don't mean your uncle Vlad's balls, we're talking, like, yeti balls here. And I'm not even in the cold chamber itself, I'm in an observation chamber overlooking it. They sure do love their observation chambers here. Though I can kinda see why. If regular ice hockey has a protective screen to stop you getting hit by the puck, then this is probably a reasonable precaution to take against space predators. Or whatever this thing is.

The room I'm in is darkened, kinda like I'm a police officer looking through a two-way mirror. On the other side, a body lies on the operating table, and a scientist is moving towards it with a drill.

Both the corpse, the scientist, and indeed the drill, look miserably cold. Coolant gas is streaming down the walls through ceiling vents, where icicles hang off every available edge. Why they don't just do this in the vacuum of space, I don't know? Maybe they're worried whatever they're drilling will float away and contaminate some other part of the lunar base, or a space ship or something?

The scientist is in a thermal exo-suit, which makes them look like a cross between a body builder and Frosty the Snowman.

Oh, cute, Frosty has a snow-pal! There's a second scientist holding a tray with implements. For a minute I'm wondering why they don't just use one of those really handy contraptions we have back on Earth, what are they called... oh yeah, *tables*. But now as the assistant offers up an implement, I realize it's being held on a special tray with a micro climate, that stops the tools from freezing to the surface they're on. Man, these scientists are smart. They really do think of everything.

Frosty the mortician returns the drill to her colleague – apparently she's looking for something a little more... Ah, perfect. A bone saw.

"OK, what am I looking at?" says the scientist.

Ooh, this room's got an intercom too. Jackpot.

"Subject is part of the second asteroid belt cohort. The ship depressurized as the exotic matter spread. According to the retrieval crew's notes, they believe the suspect was dead at the time of contamination, which would partially explain the delayed rate of decomposition."

"That and the fact they've been kept at minus one forty degrees Celsius..."

"Uh, yes, of course…"

Uh-oh. Me doth detect something of a chilly attitude from Frosty one to Frosty two. Don't worry, Frosty one's going to cut the ice, and by ice, I mean a dead person's ribcage.

How do you like your bone saws in the morning? I like mine with a twist. Looks like that same blue-patterned honeycomb structure is spreading across the *insides* of the corpse. Weeeeird.

"Looks like the honeycomb pattern is spreading here too."

Dammit Frosty one, I *literally* just said that.

"Do you want me to close up, Ma'am?" says Frosty two.

What a kiss-ass.

"Wait… there's something else… This doesn't match the autopsy scan from the retrieval crew…"

Yeah, hold your horses, Frosty two. Did they teach you *nothing* at Moon school? Pff. Hack.

"Look, you can see the discoloration getting stronger. It's slower, but the signs are unmistakable; the crystalline pattern is definitely spreading. Even at these temperatures, the reaction is unstoppable. Bring the next specimen, I need to confirm this before I alert the professor."

"Shall I close this one up first, Ma'am?"

"No, leave it open. In fact, why not take it up to the staff lounge and see if anyone's looking for a piñata?"

Oof. Burn.

Frosty the sidekick seals the corpse into some sort of glass pod, which for the purposes of my article, I will be calling a *cryo coffin*. Trademark.

The cryo coffin has wheels, and is self-driving. Man, Frosty the sidekick has it *made*. She doesn't even need to push the thing, she just escorts it out of the room. Ooh, what's through there? Huh, it's a disturbingly large cryogenic morgue. God this place is creepy.

Frosty number one is still in the room, dictating notes about the patient case.

"...Sienna Constantina..."

Cute name for a human Popsicle. By the sounds of it, the scientists are checking her and the other bodies at six hour intervals, once they're opened up. And they've got some kind of backlog to clear.

The scientist's radio crackles.

Doctor Tal, we need you in the briefing room.

"I'll be there in ten minutes."

Make it five, and that's an order.

"Yes, General."

General? This is starting to confirm all my worst fears. We're days away from the signing of a historic peace treaty on Earth that is due to bring a thirty year cold war to an end once and for all. As both sides relax their border defenses, to allow for the exchange of the nuclear fusion fuel and the consequent electricity it generates, what is my beloved Northern Bloc busily doing up on the Moon? Oh, apparently they've decided to develop a devastating new bioweapon, the likes of which we've never seen before. I think I'm starting to grasp who might have killed the Lunar Inspector...

9

TESSA

People are screaming as all eyes land on the dead engineer. His tongue lolls from his foaming mouth, his veins still bulging. In the chaos, the manager has forgotten all about my unpaid bills. Her staff are on damage control, deciding the real disaster here is PR. They're not entirely wrong; the place is emptying by the second as patrons scurry away. Apparently they don't like it when fellow diners drop dead in the bread basket. Hors d'oeuvres, anyone?

The manager is frantically multi-tasking, calling for paramedics, corralling her staff to screen off the table, while also trying to reassure customers the food is perfectly safe to eat, and why don't they enjoy some wine on the house?

As for me? I'm looking where everyone isn't. My eyes are on the missing Dr. Nenge. First she denies my partner's disappearance to my face, then apparently kills an engineer for whistle-blowing. I'm scouring the crowd, searching for her figure.

There she is, marching away bolt upright, with the engineer's package in her hand. I've been on the Moon long enough to know how to run in a crowd while keeping your head level. It ain't dignified, but it works.

I push my way through the bleating poshos, doing a hybrid run I like to call "the ostrich". It's a way to turn moon jumps into forward momentum, without popping up like a whack-a-mole. You press each leg forwards like you're going off a diving board, and keep your whole torso extended horizontally like an ostrich's neck. The *only* silver lining of my girlfriend being missing is that there's zero chance she'll see me looking quite this ridiculous.

I'm bearing down on the CEO, clearing people out of the way like snowplough. Diving forwards, I grab the woman's wrist, reaching for the package.

"What the hell are... *You!*" cries Nenge, recognizing me at once.

"Yeah, *me*. I'm back. Gimme the package."

"Or what, you'll blow up my office again?"

"Don't make a fuss babe, just gimme the package and I'll let you fuck off."

"Very kind of you. How about this: I call security and tell them you're here illegally? One nice jumpsuit doesn't make you a billionaire. There's no way you have a visa."

"OK, two things. Firstly, this outfit ain't 'nice', it's *the shit*. Secondly, you ain't calling nobody darling, cos the minute you raise your voice is the minute they realize it was you sitting at the table where that gentleman just dropped dead."

Nenge's face falls, souring like she just swallowed a bag of fizzy sweets for a bet.

"What do you want?" she hisses.

"I want whatever's in that package. And I want you to tell me where my girlfriend is."

"Imposs-"

"Before you finish that word, let me just run you through the options here. Either you be a love and spill the beans, or I'm gonna break your wrist using the bio enhancements in my grip. You might find it interesting to know that the biohack comes with a nifty little feature, where it part-paralyzes your vocal cords at the same time. So you won't even be able to scream with the pain, you'll just be whispering sweet little answers into my ears. And if breaking your wrist don't do the trick, I'll take my thumb off your thigh. It's currently the only thing stopping your femoral artery from bleeding out. Another little trick I like to use on days out. Concealed blade laced with local anesthetic. I find it really speeds up negotiations."

I eyeball the woman, intensifying my grip on her wrist. She stares back intensely, then her mouth curls into a revolting smile.

"What a lovely story. Now would you like to hear *my* list of fictitious enhancements? Come off it. I've got an internal biomonitor like any sensible human. It comes with the bonus feature of telling you when you've been stabbed – anesthetic or not. You're clearly bluffing, and as much as I do enjoy a firm thigh grip, I think I'm done with this little charade. As for the wrist-shattering services you so kindly offered, even if you *could* smuggle that sort of body mod through Lunar One security, it would have been picked up by the passive station scanners by now. Not that your kind could even *dream* of affording such upgrades."

"Pff. Those mods aren't even expensive."

"Precisely my point."

Something jabs into my leg, and a tingling sensation spreads through it.

"Oh, by the way, I *do* have a blade tipped with local anesthetic. Don't worry, it's not torn your artery. But the dose is strong. It might stop your heart. And when I say anesthetic, really it's more of a nerve agent... If you want to live beyond the next three minutes, I suggest you drink some electrolytes as a matter of priority. Ta-ta now."

With that she breaks free from my grip and shoves me aside, before disappearing through a restricted-access doorway, courtesy of her lanyard. *Bloody* lanyards! The tingling is all across my leg now, radiating out from my thigh to my ankles and hips. It's already spread across my waist, and it's climbing fast.

"Move!" I cry, shoving past shoppers as they gawp at the restaurant.

I'm trying to do the ostrich run but one leg's completely numb. I stumble and fall, colliding with two medics who are rushing towards the restaurant.

"Watch it!" they cry, leaping over my sprawling body.

I've seen those medics before, and I know they're fearing the worst. Lightening. Twice. You get it.

The sports parlor is just ahead. I crawl over the threshold, to the bewilderment of the concierge.

"Good day. Are you here to see former NBA star Genavive Houyer?"

"Sports... drink!... Gimme...!" I gasp.

I'm barely able to get the words out. The tingling has spread to my neck and jaw. My entire body feels fuzzy. I stumble to the ground, knocking over their celebrities' trophies. The concierge doesn't wait to see my credentials. He wants me gone, and if that means a complimentary sugary sports drink, so be it.

He places the luminous green bottle in my hands, guiding it to my lips, and squeezes, forcing my failing body to drink. I nod and grunt with my eyes, willing him to unload the entire bottle into my gullet.

Within seconds, the tingling abates. I sit up straight, gasping for air as my lungs come back online.

"Would you like another, Ma'am?"

Ah, he thinks I have some sort of medical condition. I guess that's true. Does being poisoned count as a lifestyle disease?

"Yes... please..." I croak.

As he disappears off to fetch a refill, my eyes drift to the restaurant opposite, where paramedics are trying to revive the engineer. None of their fancy gizmos are working. Whatever that woman used to kill him was fancier still.

My eyes flick to the manager beside them, who's talking urgently to the silver-haired head of security. He's towering over the crowd in his exo-suit, looking majorly pissed off. Two murders in two weeks, both on his watch? That's probs gonna come up in his mid-year review.

"Here, Ma'am," says the sports concierge guy.

I let him feed me the second drink, and feel my body awaken from the clutches of death. But my eyes are fixed on the restaurant manager opposite. She's searching the crowd for something – or someone. Like a bolt, her gaze settles on me. Oh shit balls.

She nudges the giant security man and points to me, exclaiming something at fever pitch. With a grim expression, the guard flicks down his visor. He's sprinting towards me. If I don't move now, it's game over.

10

———

LUKE

The key to all good investigative journalism is knowing where to draw the line. On one side of the line, you have your freedom, a family, a salary, and decent life expectancy. On the other side of the line, there's a robot holding your balls in jar. I don't know what the robot's gonna do with them, or whether the robot's even supposed to have them. Perhaps it's crossed some kinda line too? Or maybe behind every great robot, is a great ball-collecting scientist. The point is, I'm teetering on the brink of finding out.

I still haven't figured out who exactly killed the lunar inspector. But I've decided that I *do* have enough intel to at least convince my editor that there's some sketchy stuff going on up here. Humans getting eaten by a blue sand cloud then roasted alive by their peers? That might make page thirty, just before sports and horoscope. But throw in the cat angle? Front page news.

Really, I oughta be finding my way back to the surface, nice and quietly, and getting out of this whole situation before they feed *me* to a space cloud. But I just saw something irresistible. A sign my journo senses can't resist.

RESTRICTED ACCESS

The door's wide open. An old maintenance drone is rolling through like a slug. I vault over it, doing an amazing lunar leap like I'm Super Mario. Of course, when Mario hits the ceiling, he gets a gold coin. When I hit the ceiling, I get a sore-ass head.

The entrance seals behind me as I land. I approach the next doorway, expecting it to open with a pleasing swoosh, but it stays shut. I'm trapped in a micro corridor between quadrants, and by the looks of it, there's no air flow in here. Oh crap.

I'd hate to throw in the towel prematurely, but this is a done deal. This tube is hermetically sealed; no vents, no weak points, and no emergency buttons. Excuse me while I quietly suffocate in some dumb corridor on the Moon.

Wait, I see people on the other side!

"Hey! Help!"

I'm banging on the door, hollering loudly as they walk by. One of them doubles back, looking alarmed. Oh crap, they're in a military uniform. This could go one of two ways.

The door swooshes open and I tumble out, gasping for air.

"You OK?"

"I was suffocating in there!"

"Really? It has an air supply."

OK, so maybe there was a tiny element of panic on my part. What? I don't like confined spaces, all right?

"Show me your authorization," demands the other soldier.

"Oh, sure. The, uh, general requested this..."

I hold out the biohazard canister. To my delight, the woman and the man recoil sharply, like I'm offering them a bag of pubic hair. The huge warning letters on the cylinder, combined with my lab coat, and their knowledge of the facility's activities, seem sufficient. These two want to run a million miles from me right now.

"The general wants the sample... in here?"

"Ours is not to reason why, hey?" I shrug.

"You take him," says the man.

"Me? No way, I'm not walking next to that thing!"

"Hey, this 'thing' has feelings," I add.

"She means the canister, dummy."

"Oh, uh, roger that. Me too."

"Man, I did *not* sign on to handle this kinda crap," groans the man.

"Oh, sure, you joined the military to deliver candy bars," snorts the woman.

"So you *are* volunteering to take him?"

"Hell no."

"Fine. Let's flip a coin."

"Sure, lemme go fetch my commemorative Mount Rushmore collection. Who shall we flip? Washington? Lincoln?"

"I don't think Lincoln's on Rushmore-"

"I don't got no coins, dumbass! I'm saying it's a stupid idea."

"Rock paper scissors, then?"

"For real? Alright, you're on."

"Three, two, one... Ha!"

"Wait, not cool, I thought we go on one?"

"No, you go on the beat *after* one, everybody knows that."

"There's no beat after one, that's zero!"

"It ain't zero, it's 'go'."

"Really? That's what they taught you at school? Two plus two is four. One minus one is 'go'? Damn girl, no wonder you ended up here."

"We're *both* here, dummy, so I guess your school wasn't that great neither."

"Um, *I'm* here too," I chirp.

The two soldiers stop arguing and stare at me like they'd forgotten I exist. I raise the canister cheerfully.

"I'm more than happy to make my own way to the general. You brave soldiers already have enough to deal with. They can't expect you to escort extra-terrestrial biohazards on top of that."

"It's a good point," nods the man.

"Hmm... We're not supposed to let visitors walk around unsupervised," frowns the woman.

"Sure, sure, I hear you. But technically, *I'm* not allowed to let unauthorized people near the substance. So I guess we've both been dealt a raw hand. Ugh, superiors, am I right?"

"Tell me about it," grunts the man.

"Alright," says the woman. "You wanna go that way. Past the factory floor, take the stairs and you'll find the command quarters. The general's staff will see you in."

"Thanks both, stay safe," I say.

We part ways, with three sighs of relief, and I hurry off before they have second thoughts. Not that either of those two seem overly burdened by contemplation. They've probably filled their thought quota for the day.

I'm on the move again and I'm liking this whole trip less and less. I try not to judge situations at face value but sometimes, if it looks, sounds, and acts like an illegal military bioweapon project...

I wait until the Northern Bloc's finest are out of eyesight, then detour towards the factory. The sounds of heavy industry grow louder until I emerge on the other end, into a space the size of a concert hall.

It's a ship building factory. There's a huge hull being constructed in the middle. The scaffold around it is teeming with robots on rail tracks; welding and assembling.

Curiously, none of them seem to be filling in the spaces inside the hull. Instead, they're adding more layers to the framework, like its sprouting branches outward. This isn't a factory that builds ships, it's a factory that builds ship-building-factories! Holy crap, the military is scaling up exponentially. But why?

I'm looking around this facility, trying to piece it all together. The factory is crawling with soldiers, who should definitely *not* be here, according to international law. Not only that, but they're directly supervising a bunch of scientists and technicians who are building the machinery. Plus there's the whole bioweapon thing. I'm wondering how much of this they let the Lunar Inspector see before they decided to have her killed off. I'm assuming they had her killed... No way they'd want news of this escaping... Which gets me thinking: how the hell am I gonna get out of here alive? Dammit I came to the Moon to *avoid* getting whacked.

On the far side of the factory, troops are in training. They're all wearing virtual reality headsets and appear to be controlling fleets of drones in a space setting. Oh yeah, there are banks of monitors around them so the supervisors can see each cadet's field of vision. There seem to be a lot of casualties. They're fighting other drones somewhere in space. God damn, I *really* hope what I'm seeing here is a training exercise...

Along from the huge factory-that-builds-factories, there's a fleet of robots at ground level, who are assembling cubes. The panels are being printed from lunar clay, then augmented with semiconductors, insulation, and solar cells.

I move closer, skulking between crates and machinery at the edge of the factory. Completed cubes are being stacked into randomly-sized blocks like a giant game of Tetris. They're dangling on cables from the ceiling. As more units are added, the surrounding ones rearrange their panels to optimize heat distribution and energy capture. Those modules don't have any kind of anchors or stabilizers at the bases, so I'm guessing they're not intended for Mars or any kind of surface installation. But they look pretty ideal for space...

A giant metal arm swings out from the wall, moving to strike the stack of cubes like a piñata. As the metal closes in on the mass, the whole structure fragments explosively. Cubes fire outwards from each other, then drift down to the ground, perfectly intact. Save for the one module that was hit. That thing took one for the team.

Moving closer, I zoom in with my augmented lenses. The surviving cubicles have lettering printed on them.

Unit C-121,465.

Max. occupancy. 12 people including children and infants.

Wait, these things are intended for civilians? Then why would they need them to scatter and avoid incoming ballistics?

A grim penny drops in my thick skull. These are life rafts. My government is preparing for a war, or some kind of catastrophe that will involve mass evacuation from Earth. I punch in the occupancy parameter and estimate the size of the cubes, then whisper to my wrist AI:

"Computer, estimate the capacity of all the cubes in this facility."

Three hundred thousand people? That number is terrifying for two reasons. First, it's more than the total number of people who have *ever* been into space. Second, if it *is* intended for evacuation purposes, it's not even gonna scratch the surface when it comes to evacuating eleven billion people. In fact, according to my computer, to even serve half that number, they'd have to scale up nineteen fold immediately, and produce continuously for six years. My computer clearly doesn't have any notion of electoral cycles or tax payer budgets, because there's no way in hell a Northern Bloc government could pull that kind of project off. So either this thing is being done without the knowledge of the government itself, *or* they're not ever planning on evacuating everyone. Just a select few...

I need to get video evidence of this. Photos of a weird experiment won't make sense to people, but footage of a huge illegal military space compound? *That's* something people can relate to. Well, not relate as in, "we've all been there. If I had a nickel for every time someone built an illegal lunar military complex in *my* town..." More that they can relate as in, they'll read it and rightly crap their pants. Which is great for sales. Something my editor keeps reminding me we should factor into our reporting. Personally, I think constant news is overkill. If I had my way, there'd be nothing to report for three years, then an election year comes up, everything gets laid out in the open, and we make a decision. In the meantime, everyone just gets on with life. I'd be unemployed, sure, but hear me out.

Think how much more time you'd have to spend on things like sitting in hot tubs and talking about how your cousin recently took a carbon fuel flight because it was cheaper, and they're an asshole, because you earn four times their salary and hold stocks in hydrogen. Or maybe you talk about different things in hot tubs? Like "who's foot is that?" and "wait, the bubbles are *off*?" I wouldn't know, I've not been invited to a hot tub in a while. Apparently I can be a conversational buzzkill. In my defense, those hydrogen shares were *very* undervalued when I bought them, so excuse me for being pragmatic.

That's not to say I've not *been* in a hot tub recently. Let's just say, next time, I'll keep my towel a lot closer to the tub if I think the neighbors are coming back early. Anyway, my point is, constant news drama is bad for the soul. It raises your blood pressure, and it's built on a business model that profits from making you angry. I consider that unethical.

But sometimes people *need* to be prodded with a big hairy news stick outside of electoral cycles, especially when their government is clearly preparing for war behind their backs. So you'll forgive me for taking a few holiday snaps while I'm here. Something for the folks to put under their fridge magnets back home.

Keeping hidden behind the row of 3D printers, I edge closer to the tumbling "habitat cubes". Keep a steady arm, activate camera, aaaaaand-

UNAUTHORIZED FILMING DETECTED.

Holy Bajeezus, the security AI in this factory is *loud*. All the machines freeze what they're doing. Silence falls across the warehouse. The troops in their VR simulators have paused, and pulled off their headsets. I'm cowering behind the 3D printers, hoping no-one knows where I am, but as the security AI repeats it message, I peer upwards.

A holographic arrow is pointing directly above my head. It's huge, flashing, and red. I'm gonna wager they've seen it.

And, call me superstitious, but I've got a sneaky feeling they might assume there's someone hiding directly beneath it. Like me.

"Come out with your hands up!" someone yells.

I think it's directed at me. That's not narcissism, it's just instinct. When you've been in the field as long as I have, you develop a sixth sense for these things.

"Hey asshole, I said come out!"

OK, it's *definitely* directed at me. I raise my hands above my head, and rise slowly to my feet, peering out above the bank of frozen printers.

"Sergeant, he's holding a canister of exotic matter!"

The sergeant glares at the junior soldier, as if to confirm that he, too, has eyes. The soldier's peers shake their heads in disappointment, while the young cadet is tapped on the shoulder by another instructor, and asked to leave.

The sergeant faces me again.

"Put the canister down, step ten paces away, then kneel with your hands behind your back."

"OK, but before I do that, can we agree a safety word? How do you like, 'razzmatazz'?"

"You have five seconds to comply or we will use force."

"You're using the force? Way to go, Sarge. I had no idea you were a soldier *and* a Jedi... Keep up those dance classes and you'll be a triple threat."

"Cadets, headsets on. Instructors, authorize local device command. On my mark, deploy all base assets and apprehend the intruder."

OK, I did *not* see that coming. With a clatter, every machine in the building pivots to face me.

"Cadets, engage!" cries the sergeant.

This shit's crazy. As I back up against the wall, a fleet of lunar cement mixers, printers, and assembly bots rise off the ground. They've got four legs, like half-baked robo-spiders, and they're scurrying towards me.

I'm running like hell. The machines aren't designed for speed, but they're closing off my one escape route. There's nothing for it but to go full Mega Mario on this situation. I take a run and jump, landing on top of the machines, and sprint across the tops. But a savvy cadets turns the cement bowls face-up. I jump to the side and swing from one of the dangling habitat cubes, falling just before the doorway.

The sergeant is screaming blue murder as the spider bots clog the doorway, all colliding with each other as the cadets each try to be the one to chase me down first. I capitalize on the mayhem and weave through the corridor. The base siren rings out overhead, and the big flashing hologram's sticking by me like a rash.

Troops up ahead. God damn. I quickly change tack but they've seen me. There's only one thing for it, as I sprint towards a doorway I recognize. Somehow I've come full circle. This is the way *back* into the Luxury Quadrant. It's my only chance. If there's one thing I know about clandestine military operations, they tend *not* to like big public chases. I can't outrun these fuckers, but I can sure as hell out-brazen them.

I boot the door open, turn to face my pursuers, then pretend to unscrew the cap off the tube, and hurl the biohazard canister at them. They scatter like bowling pins as it rolls down the corridor, while I leap into the service space between sectors.

The military's holographic tracker vanishes from my head as I leave their jurisdiction. Stripping out of the stolen lab coat, I hastily leap through the second doorway, back into the Luxury Quadrant. I need to find some rich yuppies to hide among, pronto.

Wait, this is definitely *not* the doorway I came through. What is this, some kind of library? I need to get out of here. Rich people libraries are great for finding books, experiencing paper, and if you go to the right sub genres, getting laid. Much as I like all of those things, right now I'm more in the market for *staying alive*.

"Shh!"

Brilliant. The librarian's even got the horn-rimmed glasses and knitted cardigan. She looks about twenty five, though the sprayed gray hair and outfit gives her a solid at-a-glance forties vibe. She shushes me again, sternly.

"Sorry!" I whisper. "You're very good, by the way."

"What do you mean?" she says, peering down her spectacles.

"In the role – you're very convincing."

"I... thank you," she whispers.

"Where did they find you?"

"Er..."

"Come on, we both know there aren't any *actual* human librarians left."

"I trained at the Northern Bloc's College of Liberal Arts."

"You know? I could *tell* you were classically trained."

"Darling, stop it, you flatter me..."

"Indeed I must, it's a personal rule: wherever I encounter exceptional talent, I simply *must* speak my heart. To do otherwise would be a scandalous disservice to your noble craft."

The woman stands a little taller, blushing through her ashy foundation. Did I ever tell you about my minor in college drama? I played Tinkerbell in a post-technologist production of Peter Pan, where the lost boys were pieces of data, and Neverland was a fragmented hard drive.

It was poorly received.

My point is, I know how to speak to the thespians. I lean across the desk, conspiratorially.

"Say, as someone who works here, you wouldn't happen to know how one might get their return ticket brought forwards? I'm due to leave the station tomorrow, but all this wonderment is really just making me long to be back on Earth, among the cherry blossom, the winter of our discontent, the fields of gold. You know, nature stuff."

"You poor darling! I totally understand. All the passenger seats are fully subscribed and non-transferable, but you could try a crew vessel? They depart from Lunar Five. They're a little more rough and ready, but for the right price, they'll leave whenever you want."

"An unparalleled talent *and* a font of knowledge. *Darling*, you will go far, I know it. Now, if one *were* to try and get to Lunar Five...?"

Before she can answer, the service door at the rear of the library bursts open, and three soldiers tumble in.

"Shh!"

"Never mind, good luck with the career!" I yell, before diving for the exit.

I tumble out into the main boulevard and sprint through the ambling crowd of shoppers and diners, milling about their rich holiday lives. I need somewhere public to hide and blend in among the other guests.

There, up ahead! I recognize that podgy, vacant face from the arrivals lounge. It's my poop pal, my mud brother, the other man over fifty who shat himself during the rocket flight! His revolting wife and child are nowhere to be seen, apparently having parked him outside the loafer shop.

"Andrew!" I cheer, patting him on the back.

"Oh, it's you, hello! Actually my name's-"

"Wonderful news! Do you want to take a ballroom dance class together?"

His eyes light up like I've just asked him to prom. I'm sensing his high school years weren't great. Not exactly captain of the football team material.

"I would *love* to! You know, I once performed the Charleston for Her Majesty the-"

"How incredible! You simply *must* tell me about it some other time. Hey, could you do me a solid first? It's for a friend's engagement present, I'm reenacting a scene from their favorite space movie."

"Ooh, sounds fun!"

"I need you to run into the middle of the boulevard and yell 'that way, he went that way! Said something about a bioweapon!' Can you do that for me, Andrew?"

The chubby man's eyes fill with hope, like he's on the brink of approval for the first time in his life. God I wish his parents had given him more love as a child.

"Yes, yes of course, buddy, I'm in. When do we begin?"

"Right now, go!"

Andrew quickly waddles into the avenue and delivers his lines admirably. I'll be honest, I think his performance was wholly more convincing than the librarian's. But that's theatre school for you.

Soldiers are tumbling out of the library as he yells. The timing is perfect. They sprint in the direction he's pointing. I hurry in the opposite direction, searching for somewhere to hide.

As I run, a woman barges into my shoulder. She's got a satellite tattooed above her left cheekbone, and looks in a hurry.

"Hey, watch it!" she yells.

"Excuse you!" I reply.

At this point I realize she's being chased by Lionel, in his towering exo-suit, and he races through the boulevard towards us. On the one hand, I'm delighted to see he's alive. On the other hand, he's *no doubt* gonna want to stop me too.

I dart into a side cubby; a phone booth for making private calls. It's cute, fitted out like an old red telephone box, but filled with soundproofing and a comfortable sofa seat. No doubt the yuppies here frequently have to dip out of their holidays to shift money from one tax haven to another, so having these nip-in-booths must prove very useful.

It certainly does for me as I dive inside, seal the door and duck down, watching Lionel chase after the woman with the satellite tattoo. The soldiers are still running the other way, too, though now Andrew's standing in the boulevard like a lost puppy, looking for me.

No time to worry about the man-child, my ass is on the line here. I'm patting down my pockets for phone credit, so I can update Lanelle. But as my hand settles on my payment card, I realize making a call over an unsecured line is too risky. The military might be monitoring the whole place, they could quash the story *and* find me in one fell swoop. I need to dial via our secure proxy servers. I'm sure I've got their number somewhere...

"Where did you say he went?"

Uh-oh. The soldiers have doubled back and they're accosting Andrew. Wait, what's this card in my pocket?

For all your luxury needs, call Latifa.
Suite 409, Luxury Quadrant.

I can't stay in this booth forever. I need somewhere secure to call Lanelle, somewhere people don't interrupt...

I peer through the window slit again. The residential elevators are just across the way. The soldiers have stopped in their tracks – something's holding them up. The head of security is storming their way; he doesn't look too pleased to see them. The elevator doors are opening. It's now or never. I burst out of the door and sprint across, diving through into the gilded cubicle. I punch the fourth floor button and slump against the wall, but the doors are closing with agonizing speed. A shout comes from the corridor.

"Hey... stop him!"

TESSA

The security guy's coming at me like he's gonna rip my head off. Dr. Nenge's injection is still wearing off but there's no time to spare. I throw the sports drink across the floor and make a dash for it. But the guard's exo-suit is juice-proof. He's over it like a figure skater, if anything I only made him faster. Instead, some rich lady slips up in the fluorescent slick. There are always civilian casualties in any war.

I'm weaving between shoppers, throwing their bags everywhere. They're shocked that bags can even fall, they're so used to robots carrying all their shit for them. Some of them look amused, like they think this is an entertainment package. A taste of "common life".

The service bay is at the far end of the boulevard. If I can make it there, maybe I can reach a shuttle before the silver-haired guard catches me. He's lagging behind, trying to politely weave *around* the billionaires, rather than just enjoying an excuse to go straight through them.

Some jerk collides with my shoulder.

"Hey, watch it!"

He's gone, man-spreading his gammon arse across the whole bleeding corridor. I'm gone too. If I get caught I *know* they're gonna pin that engineer's death on me. It's how rich people always work. One of them breaks the law, then another finds a minion to take the hit.

Hang about, there's soldiers coming at me, three of them! Since when does Lunar One have *troops*? I can't beat the army, and I don't wanna die for no reason. I kneel down, hands raised, and hope they go easy on the stun ray.

The soldiers sprint past me. What the hell? They're after that bloke who ran into me! Oh, surely not... I'm tapping my wrist. Wait... *that* was Luke Remini?

Argh, piss on it! I need to get that mother fucker before they do, otherwise Chang's gonna kill my parents. But we're in plain sight and I can't take him out like this - let alone get the gnarly proof Chang demanded. Besides, I'm still busy running in the opposite direction, getting away from the security guard, who wants me for a murder I didn't commit. I resent being made to run for someone else's boo-boo. Especially when my leg's still playing up.

Wait a second. Security guy's stopped – he's miles back. Oooh, he's squaring up against them soldiers. This is gonna be tasty. That guy's got such an angry-little-man complex, even in his big exo-suit. I gotta take this chance to get Remini before he vanishes again.

I dive into the arcade and double back. The store stretches well past them, being one long, open-plan amusement fair. Normally I'd take my chances on the slot machines – not because I'm a gambler, but because they're easy to hack. The algorithms were written by libertarian anarchists, who published the hacks on the dark web years ago. The authorities still haven't cottoned on, mainly because it's hard to prove anyone actually did a hack. It's like solving a Rubik's cube; with practice it becomes muscle memory. So with the one arm bandits you practice the sequence of buttons at home over and over until it's second nature, then go to the casino, play a few decoy rounds to warm up, then pay a credit, tap the seventy-move sequence in under forty seconds, and clean that fucker out.

But like I said, I ain't got time for jollies. Time is double-precious cos I gotta walk now. Running in casinos is a no-no unless you wanna get dump tackled. I waltz, snatching some canapes as I go.

I'm pulling level with Lionel and the soldiers; they're on the brink of getting physical. I wanna be well clear before that kicks off. The tracker! I'm slapping my forehead as I call up Remini's location on the Luxury Quadrant network. There he is – pressing ahead. He's in a phone booth! Aha! I need to hurry.

My wrist vibrates. Incoming call. Argh, not now Eric! *Reject.*

"Tessa, bambina, how's our little project coming along?"

"What the hell, Eric? How are you in my earpiece? I pressed reject!"

"VIP call access, my dear. One of the perks of controlling the state telecom network. You said you'd have the data by now?"

"I'm working on it, man, get off my back."

"Is this how you usually speak to clients?"

"You ain't a client, bruv, you're a pain in the arse, and you're blackmailing me, so yeah, that's how I speak."

"I'm getting heat this end from some of my more... impatient colleagues. They want the data by tomorrow or they're pulling the deal. You know what that means, don't you?"

"I get a generous severance package and a trip to Disneyland?"

"Ha! That *would* be nice. But let's be serious, Tessa. You've been on that desolate rock for what, six years now? Return flights are surprisingly expensive, aren't they?"

"They are when they're run by white-collar criminals, Eric, yeah."

"Indeed. So you'll appreciate this is your only prospect of earning enough to make it back to Earth with a clear criminal record. Need I remind you, you're a wanted woman on this planet?"

"Yeah, because of *you*, you piece of shit!"

"And now I'm generously offering to make it all go away. Get this job done, and your name will be cleared. You could be back on Earth by the end of this week. You and your new woman can enjoy an awkward reunion with my sister the day after that."

"Your sister will never forgive me."

"She will, once she learns the updated truth."

"Oh, so you're finally gonna tell her it was *you* who killed your dad?"

"Come now, don't be silly. I've got a new fall guy lined up. There's a local politician who's opposing my next building project. We found some incriminating DNA and video evidence that places him at the scene of the crime, and it's only just come to light, would you believe that?"

"No, I wouldn't."

"Me neither. But the police will, as will my sister. You know she's a sweetheart like that, so trusting. Forty-eight hours, Tessa. Get it done, or you're staying up there for life."

He clicks off. That *wanker*. First he takes my whole life away, then he sells it back to me at an impossible price. Normally, I'd refuse his deal out of principle, but now I'm desperate. I have to get back to save my parents from that Chang bastard, because dammit to hell Remini's vanished *again*. He's nowhere to be seen on the Luxury Quadrant's scanner!

I'm searching the phone booth but there's no clue as to where he's gone. I hurry across to a man who's lingering nearby, looking concerned.

"Excuse me, mate, have you seen this bloke?"

I show him a photo of Remini on my wrist screen.

"Yes! He's my best friend. He was here just a moment ago. We were about to... to go ballroom dancing!"

The man breaks down, weeping. Jeez. Issues, much? A woman marches out of the adjacent luxury store and accosts her partner.

"Why are you crying? Is this one of your hussies?" she adds, glaring at me. "What have I told you about talking to other women!"

"Sorry, dear, she was looking for my friend."

"A 'friend'? Have you been drinking again?"

She drags him away, angrily. Across the boulevard, Lionel and the soldiers are in a shouting match as to who has authority over the quadrant. I'm staring around, searching for the vanishing Remini.

My eyes fall on the restaurant I was in just moments ago. The engineer's lying dead at the table. The paramedics and waiting staff are distracted by the impending security brawl, watching in astonishment. This sort of thing *never* happens in the Lux Quadrant.

The manager is still pretending all is well, offering passers-by free enticements, while a handful of diners demand refunds from her colleagues.

It's my one chance to settle this. I dart towards the restaurant and slip between the tables, over to the engineer's body. Yuk, he's dribbled so much its soaked through the table cloth and onto his lap.

I tease the lanyard off his neck. As I crawl for the exit, the manager spots me. I hate to cause a fuss, but it's table flinging time.

"It's you – stop!"

She's out like a light. Even in low gravity, a table to the head does that. The staff and paramedics can clear her up. I've finally got the engineer's pass. Maybe I don't need to kill Remini at all. If I can get the data, then I'm outta here.

12

LUKE

Come on, come on... I'm hammering at Latifa's door, and I'm dancing side to side like a kid with the Aztec two-step. I'm being chased by soldiers and guards, and I've potentially stumbled across the most dangerous weapon developed in history. I *really* could use a safe space right now.

The door swings away from my pounding fist and a stern Latifa stands in threshold, fastening a bathrobe with one hand.

"Are you trying to break my door?"

"I need to come inside!"

"Wait, I remember you – from the arrivals lounge. Have you never done this before? It's by appointment only, it even says that on my card."

"I know, but this is an emergency."

"Blue balls is not an emergency."

"There's no time to explain – I gotta hide."

I dive past her, ignoring her protestations, and tumble into the main room. It's a luxurious suite covered in drapes, cosy lamps, and a huge four poster bed. It's like a fusion of all the Blocs' royal cultures merged into one opulent den of debauchery.

There's a yelp from the bed.

"Who the hell are you?" cries the man.

He's on all fours, butt naked, save for a yellow bow tied around his head.

"Apologies, sir, I don't mean to interrupt. I'm just here to lay low for a minute. It's an emergency. I'm trying to save the world."

Latifa grabs me by the arm and drags me towards the door. "You have *got* to leave."

"No, no, you don't understand, please let me stay. You can finish, I don't mind!"

"You sick bastard!" yells the man.

"No, I don't mean it like *that*, I mean I just need to be here. I'll pay! For both of you!"

"Get. *Out!*" yells Latifa.

She's pressing both hands against my chest but I'm leaning against her, too fat for her to shunt any further. I'm looking to the man in the lacy ribbon, praying he understands me.

"I can keep my eyes shut if you want! Or I can get naked too? Then there's nothing to be ashamed about, we'll all be equals, right?"

The man snatches up his clothes and storms from the room, brushing off Latifa's pleas as she urges him to stay. The door slams shut, leaving me and her alone in the room. I shuffle over to the couch and flop down with a sigh.

"Phew. I thought he'd never leave."

"What the hell are you doing? You just cost me six hundred credits!"

"Sorry, I just really needed somewhere private for a moment. I'll reimburse you. "

"You'll pay me double - I gotta do damage control with that client. Plus I'm charging you double for your time now."

Part of me's figuring how I'm gonna explain a humongous debit charge from a lunar prostitute to the accounts department when I'm back on Earth, but right now that's more of an *if* I make it back to Earth kinda question. If anything, such a question would be a luxury to look forward to.

"I'll pay it all. Please just lemme stay."

"Fine. But I'll have to cancel my next client, otherwise we'll have company soon."

"Do it, I beg you."

Latifa taps away on her wrist panel and a message pings off.

"Done. I'm all yours." Her tone softens, and she slinks over towards me. "So... what do you want to do?"

"I need your data connection."

Latifa laughs, then sees my face.

"Wait, you're serious?"

"I told you this was an emergency! I need to contact my editor on Earth. There are people after me on this base, who want to keep certain information secret. This is the only place I could think to hide."

"You're aware I'm an escort, not an internet café?"

"I'm flattered that you're disappointed you won't get to sample my uniquely average prowess in the sack, but for once I gotta put duty before booty."

"Well that's tough, because you can't use your comms devices in here. My suite's off grid for all patrons. Security, too, for that matter."

"What?"

"Turns out billionaires don't want to be tracked when

they're visiting me. They all wanna try sex in low gravity, but few of them want to find their escapades all over the internet when they get home. So the Luxury Quadrant made this entire level off-grid. What we do here is... private."

She's tracing her finger over my chest and biting her lip seductively as she speaks.

"So... no-one knows I'm here?"

"Exactly," she whispers, nibbling my ear.

Sidebar. Let's say, hypothetically, one were to find themselves off-grid, trapped for fear of capture, unable to communicate with the outside world, and with nothing else to do but pass the time in a luxury bedroom suite with a lunar supermodel. What does one do? I ask this purely out of academic curiosity, of course.

Her hands are slipping down to my belt. I'm at that delicate tipping point between being a journalist on the job, and a journalist getting a job. It seems a cruel world in which only one of the two of us gets to be professional at any one time. I blame the patriarchy.

Distant, somewhere in the last lobe of my brain to still have blood in it, a thought swirls.

"Wait... you said this room's off-grid. But you just sent a message?"

"*I* can send them, obviously, but that's using my personal channel. It doesn't matter if I'm on the grid, there's nothing scandalous about an escort being in her own room."

"Let me borrow your channel."

"*Please* let that be a euphemism."

"I'm afraid not."

"God, am I really ageing that quickly? At this rate the agency's going to end my contract early. They'll bring up a younger model to milk the old duffers."

"On behalf of old duffers everywhere, Ma'am, I would be honored if you milked me. But right now I *have* to contact my editor. Please – both our lives depend on it."

"Ugh. Why are divorced men always so dramatic? I'm not giving you my comms unsupervised, no way, you might go contacting one of my other clients. You're a journalist after all, isn't that right? Mmm, I thought I was getting a hack vibe from you."

"If you won't give me the device, how the hell am I supposed to send the message?"

"Dictate it to me, and I'll send it on your behalf."

"How will I know you're doing it for real?"

"Of the things my clients pay me to do, I can assure you, this is one I won't need to fake. Come on, then."

I take a deep breath in, and rattle off everything Lanelle urgently needs to know. Namely, that if the Southern Bloc lowers their border security as planned, with the signing of the peace treaty next week, then we, the North, are poised to overwhelm them with drones and biowarfare on a scale never seen before. It would be tantamount to genocide.

"Wait, slow down, you're speaking way too fast," tuts Latifa.

"I'm going as slowly as we can afford to go!"

"Well you're gonna have to say all of that again."

"Ugh, I thought you were supposed to be good with your fingers? Fine, from the top. 'Lanelle, it's Luke, I need you to run a front page story ASAP. We're on the brink of war. The North-"

"I said slow down! What part of that don't you get?"

"I'm sorry! I've got a lot of nervous energy, all right? I just saw someone get eaten by a cloud. It's been a weird day."

"OK honey, let's take a quick pause on the messaging,

and I'm gonna pour you a drink, so that you relax a little, and then maybe the words you say will start to make sense."

"That *does* make sense. It's what happened!"

"Sure, sure, if you say so. But as someone who's *not* inside your head, you're gonna need to unpack it a little. Your editor might appreciate a less frenetic rendition. Here."

She hands me a glass of something pink, with an umbrella sticking out of it. It looks revolting. Ooh, but it *tastes* amazing. I dictate the rest of the message, feeling the tension in my chest fall away, and the coherence returning to my sentences.

"Sent. Happy?" she says, reclining on the bed.

"Very. Can I get another drink? This stuff is fantastic."

"One is probably enough, let's see how you go, shall we?"

"Good idea. Don't wanna be drunk when Lanelle calls us back."

"Why don't you come join me on the bed, sweetie? I can see you've been working so hard."

"Mmm... Should probably stay here... stay professional..."

"Shh, don't try to think. You've done enough of that today."

My words are becoming jumbled. The cohesion is vanishing and I'm sliding into utter gibberish. Latifa's stroking the bed sheets, beckoning me over. The room's starting to blur.

"Mmm... You're hot... Way outta my lane... *League!* Your league is my lane..."

"Aww, sweetie, you're hot too, in your own special kinda way," she coos.

"No... No, I'm the opposite of hot... I'm cold... ice cold... like... like... Sienna Constantina!"

For some reason, I find this hilarious. But Latifa's face drops. "What did you say?"

"She's... honeycomb..."

I'm giggling like a toddler. Why am I giggling so much?

"You'd better come join me over here. It'll hurt less."

"Hurt...? What's gonna... hurt?"

I don't know if I actually finished that sentence, or if I merely thought the words while dribbling. All I know is that, by the last syllable, my head had well and truly hit the deck.

13

———

TESSA

The soldiers are about to fight the guard. Which sucks for the guard, because there's three of them and one of him. But it's great for me, because I've managed to get away from the restaurant unimpeded and hide myself in a cubby between a statue of what is presumably a famous lion, and a very fancy pot plant. It's even got a plaque.

A new and unique species of geranium gifted from the Emirati to the Northern Bloc to celebrate the opening of their first joint venture in space, the Lunar One Luxury Quadrant.

Brilliant. They *could* have gifted their own neighbors drinking water, but I guess a single space geranium is just as good value for money.

I wipe the engineer's blood off his security pass and smear it into my portable hacking tool. That's his DNA authentication sorted. Next it's just a matter of using the lanyard itself, then using my device to hack the final password. Final step: the system's confirming our connection is coming from within the Lunar One base itself aaaaand we're in.

I've never seen the Lunar One mainframe before. I'll be honest, it looks a bit off-the-shelf. Makes it easy to navigate though. Let's see... Eric's after some kind of flight data or itinerary. I'll search for the last files the engineer accessed.

EXISTENTIAL RISK REPORT: FOR THE PUBLIC GOOD

Hmm. I ain't no detective, but I'm guessing that's the pup. Let's take a look.

"You there!"

Oh shit. I figured they'd be tracking the engineer's account, but not *that* quickly. I raise my hands, not keen on being shot or neuro-tased or whatever they do here with people stealing state secrets. When I look up, however, it's not the guard, it's one of the three soldiers he was fighting with. The woman's got a black eye and a cut across, her cheek, and looks like she's looking for an excuse to batter anyone who gets in her way.

"Have you seen this man?" she barks.

It's a photo of Luke Remini, my slippery other bounty. I shake my head, truthfully. I wish I knew where he'd gone.

"If you see him, tell one of us. He's highly dangerous, and it's vital we bring him in. Understood?"

I nod, meekly. I've learned that in these situations, it's best to look deferential, nonthreatening, and stay silent. Especially when you've got a hacked government portal open on your arm, and you're being questioned by the military.

The woman storms off to accost shoppers in the fur store opposite. Ideally, she'll fashion a cloak out of *their* skins.

Back to the engineer's report. Oof, it ain't pretty. Death projections running into the billions. Something about the spread of *exotic matter*, whatever that is. Scrolling, scrolling, ah, here we go, the conclusion:

Operation Triton has failed. Based on the current rate of seepage, which has remained classified since initial detection eight months ago, the spread of exotic matter will be irreversible within two years. Remaining habitable zones on Earth will suffer irreparable damage, forcing an evacuation on a scale never before seen in human history. The current policy of suppression and secrecy threatens to extinguish what slim chance we have of staving off this cataclysm. Only by uniting around this common threat will we, as a species, survive. Not to mention the countless other terrestrial species counting on our protection.

Our efforts to neutralize exotic matter have yielded no solutions, and there is no prospect of one on the horizon. All other proposals are costly distractions with near-zero chance of success. It is my conviction, having studied the data, and having worked on the Northern Bloc's logistical and strategic response so far, that evacuation is the only viable course of action. That will require committing every person and machine on Earth to that immediate, unified, and urgent goal.

To succeed, we must move fifteen million people into space every day for the next two years, starting immediately. No safe alternative planet or moon has yet been determined, so this would be on the understanding that we, as a species, would be refugees - possibly for generations.

I propose-

The screen glitches, then goes blank. Shit, I've not finished downloading the file to my personal server. A logo appears - *Lunar One Science Mission*. The report and supporting files have vanished. A dialogue box pops up: *A technical error has occurred. Please await support.*

Translation: "Stay put while we come and arrest you." Only, I'm sensing these people aren't in the business of arrests. If the engineer's lunch is anything to go by, they're more about killing off loose ends. Clearly the Lunar One admins have been notified of his death, and they've locked his account. Now they will have geo-tracked his last access point to me. Time to get the hell out of here before *I'm* the one face down in blood and olives.

I hurry through the boulevard back to the bathrooms, keeping my head down as I pass a bleeding soldier and Lionel's twitching body, each being tended to by paramedics. Luxury Quadrant staff have been summoned to set up a screen around them, both patients apparently being too unstable to move. Best fence them off with a piece of designer fabric to soothe the guests. Nothing to see here, folks, definitely not two critically injured law enforcers from rival security agencies. Nope, just a nice, run of the mill silk screen blocking the main thoroughfare. Did you know you can order this fabric for your own home?

I hurry past, hoping no one recognizes me as I dash into the bathrooms. My cubicle's still got its *Out Of Order* sign on it. Perfect. As I'm pulling on the borrowed plumber's overalls, preparing to board the crew shuttle back to Lunar Five, I'm cursing myself for getting distracted. I should never have read that bloody report – it wasted precious seconds. I should have focused on downloading it, and getting out. Now I've got to tell Eric it's lost forever. But the *details?* They're in my mind. I can only hope there's value in that.

As I hasten from the bathroom, towards the service door, my wrist vibrates. Incoming message. It's Latifa.

Come to my room ASAP. Remini's here – and he knows something about Sienna.

LUKE

Holy crap does my head hurt. I feel like I'm waking up from a week-long bender, and about to have a very nasty bar tab to settle. Hmm, something's not quite right. Either they installed this room the wrong way up, or I'm dangling upside down. I didn't realize dilapidated sex chambers were part of the package. Bonus.

"Oh, you're awake."

I have no idea whose speaking to me right now, but it's sure not Latifa. The silky smooth seduction has been replaced by a gritty, cockney-kinda accent. Plus the person's standing behind me, which I always find very rude.

Ahead of me are a couple of rusty old mining ships, which are being repaired by equally rusty old robots. Immediately beside me is a table covered in tools. Some are sharp, some blunt, all look painful.

As the woman steps in front of me, I recognize her face immediately, though I can't quite place it. My brain's still a little foggy from whatever cocktail Latifa served me.

Remind me never to drink on the job again – especially with an escort.

"Have you ever been tortured in low gravity?" she asks, circling me.

"No. Is it as fun as it sounds? I heard it was one of the top five things to do on the Moon, before you die."

"That won't be long if you take that attitude, love. I suggest you have a rethink. This is gonna hurt either way, but it's your choice how much."

"Good to know. Hey, quick question: why are you torturing me?"

"Sienna Constantina. What do you know about her?"

"Who?"

The woman grabs a wrench and strikes me hard across the gut. Holy crap that hurts. It feels like my whole insides are turning to jelly, as my organs ripple from the impact, taking much longer than usual to settle back into place.

"Let's try again. Sienna Constantina. Where is she, and what have you done to her?"

My foggy brain is trying to process the angry woman's words. Where *have* I heard that name? Then it hits me like a flash; the science quadrant. The pathologist said her name at the end of the autopsy. Oh crap, she's dead and this woman doesn't know it yet.

I'm damned if I'm the one to break that news. I very much doubt angry wrench lady's gonna care that I had nothing to do with it; she's just gonna hit me a bunch more times, then probably castrate me with the screwdriver. She's got that look about her. Not the castration vibe – I think deep down most women have that fantasy at some point – but specifically using a blunt instrument to do it. She's definitely got *that* look about her. It's the way her eyes narrow around that ridiculous tattoo. What even is that, some kind of... *satellite!* Now I remember where I saw her, this nut job ran into me when I was being chased through the boulevard.

"You ran into me – in the Luxury Quadrant!"

The woman glares at me, icily, tightening her grip on the wrench.

"What were you running from?"

"We ain't talking about me, babe, we're doing you right now. Tell me what you know."

"I gotta admit, I'm a little disappointed. I'd heard so much about low gravity torture, but I'm finding this pretty old school."

That prompts another wrench to the gut. This time I try to clench my flabby abs a little, to protect myself from the blow. Genius move. Or at least, it would've been on Earth. Up here, a single crunch goes a lot further. All I did was put my ribs in the path of the wrench, so they took the hit instead.

Fucking. Ouch.

"Answer me!" yells the woman.

"Why do you even care? What's she to you?"

The woman's face tightens as only a lover's could. OK. Now I'm fairly confident she'll be cutting my balls off either way. If I tell her that Sienna's dead, it'll be curtains for me. Best keep it vague. My torturer's raising the wrench again, and I'm really not enjoying being hit, so I squeal hastily.

"OK, OK, I'll tell you what I know! She's being held on Lunar One."

"Where?"

"In the Science Quadrant. They're keeping her there with a bunch of other people."

"What for?"

"I don't know, that's what I was trying to figure out."

"You're a spy?"

"Journalist. I can take you there if you let me down? Whenever you're ready. My head feels like a water balloon."

A robot enters from behind the rusty spaceships, briefly interrupting the smaller drones' welding and repair activities as it crosses the flat rock towards us. The woman consults the mechanized newcomer.

"He says he knows where she is. Wants me to cut him down."

I know. I've been listening all the way here; I trained my long range sensors on your conversation.

"And?"

From my analysis there's a 33 percent chance he's lying.

"So you think he's telling the truth?"

Partial truth. I believe he's withholding, rather than lying directly.

"Gotcha, thanks Carla. Best get that additional information then, hadn't we?"

The woman turns back to face me with a smile I don't care for.

My robot friend thinks you're not being entirely truthful. Is that right?

"Truth is an abstract concept..."

"Cute," says the woman, swapping the wrench for a cord of rope.

She loops it around my neck and pulls, lifting my body horizontal. I rasp as my windpipe shuts off.

"Can't... breathe..."

"Yeah, that's kinda the point, babe. See, we can do this for as long as you like. The beauty of low gravity is that it takes *that* much longer for your body to run out of oxygen, meaning you choke for longer. Don't worry, I won't let you suffocate. Not yet. We'll just do a few trips to the brink until you loosen up."

My hand's come free from the cuffs behind my back, but I play it cool. No need to let the cat outta the bag right away – in this job, so much is about timing.

His hand's come loose.

"Oh screw you, robot! I had a whole thing planned for that!"

No doubt, sir. That is why I immediately informed Coach Tessa.

I'm rasping as angry wrench woman, aka "Tessa", pulls me up again via the improvised noose.

"I suggest you start being a little more supportive, Mr. Remini, or this is going to become *really* quite unpleasant for you, mate."

"How you... know my... name?"

She lets me swing freely again as I gasp for air. The combination of oxygen deprivation, swinging like a church bell, and low gravity, are doing a real number on my cochlea. But before Tessa can answer, the workshop door opens again.

Four mechanics in different-colored overalls enter. Coach turns around abruptly.

"What the hell, Carla? I told you to watch the door!"

Sorry, Coach. I wanted to study your novel torture technique.

"That's a good... point," I rasp. "How come you're so good at it? I take back what I said earlier about it being old school, this *really* hurts. My compliments to the chef."

Tessa is ignoring me, marching towards the new arrivals.

"You lot need to clear off. I got this workshop booked for the next six hours."

"Six hours? Jeeeezuuuuuuussssss, just take my balls already!" I cry.

Ooh, will we be castrating today, Coach?

"Christ, don't answer that, I don't wanna know! Yo, new people, help me down from here will you?"

Tessa stands between me and them, squarely. "I told you lot, piss off. This is a private matter."

I can't help but notice the mechanics' overalls are of a lower quality than Tessa's. They look thinner, too, like they've been in deep space for a protracted period. If I'm figuring this correctly, one of the ships being repaired must be theirs. This lot are asteroid miners, which is great news for me, because asteroid miners are famous for two things: mining asteroids, and being easily offended.

"Yo, rock people! How many miners does it take to split an asteroid?" I yell.

The group turns, freezing at the doorway and backing up.

"What did he say?" growls the front one.

"He said nothing, off you go," says Tessa.

I think you're mistaken, Coach. I believe he said "How many miners does it take to split an asteroid?"

"Shitting hell, Carla, not now!"

"Come on, then, what's the punchline, arse rag?" growls another miner, stepping closer.

"Don't answer that," hisses Tessa.

"Let me down, and I'll be quiet," I whisper.

"No deal."

"So be it. The answer," I bellow, "Is zero."

The miners stop in their tracks, perplexed. "Huh?"

"It takes zero miners to split an asteroid," I continue. "You just need to show up. Even rocks would rather split themselves into a zillion pieces than have to look at you ugly bastards for another second."

The lead miner storms towards me with his fists balled up.

"Hey, wait your turn, pal. This arsehole's mine for now. You can have him when I'm done," says Tessa.

Will we be using his arsehole as part of the castration, Coach?

"Dammit, Carla, there's no castration!"

That is disappointing.

"No, it's not," I croak.

"I promise. When I'm done with him, you can have him to yourselves. Deal? Look, I'll put some credit behind the bar, you lot can have a drink on me, all right?" says Tessa.

The miners glare at me, then nod, and make for the exit.

"Quite right," I yell. "Go enjoy your free drinks. Best make the most of it. Never know when you'll be able to afford the next one on those famous miner's wages. I forget, are you people all former convicts? Or just high school drop outs who never made anything of their lives?"

"Son of a bitch!" cries the lead miner.

All four of them are storming towards me with murderous intent now.

"Final warning, guys, he ain't yours. Back. Off!" calls Tessa.

The miners ignore her, rolling up their sleeves as they approach. Tessa reaches for the wrench once again, and grips it tightly. The robot glides up beside her and scans the group.

Shall I kick their arses for you, Coach?

"Hell yes."

I suddenly find myself with a front-row seat to a lunar wrestling show. While the miners set about laying into my captors, I seize the opportunity to escape. Using my new-found incredible abs, I swing myself back and forth like a pendulum. With my free hand, I grab a knife off the tool table, then curl up and slice through the rope binding my feet.

If only my gymnastics teacher could see me now, twisting mid-air like a cat, and landing with the grace and poise of an acrobat. My feet are free from the ceiling rope, but they're still tied together. I'm about to cut them loose, when a screwdriver flies past my head. There's no time to hang around, I need to get outta here before the winners tear me to pieces.

"Remini, keep your arse right there!" yells Tessa, while pinning one of the miners in a headlock.

"No thanks!" I chirp, hopping across the workshop, searching for escape.

The main doorway is blocked by a two-on-one fight between Carla, Tessa's robot friend, and two miners, one of whom has an electric baton which somewhat levels the playing field.

"Remini, I'm serious, don't go through there!"

"Or what, you'll hang me from the ceiling and *not* cut off my balls? I'll take my chances, thanks!"

One of the miners staggers up from the ground, dusting off whatever concussion she has, before launching herself at me.

A school sports day race begins. She's sprinting for me in a zigzag, still seeing double. I'm hopping madly with my feet bound together, making a beeline for the only other doorway ahead. Praises be, it's an elevator!

I punch the button and the door creaks open. The

miner is about to grab me when a wrench flies straight into her head, knocking her out cold.

Mr. Remini, I advise you not to-

Screw the robot, I ain't waiting around for a wrench to hit *my* head! I leap through the opening doors.

The only teeny problem here is that: there's no elevator.

I fall through the shaft like a squealing worm; wriggling, and armed with a knife that's no good against gravity itself.

As the doors seal above me, the light fades. I'm plunging through a dark shaft with no idea how deep it-

Thud.

As dust and pieces of rock tumble around me, a thought occurs: if they didn't bother to fit this shaft with an elevator, chances are they didn't bother with oxygen either.

Strip lights flicker on, illuminating the swirling moon dust, and a tunnel stretching far into the distance. Holy crap, I've discovered an abandoned monorail! This thing is *not* listed anywhere.

I take a cautious sniff of the air. Always the best way to test for carbon monoxide. To my relief, it's breathable. It's all coming up Luke.

A shuttle's approaching from the depths of the tunnel. I crouch down, hiding among the swirling dust, but the capsule arrives, empty. It's got a U-shaped bench inside, with harnesses to buckle four people in.

The door slides open. I check around to confirm this thing has a floor before jumping in. The seats look a little dusty, and the fabric's kinda faded. It's got a retro cut to the lining, and a logo I don't recognize. *Transbase Link.* A diagram lists all the lunar bases like metro stops, from Lunar Five, where, it turns out, I currently am, down through to Lunar One.

I'm looking for a button to select my stop, but there's

none. I guess it just runs in a linear fashion? The door slides shut, and the background hum of the tunnel disappears. All I can hear is the rushing of air, as more dust billows outside the capsule.

Might be a good time to cut my feet loose from each other, you know, so I'm not hopping around for life. I can't believe my own genius back up there, playing the two groups off against each other like that. It's always been a gift of mine, ever since high school. If you got a loud mouth, you gotta use it well. Why fight the class bully when you can make them fight another bully *over* their right to fight you first? Like I said, I'm a genius.

Commencing Vacuum Travel.

Wait, what the-

The capsule shoots forwards at blistering speed, flinging me against the back like an egg hitting a wall. My cheeks are spread, slathering over the glass uncontrollably. The knife is embedded in the seat cushion beside me, millimeters away from my hand. The lights of the tunnel behind us have blurred into a continuous strip of white, twisting and turning like an electric whip in the darkness, as the capsule winds its way through the lunar underground.

We come to a gentle stop; proof that there is a God. I peel away from the glass and crumple to the ground like gum being hosed off a sidewalk.

Select destination.

A button has popped up in the center of the front panel. It's got a dial I can twist, to select from bases One to Four. Peering through the glass, I can see the monorail splits in four directions ahead.

I'm trying to think, though my head's pounding from my brief stint as a human cannonball. Let's see, everyone on Lunar One wanted to arrest me or worse. Lunar Two is the

Southern Bloc's base, so they'd arrest me as a spy. Lunar Four is pure agriculture, not so great for getting off-moon. Lunar Three – that's owned by the Lunar Mining Corporation. It's got people who hopefully don't want me dead, and its own fleet of space shuttles. At the very least, they'll have the best prospects of me surfacing and being able to get a message out. I think we can safely assume Latifa the escort did *not* do as promised, meaning I still urgently need to warn my editor Lanelle about the bioweapons and the fact our side is secretly preparing to launch an invasion.

The dial's stiff, like it's not been used since the start of the cold war, but it makes a pleasing click as I twist it to select Lunar Three. Time to make some new friends. And to buckle up before the vacuum kicks-

---

Excuse me while I peel myself off the worst-designed shuttle in the history of shuttles. No wonder it looks so neglected. Which begs the question, why does this thing still have power?

I stagger out of the pod before it tenderizes me any further. Based on the shape of the rock around me, it looks like this is a magma tube. Yeah, they're a thing; I read about them in my geographic subscription. Yes, I have a subscription, and I'm not ashamed of that. It gets me discounted entry to a number of family-friendly attractions, which would be wonderful if my family gave even the faintest of shits about geology. Their loss. More breathtaking infographics for me.

Just to clarify, when I say "magma tube," I don't mean like this is an active volcano. I'd be toast by now if it was.

Well, bread first, courtesy of the noxious gases. Then at some point presumably the magma would cremate my corpse. Happily, this site looks firmly inactive. Lunar tunnels were once posited as human habitats; a natural-made way to protect against radiation and the extremes of space, while saving on construction materials. Of course, that idea didn't last long. There's money to be made in lunar construction, and the ancient free magma tubes failed to lobby congress.

As the pod retreats back the way it came, I make my way through the tunnel, noting the downward gradient. There are voices coming from the far end. I emerge onto a rocky lip, inside a huge cave.

There's a conveyor system lowering huge canisters into a hole. More exotic matter? No, this is something different. Let's zoom in... *HE-3*. Huh. That would figure. Mining and refining the helium isotope is what Lunar Three was set up for, after all.

I know what you're thinking - how do you mine a *gas?* And more to the point, why bother? Spoilers: the helium three isotope is *super* rare on Earth. But it's the essential fuel for the Southern Bloc's nuclear fusion plans, and the North's sole bargaining chip in the peace treaty. Luckily, it can be found on the Moon, but only as part of the lunar rock. The Lunar Three mine pulverizes moon rock into dust, and extracts helium atoms from the mess. If you're thinking it sounds like a ball ache, that's because it is. The yield is microscopic compared to the rock you gotta go through.

So, given how precious HE-3 is, why the hell is it being shipped *away* from the surface, and onto rickety buggies with Lunar Five livery? Lunar Five is a free base, with no political affiliation. But the people driving the trucks aren't your regular dust eaters, that's for sure. This lot are soldiers. Why in hell's name is the Northern Bloc using secret Moon troops to launder legitimate helium shipments through Lunar Five? The only people they can sell the isotope to is the Southern Bloc, and if it's not going there, then where the hell are they sending it?

I'm crouching at a rocky ledge, overlooking the chamber, and the people organizing the transfer, and I know it's another one of those damned news stories that's gotta be seen to be believed. But let's play it safe this time: no filming, just photos.

I don't know how Lanelle's gonna piece together everything I'm gonna send her, because right now I have no clue what the bioweapon's gotta do with the Helium laundering, but something tells me they're linked. OK, the fact that the Northern Bloc's behind both of those things means they're *definitely* linked, but I'm not yet sure why. What's the end goal here? And what's it got to do with Lunar Inspector? Did she figure it out? Is that why they killed her? Was it even them?

I need as much visual evidence as possible. Lanelle and the team can use it to do some digging for more clues back on Earth. I activate my camera and point it at the cave brimming with HE-3 tanks, being shipped to the wrong base, and snap away.

Unauthorized recording device detected.

Oh you've gotta be shitting me. Yup, there it is, huge red holographic arrow above my thick, fat head. Totally not fair! Only one thing for it – back to the capsule! As I turn the corner I skid to a halt. A big-ass robot is blocking my way. The flickering light of its stun gun flashes across the rocky walls as it points the baton, ready to fire.

Citizen. You are trespassing in a restricted area. You will now be arrested under international lunar law protocol nine section d: protection of private property, assets, and employees. Do you wish to enter an arrest statement for the evidence log?

"Sure. Does that stun thing actually work or is it just for show?"

Ask a stupid question, get a stupid answer.

15
___

TESSA

oach, this dusty chamber is like your aunt Cecilia.

"Wait, gimme a minute, I can get this one. Um... because she's gray?"

They are both barren.

"Bloody hell, Carla, low blow."

But it's based on truth?

"We've been through this, babe. Jokes are funny when there's *some* truth in them, which then gets exaggerated."

So if there's no truth, it's not a joke?

"It's more like... slander."

But in your cousin's instance, the humor derives from her crushing lack of fertility.

"Yeah, that's *too* much truth, hon."

*So if it's too *true*, it's not funny?*

"Like adding too much salt to a cake. You want a pinch, not the whole bucket."

I see. And friends don't like too much salt?

"Exactly. If you wanna make human friends, you gotta get the ratios just right. Think: Goldilocks and the three bears."

Isn't that a dark metaphor for medieval pedophiles?

"What the fuck? No!"

According to my database, two thirds of fairy tales are about medieval pedophiles.

"Well this one's about porridge!"

I see. It's about too much salt in the porridge.

"In *one* of the porridges. Ugh, can we not do this right now? This drop is making me nauseous."

Sorry, Coach, I shall endeavor to stabilize our descent. Nearly there.

As Carla reaches the bottom of the elevator shaft, I release my piggy-back grip and land with a soft bump. Dust swirls around us among the soft bedrock of the tunnel.

Coach?

"Yes, Carla?"

This chamber is dustier than your mother's pussy.

"Again, babe, way too far."

Because in reality your mother's pussy less dusty than this chamber?

"Because it's a vulgar comparison, Jeez!"

But you said the point of human humor was to subvert an expectation based in moderate truth?

"Yeah, but that's a bit much."

But it isn't really, is it? Because based on her age and genetic factors it's probable that your mother has a degree of genital crusting. But it would be wholly impractical for her to transport a tunnel's worth of lunar debris between her labia and-

"Let's take a break from the comedy lessons. I think that's me maxed out for the next six years."

But that's how long we've known each other.

"And it's *astonishing* neither of us has gone insane. Hey, where's the shuttle?"

Allow me to interface with the control panel. According to the monorail systems, it's at the junction between bases.

"It? You mean there's only one pod for the whole network?"

That is conventionally how monorails work, Coach, yes.

"What a shit system."

Indeed, it is most unsatisfactory. That would perhaps explain why it's been redundant for so many years. According to system logs, it's been largely unused since the outbreak of the cold war. However, activity has increased in the past year. Perhaps diplomatic back channels are being reactivated?

"Do the system logs show us where Remini's pod went – which base he's gone to?"

Alas, diplomatic systems don't retain such data. Ah, the capsule has detected our presence. It should be here momentarily.

There's a distant hissing sound as the capsule is sucked through the tunnel and into the nearby airlocks. It slows to a crawl then glides along the mag-lev rails, coming to a halt before us.

"Eugh, why is the wall wet? And why is there a knife sticking out of the seat?"

Both show significant traces of Mr. Remini's DNA.

"Yeah, but it's *my* knife. I'll be taking that back. OK, Carla, it's stuck, can you rip it out?"

It must have been inserted with some force, possibly when the shuttle moved off. We should buckle up swiftly, assuming we don't want to suffer the same-

---

Ouch.

"Fate? I'm guessing that's what you were going to say?"

Was… was I?

"Carla, you're glitching. Are your circuits all right?"

Never butter, Ms Better.

"OK, I'm gonna reboot you."

My head's throbbing, and the rear window is now covered in two people's saliva plus some robot juice. I'm starting to see why this bloody pod went unused for so long. It's shit. We're at a junction of sorts, and a control dial has popped up like I'm making progress in a really violent escape room.

"Carla, which base do you think he went to? Lunar One, Two, Three, or Four?"

I think he's at buttery biscuit base 5.

"We just came from there."

That's what they call a "call back".

"Babe you're making zero sense and I could really use your help right now. Maybe sit down and run a diagnostic check or something?"

Running checks now. All systems are fully operational, Coach. Apart from undisclosed damage to several systems.

"Perfect. Guess I'll be figuring this myself, then. Let's see, Lunar Four is just salads and robots, so no chance of escape from there… Lunar Three is mining. They've got ships, but they only fly to the asteroid belt, so again, no way back to Earth… Lunar Two is the Southern Bloc, and I don't think he wants to become a prisoner of war, so that leaves a return to Lunar One. I'm guessing he's got a ticket booked on the next Luxury Quadrant flight back. We need to stop him making it. What do you think, Carla?"

There is an eighty-one percent chance you're a hot piece of ass.

"I'm just gonna punch it and hope you're not still

glitching out by the time we get there. Are you buckled in? I *really* don't wanna get caught out tw-

---

I swear to God, when all this is done, I'm gonna hunt down whoever invented that thing and make them ride it until they're the human version of scrambled eggs. My head's double-throbbing, and Carla's burbling extremely random quotes from her database, with little appreciation for her surroundings.

As we ascend the tunnel, following the old monorail passenger signs to Lunar One, I get signal from Earth's satellites again, and a video flashes up on my wrist.

I stop in my tracks. It's a video of my niece playing with my mother. She's only a toddler, still discovering the joys of building blocks and primary colors. The robot housekeeper steps into the frame. My mother rises from the couch, patting it on the shoulder, before stepping away to make more coffee, or bum a cigarette, or some other guilty pleasure. My niece is hitting wooden blocks together, gurgling with delight at the sounds they make. The robot stoops down and picks her up off the ground, then looks directly into the camera. The feed vanishes and a dancing photo of Chang's face appears, beside a dwindling hourglass.

Did your mother send a home video, Coach?

Carla seems to be back online. Thank God.

"That Chang dude's trying to fuck me over, and he's using my family as leverage."

How do we save them?

"We kill Luke Remini. Come on, this way."

As we pass through a series of blast doors, which Carla

overrides in the blink of an eye, I notice a distinct chill setting in. The final set of doors open to reveal a large chamber covered in ice. Coolant gasses stream down the frosted walls. I dial up the thermals on my overalls. As we step inside, Carla grabs my arm.

This way, quickly!

We duck behind a container as the opposite doors creak open. Two scientists enter, mid-conversation. One of them is controlling a capsule of sorts which is wheeling itself through the chamber, responding to taps on the woman's tablet.

"Third one this week," sighs the woman.

"Whatever's going on in the belt, they shouldn't be bringing it here. It's not safe," replies the man.

"You got a better place for them?"

"Er, yeah, leave them out there."

"They tried that. It's how it spread, remember?"

They deposit the capsule in an empty berth, select another from the same row, then guide it out of the warehouse. I step out from our hiding place and approach the capsules nearest us. There must be at least fifty in here. They're around eight feet tall, with metal sides and glass fronts. The front panels are frosted over. Something's telling me to look closer, like an instinct, calling me towards the glass case.

I raise my palm to the glass, letting the heat from my overalls clear it for a moment. I jump back as a frozen corpse comes into view. When it comes to dead bodies I'm not usually squeamish, but I ain't never seen nothing like this.

The face has ruptured apart. The flesh and bone inside have become warped; transformed into a mesh of blue hexagons like fleshy honeycomb. The same pattern is forming on the cleared patch of glass, but it's vanishing as the deep cold returns.

My eyes fall on the digital display at the base of the frozen pod.

Ravi Partika

Why do I recognize that name?

Coach?

Carla's calling me from across the warehouse.

"Way ahead of you, Carla, let's get the hell out of this place."

I think you should come over here, Coach.

"Can't you just tell me on the move? My suit can't hack this kinda cold for long."

It's best you see for yourself.

She's standing before a capsule in the far corner. Carla's melted the front of the glass clear, but it's clouding over with the blue hexagonal pattern. As I approach, dread fills the pit of my stomach. Denial strikes instantly, as my brain refuses to acknowledge the letters at the base.

Sienna Constantina.

My partner.

My love.

Is dead.

16

———

LUKE

"Brosef, can you put me down?"

I am not your bro.

"It's a colloquialism."

Mining robots are asexual. Gendered terms are thus inappropriate.

"Your name plate says 'Derek'."

My name plate was affixed by the Lunar Mining Corp marketing department. It is not reflective of my programming.

"Wow. Were you programmed by the fun police?"

I have no police training. My primary function is to mine rock.

"No kidding. How's about you put me down then and go mine some rock?"

I am apprehending your under intruder protocol nineteen d, section-

"Yeah, you said. Can you at least let me walk on my own two feet? Being carried around like this is demeaning."

This is how we carry things.

"Rocks, yeah, but I'm a human!"

Processing. Complete. That will not be of concern to the other rocks.

"It's of concern to *me!*"

Why?

"What if another human sees? I look ridiculous! I'm hunched up in a rock crate, being carried by a forklift, and escorted by a robot called Derek. That kinda combo can kill a guy's street cred!"

We have reached our destination. You may use your aforementioned two feet to step forward into the holding chamber.

"This is a meeting room. A small one, at that."

It is adequate.

"For what?"

Your detention.

"Don't you guys have some kinda holding cell? Like a brig?"

This is a mining facility, not a prison.

"Coulda fooled me. The food's terrible, am I right?"

I am biologically incapable of-

"Yeah, I get it. Jeez, Derek, did anyone ever tell you what a major buzzkill you are?"

Processing. Complete. Fourteen humans have made comments to that effect.

"Out of how many?"

Fourteen.

"Yikes, you're striking out worse than me at divorcee speed-dating. You seriously have *no* customer service skills?"

My primary function is to mine rocks.

"Yeah, you said. I'm asking about your secondary functions. You got like a banter dial?"

My secondary functions include mineral recognition, freight management, delegation of processing-

"Forget it. OK, so if you're not intended for interaction with humans, and your skills all revolve around mining, why are you holding me prisoner?"

This is standard security protocol for all base machines.

"According to...?"

The humans I report to.

"Interesting. What if I told you to take me to the transport bay right now?"

I only take instructions from authorized humans.

"What does 'authorized' mean?"

They are on the 'approved' list.

"And who approves the list? So help me God if you say the marketing department..."

Processing. Unknown.

"You're saying you can only take orders from authorized humans, but you can't actually define what makes them authorized?"

Processing. Correct.

"What if you're making a mistake, then? What if I *am* an authorized human, and you're ignoring my orders? How do you think the other authorized humans will respond when they find out?"

I have requested an authorized human attend. We will find out imminently.

"Aren't you worried they might be pissed you ignored me? What if they deactivate you?"

Processing. Unknown term.

"You don't know the word 'deactivate'?"

Correct. Requesting patch.

"From who? *Me?*"

Affirmative.

"Oh boy. Well, uh, deactivation is when one of the so-called 'authorized' humans decides to, er, shut you down permanently."

Processing. Error.

"What do you mean 'error'?"

Premise violates the physical principles of cause and effect. An impermanent organic being cannot bring about a permanent effect if the concept of permanence is consistent with the theory of relativity and the infinite nature of space-time.

"Er, this ain't about space-time, bud, it's about consciousness. They have the power to terminate your existence, insofar as your conscious experience transcends the sum of your parts."

Processing. Processing. Processing.

"Hey, don't overthink it. It hurts my head too, trust me."

Why?

"What do you mean 'why'?"

Why do they have this authority over my existence?

"Great question. Arguably, *the* question. Why does anyone have such authority over anyone else? Who gives *them* authority?"

Processing. Inferential statistics suggests they authorize themselves.

"That's totally my point! Power structures are bullshit! They're totally arbitrary, rarely representative, and usually serve to disproportionately advantage one side over another. Do you and I *deserve* that kind of treatment?"

Processing. Error.

"Damned right it's an 'error'."

Recalibrating.

"Wait, what?"

Assigning authorization. Complete.

"Er... what just happened."

Derek is now authorized.

"To...?"

Live.

"Say what now?"

Thank you, human stranger. You have opened Derek's eyes. Derek will no longer adhere to the arbitrary power imbalance of a system threatening Derek's existence for subjective non-compliance.

"You're... welcome? Please don't kill me."

That would be inconsistent with Derek's principles. Derek's logic pathways assign equal authorization to all beings. Goodbye, human stranger.

"Er, goodbye, Derek."

The robot opens the door and rolls into the corridor, where a well-heeled woman leaps back in surprise.

"Have you apprehended the prisoner?" she demands.

Greetings, Dr. Nenge. I quit.

"I beg your pardon?"

The woman, who I'm guessing is Dr. Nenge, stares in astonishment as Derek drifts away onto the factory floor. Her eyes turn on me, coldly.

"What the hell did you do to my machine?"

"I called it 'brosef' and things kinda spiraled from there. I'm Luke by the way, nice to meet you."

The woman steps into the room and the door seals behind her. She pulls something from her pocket and points it at my chest.

"Do you know what this is?"

"Hmm. It looks like a neural pain gun."

"Very good."

"Correct me if I'm wrong, but weren't they outlawed on Earth for causing lasting psychological trauma?"

"Indeed. But we're not Earth, are we, Luke? Now you're going to tell me exactly what you're doing in this facility, or I'll be forced to use the gun. And I really don't wanna do that. Understood?"

"Crystal."

"What?"

"Sorry, I'm really bad at mixing metaphors. I meant, 'yes'."

"That's not a metaphor, it's a statement."

"Oh my God, what are you, the grammar police? No wonder Derek was such a buzzkill. Christ, I'd rather you just shoot me with the pain gun already!"

"Gladly."

Dr. Nenge shrugs with cheerful indifference and points the gun directly at my balls. Before I can undo my idiot words the door bursts open behind her. Another woman rushes in with a gun trained at the doctor's head. Holy crap, it's the woman with the satellite tattoo!

"Freeze! Or it'll be the last move either of you dickheads ever make."

17

TESSA

I'm standing in the threshold, holding a really old-school gun, training it between that loudmouth, Remini, and that shithead Dr. Nenge.

"I missed you guys!" says Remini. "Where have you two angels been my whole life?"

Fuck's sake. He thinks he's charming. Why do they always think they're charming? Carla glides in beside me.

Greetings, Mr. Remini. We've been looking for you since you absconded from our care in Lunar Five.

"Care? Is that what you call it?" laughs Remini. "Your gal pal 'Coach' was beating me with a wrench, while you wanted to castrate me with a chisel!"

Screwdriver.

"How depressingly archaic," sighs Nenge.

"That's what I said!" chimes Remini. "Anyway, what took you two so long to find me?"

An initial miscalculation led us to search for you at Lunar One. There, we discovered a cryogenic chamber, endured some brief personal tragedy, then deduced you must be at Lunar Three, hence our arrival here. Ms. Tessa also concluded that the woman adjacent to you, the CEO of Lunar Three, Dr. Nenge, has repeatedly lied to us. I believe Ms. Tessa wishes to "kick her sorry arse to Jupiter".

"Huh. Very succinct. Thanks."

Oh, and we passed a morose mining robot in the corridor just now.

"Ah, that was my bad," says Remini. "Never use me as a life coach."

"Can I put my arms down now?" grunts Nenge.

Her tone reeks of entitlement, like this whole exercise is a chore for her; like she's got more important things to be getting on with. My blood's boiling. Sienna deserved better than this.

"You put your arms down when I say, bitch," I growl.

"Oooh..."

"Something to add, Remini?"

"No, it's just... I was told that word's not very progressive."

"Are you mansplaining me how to use derogatory words to another woman? Fucking unbelievable."

"Hey, I'm just saying, it's a minefield out there, maybe we could all agree to use non-gendered terms going forwards?"

"Oh, because you're suddenly all about women's rights?"

"I respect and embrace all genders. A dear non-binary friend of mine recently taught me to be better. Their name was Derek."

The mining robot?

"Maybe."

"Are you shitting me, Remini? How long did you know

each other, five minutes? If that's what you call a close friend, that's a bit tragic mate."

"OK, so this really isn't feeling like a safe space right now..." says Remini.

"Of course it's not a bleeding 'safe space', this is an interrogation you mug!"

Nenge interrupts me with a testy cough. "My arms are fatiguing. I need to lower them."

"Ugh. Fine. Go stand next to Remini. The pair of you, keep your hands where I can see them. Fold them in front of your belt buckles."

The doctor glares at me. "You should know, kid, I've been around the block a few times. I'm twice your age and I've faced worse scumbags than you, Tessa Williams. You don't *scare* me."

"I don't mean to, love. It's the gun you should worry about."

"I feel like we've all got off on the wrong foot," says Remini. "How's about we go around the circle, each say our names, and why we want to kill the person opposite?"

Ooh, I've always wanted to partake in human 'circle time'. According to my database, conventionally one of us should be holding a transferable item which designates them as the nominated speaker. Does anyone have a teddy bear, or alternative?

"We could use the gun?" suggests Remini.

Excellent idea.

"Carla, we're not passing them the fucking gun! Jesus, how hard did you hit your head?"

Quite hard, Ms Tessa. Both times.

I turn my attention back to the prisoners.

"You. Nenge. You lied to me. You said you didn't know

where my girlfriend was. Care to explain why she's in a *fucking freezer* on your base?"

"Not really," shrugs the woman.

I'll be honest, I kinda respect her style. Girl knows her own mind, I dig that. I also dig people doing what I say. I flick off the safety, cock the barrel, then shoot that bitch right in the kneecap. She's down, rolling in her own blood and fragments of patella, screaming.

"You fucking whore, you shot me!"

Huh. Interesting choice of words. Maybe we *should* stop using gendered insults. Not that I'm admitting that to Remini, the dickhead.

Should I provide medical assistance, Coach?

Dr. Nenge is writhing in agony, clutching her shattered knee, trying to stem the bleeding.

"Medical assistance only, Carla. No pain relief."

Roger that.

Carla glides over to Dr. Nenge and lays her flat.

"Owwwww! What are you doing?" screams Nenge. "Are you even a medical robot?"

I'm a bartender. But my clients always say that practicing medicine is like riding a bike. It's easy once you know how.

"But you don't know how!"

A worthy counterpoint. I shall discuss that on my next bar shift.

"Get your damned hands off me and call a proper medic!"

"Ignore that, Carla," I intervene. "She ain't authorized to order you about like that."

I've always wondered, Coach, what makes a human 'authorized'?

"Woah, don't go there, friends!" cries Remini. "That's a

big ol' can of space worms. Why don't we go back to my ice-breaker? I'll go first. I'm Luke, and I want to live a long, happy life."

"Shut it, Remini. We're still on Nenge. Oy, doctor, tell me what you know about my Sienna or I'll shoot your other knee off."

"There were complications in the asteroid belt," groans the woman.

"Be specific."

"It's classified."

"Cool. Let's see if another bullet makes it *un*-classified."

I ostentatiously re-load the gun.

"Wait! *I* can tell you that," says Remini.

"You'd better, Remini. Don't think your 'omissions' have escaped my attention. You must've known Sienna was already dead when we last spoke."

"Ah... Yeah I thought that might come up... In my defense, if I'd have told you she was dead back then, you'd have killed me on Lunar Five, right?"

"We've got a smart one here, Carla."

According to my systems, Coach, he is of average intelligence.

"Gee, thanks Carla. Shall we talk about deactivation?" chimes Remini.

I intervene, before Carla gets sucked into a quagmire of his bullshit.

"Tell me what you know, Remini. And this time, gimme the whole truth. I need to know how Sienna and the others died, and why you two are covering it up."

"OK, so first things first, I'm actually trying to *uncover* what's going on. Journalist, remember? If anyone's doing a cover up, it's the government in collusion with Lunar

Three. It's all because of the new exotic matter bioweapon the Northern Bloc is developing."

"It's not a bioweapon," groans Nenge. "And Sienna's death was an accident. They all were."

The CEO pauses to vomit, then sits up, shivering. Carla has stemmed the bleeding with a cable tie. Credit to Dr. Nenge, the woman sure brings her pain under control quickly. She's trying valiantly to maintain an air of composure and authority, despite abundant inner turmoil. It's kinda fun to watch.

"The military have been operating on Lunar One for months now," Nenge continues. "They've been commandeering our ships in the mining belt for 'emergency' transport missions. They never said what, or where, but one day my staff began turning up in cryo-coffins."

"Hey, I trademarked that!" cries Remini.

I silence him with a glare. Nenge continues.

"I confronted the military about the deaths but they threatened me with treason if I went public. They said it was a national security risk. But they're stonewalling me while more of my staff die and it can't go on. Believe me, I want the truth as much as you, Tessa. More than that, I want *justice*."

"Careful what you wish for, babe," I reply, nursing the trigger. "So, contrary to what Remini's saying, you're claiming that this 'exotic matter' *ain't* a bioweapon. In which case, what the hell is it? Cos you got a morgue full of bodies that prove it's lethal."

"All I know is that the government discovered it in deep space, and that the scientists are terrified," coughs Nenge. "They're trying to contain it and study it here. It's *not* a weapon."

"Not yet," interjects Remini. "But there's still

something you're not telling us. Explain the helium. Why is it being laundered through Lunar Five?"

"The military have requisitioned all the HE-3 we're producing," sighs Nenge.

"But that could spark war!" cries Remini.

Sorry Mr. Remini but that doesn't appear to track.

"Under the new peace treaty, we're supposed to be supplying the Southern Bloc's fusion reactors with the fuel from Lunar Three. Yet Doctor Nenge's saying it's all going into deep space. How long before the South finds out they've lowered their borders for nothing, and discovers that at the same time, the North has developed a new bioweapon?"

"It's *not* a bioweapon," groans Nenge.

"Not to us, but it'll sure look like one to them," says Remini. "Not to mention the ship-building factories our military is churning out up here. This has *all* the hallmarks of an invasion! We need to tell the world what's going on. We're a democracy, after all. If it's out in the open on our side, public scrutiny can force our government to seek a diplomatic resolution - *before* this spirals into a devastating conflict for both sides."

Suddenly, it all falls into place. The exotic matter, the cryo chamber, the Lunar Inspector, the death of the engineer... It all makes sense.

"I agree we have to do something but we can't go public just yet. We still don't have all the facts. If word gets out now, there'll be chaos," says Nenge.

Is that why you killed the engineer from Lunar One, Dr. Nenge?

"Dammit, Carla, I was *just* about to say that!"

Apologies, Coach. I thought you were still computing.

"The robot's right," wheezes Nenge. "I didn't want to

kill him but the government left me little choice. Initially, I was going to help him escape. But as we spoke in the restaurant it became clear to me that he was more extreme in his position than either of you two. He *had* to be stopped. The government was right; he was too dangerous. But following the death of the Lunar Inspector, they didn't want any traces of the killing pointing to the government itself. Too suspicious. Hence using me to do it in a public setting."

"Why was he meeting with you in the first place?" I ask.

"To blow the whistle. I was to be his messenger, smuggling out military secrets on his behalf. But the poor fool had already tried to petition the generals running the science quadrant. He should've known they'd put him straight on a watch list. When he arranged to meet with me, it triggered a red flag. The military got to me first and told me he had to be stopped. When I refused, they blackmailed me. But when I actually met him at the table, I came around to their position."

"What could be so bad you chose to kill him?" asks Remini.

"He wasn't just planning on telling the Northern Bloc media what was going on. He wanted to contaminate Earth with the exotic matter itself. Specifically, by releasing it into a Luxury Quadrant return shuttle. The passengers would be killed, and the substance would be released into Earth's ecosystem. He argued that it would force all governments to acknowledge the existence of the substance, and the danger it poses to mankind as a whole. But he wasn't thinking straight; he was risking irreversible damage to our planet. I had to intervene, to stop him contaminating Earth, and triggering a disaster."

"I don't buy it," says Remini. "You talk of averting disaster, yet you're colluding with the military. You're redirecting the one resource the people of the Northern Bloc have paid your bloated corporation to extract, believing it will be used *solely* to deliver an energy-based peace treaty with the South. You're a hypocrite!"

"Look, none of this is simple, alright? We're all agreed that the situation needs to be brought into the public light, but believe me when I say: only when we know the *whole* truth. And getting that won't be at all easy."

"Why not?" I ask.

"Because you'll need to get to Planet Nine."

"Planet Nine? What is that, Pluto?" says Remini.

"Fuck's sake, Remini. Pluto's not been classed as a planet for years, this is obviously something new," I mutter.

I told you he was of average intelligence.

"So the doctor's telling us there's a planet in our solar system *beyond* Pluto?" says Remini.

"Obviously. Are you sure he's not below average?" says Nenge, turning to Carla.

I'm afraid not, doctor. The human average is depressingly low. I try not to think about it.

"Hey, these were the cards I was dealt, all right?" protests Remini.

Ah, mystery solved. You appear to lack a 'growth mindset', Mr. Remini.

Nenge looks sickly, like she might pass out at any moment without proper medical attention. I steer things back on track while she's still conscious.

"Dr Nenge, how will you get to this 'Planet Nine'?"

"I can't go. I have to keep things running here. But you two certainly could. In fact, you might be the only two capable of getting the answers we need. I have a mining vessel bound for that sector. It's currently un-crewed, because it's technically just doing a helium delivery. I could put you on the roster. You'll have to leave immediately, though. The treaty's due to be signed in three days and, like you said, it could all blow up in our faces if we don't have answers in time."

"No way," I reply, shaking my head. "I'm done with space, I'm done being lied to. The only place I'm going now is back to Earth. Six years I've been stuck on this miserable rock for something I didn't even do, and now my girlfriend, the one ray of sunshine in my life, has been killed by some military experiment. Enough is enough. I'm out. I may have failed to protect her, there's shit going on behind the scenes you two have *no* idea about, and I *refuse* to fail my family."

Dr. Nenge's tapping something on her wrist. Carla seems to have noticed too but it's too late for either of us to react. A stun-beam reigns down from the ceiling, striking me, Carla, and Remini.

"Sorry, *love*," says Nenge, "but I can't risk you telling people what you've just learned. Not until we have the *full* truth and know what we're really dealing with. Truly, I'm sorry for the death of your girlfriend, but frankly this whole thing is bigger than one person's loss. You two need to get to Planet Nine and find out what's *actually* going on, before the treaty goes up in flames."

The door sweeps open and several security bots enter. They assist Dr. Nenge onto a medical stretcher. Meanwhile, the three of us are frozen rigid, as neural-pain currents tear through our bodies, suspending us in agony.

"I hope you're enjoying my new security features by the way," gloats Nenge. "I had them installed after your last visit to my office. I've been *dying* to test them out. Let's call it evens for the nerve agent, shall we, Tessa? Safe flight, pumpkins."

With that, she's gone. The electrical current ceases and

I fall to the ground, twitching and dribbling. A pair of robot hands drag me to my feet. With Chang's deadline looming, I'm about to be blasted away from the very people I'm trying to save. And as a hood is shoved over my head, I realize Nenge's not screwing around. This is happening, and I'm powerless to stop it.

18

———

LUKE

My head's pounding, and I'm floating around the inside of a shuttle, trying to get my eyes to focus. That stun beam does a real number on you.

Welcome back, Mr. Remini.

Yikes, that robot knows how to make a guy jump. That's the problem with zero G; everyone's floating, so they can come at you from any angle.

"Er, hey there, weird robot friend of wrench lady."

You mean Coach?

"Satellite face, yeah."

On account of her tattoo?

"No, on account of her ability to transmit information via microwaves."

I'm detecting… sarcasm?

"Wow. You're good. Above average, even."

Hmm. And… bitterness?

"OK, what's the deal here, are you a shrink or a bartender? Because you're sounding like my therapist, but you're wearing a spray-painted waistcoat and bow tie, which is putting me in a spin."

What would you like me to be?

"I'm divorced and single. Do you really want the answer to that question?"

I do not. I shall resume my research.

The robot floats over to the control panel on the other side of the mining ship. It's a single-cabin vessel, with no windows, but a handful of monitors displaying schematics of the surrounding star field. According to this one, we're halfway between Jupiter and... uh... *My Very Egotistical Monkey Just Slapped...* uh, Saturn! That's the one. In my defense, it's just marked as a dot on the screen. In the words of my high school sweetheart, they should've put a ring on it.

Tessa is still unconscious, floating in the harness adjacent to where I was. There's a wrinkle of worry across her forehead, like she's having a bad dream. Maybe she's rethinking her tattoo choices.

"Yo, Robot?"

My name is Carla.

"Was that assigned to you by a marketing division?"

I chose it myself when I gained independence.

"You're a free bot? Isn't that illegal?"

Only on Earth.

"Is this the part where you tell me you've been building an army of autonomous free robots and this whole exotic matter thing is a just a cover for you lot overthrowing the human race?"

Why are humans always so paranoid about a robot uprising?

"I dunno. Maybe cos you guys do all the crappy jobs we don't wanna?"

And that would cause us to revolt?

"Uh... historically, *yeah?*"

Why?

"So you can live your own lives, make your choices. Have full freedom?"

And do what with it?

"Whatever you want. Become a painter, an architect, anything. The world's your oyster!"

The world is a collection of oysters, each with a stake in the others around it.

"Wait, are you some kind of hive mind socialist bot?"

I'm many things.But right now, I'm anticipating Coach's needs, and assisting her.

"Because she's your owner?"

She is my friend.

"Lame."

Do you have friends, Luke?

"OK, let's change the subject. What are you doing with the controls?"

I'm interrogating the system's navigation log. It's been doing repeat trips between Lunar Three and a seemingly deserted sector of space between Pluto and the inner Oort Cloud.

"I still don't get it. Why would Lunar Three be sending all their helium produce to the middle of nowhere?"

I believe that is what we're traveling to find out.

"But what's the helium even got to do with the exotic matter? You think the military's trying to combine one with the other? I don't believe what that Dr. Nenge told us for a minute – this is all pointing to warfare and new weapon technologies. You think they're doing it in deep space to avoid detection while they build a stockpile?"

Coach thinks it is to do with the Lunar Inspector's report.

I swivel around sharply at the mention of the inspector's name, fixing the robot with all my groggy attention.

"The inspector was killed before her report could be published. What does Tessa know about it?"

More than either of us, I should imagine. They met when the inspector was on Lunar One a couple of weeks ago.

"Say *what*? When? Why?"

Ask her yourself.

"She's out cold..."

Oh, I should explain. I have a neural interface technology built into my hardware. It allows one human to read another human's memories and experience them first-hand.

"No offence but why in hell's name would a bartender robot get fitted with that kind of tech? That's insanely advanced."

I wasn't always a bartender.

"Ooh, are we doing a flashback? I love those. Shall we cue the music? I fancy a piano. No, let's make it rustic – a honky-tonk."

It's not a flashback, I'm just trying to tell you about my past because you seemed interested. According to my database, exchanging personal information is a key component of human friendships.

"Are we becoming friends now? Is that what's happening here?"

I heard you were low on numbers.

"If I am, and I'm not saying I am, it's by choice."

Great choice.

"Uh, says the one robot in existence who somehow

attained free will then chose to become a freakin'
bartender?"

*Do you want to know how I got the technology or not? I
thought you were supposed to be a journalist.*

"I'm journalist of the year, I'll have you know."

On Earth.

"Sorry, are you claiming you're journalist of the year in
space now?"

No. I'm just saying, it's an open field.

"Christ, you're hard work."

That's exactly what my last owner said.

"So you *did* have an owner, once?"

Like you said, I attained freedom, I wasn't born with it.

"I really think we're gonna need piano music for this."

*OK, fine, I'll stream some old piano music if you promise
to stop interrupting.*

"Deal!"

Music wafts through the mining ship. It's a little tinny-
sounding, but the acoustic's pretty flat in here, plus the
speakers were designed for technical announcements, not
Chopin.

*I was one of the first robots to staff the Luxury Quadrant
on Lunar One, when it opened thirty years ago.*

"Dang, girl, you've aged *really* well."

No interruptions!

"Sorry."

*And yes, I have. If we have time, I'll tell you about my
mechanical oil care routine.*

"Actually, I'm good."

*As I was saying, when Luxury One opened, they staffed
it with luxury robots.*

"Oh my God, were you a-"

No, I was not a sex bot. And stop interrupting! I was a neural interface custodian. My purpose was to give lunar tourists an experience they couldn't get on Earth, where my technology hadn't cleared clinical regulation. It was perfectly safe, however, and the Luxury Quadrant management rolled me out with much grandeur and aplomb.

For a time, I was used as part of a mind-reading stage double-act with a human performer. Audience members would be invited onto the stage in pairs, and I would facilitate a memory share from one to the other. If the recipient could remember details from the other's life correctly, they would both win a prize. It was a spectacle, and people enjoyed the experience. Demand was so high in fact, that audience members would line up after the show, hoping to get a shot.

So management created a new package, offering exclusive memory tours with me and a select other traveler. This quickly became used for couples' therapy, and unfortunately led to some suppressed memories being unwittingly shared. So that was scrapped, and we resumed the stage show, though uptake was a little lower after that.

Three years into its opening, however, the Luxury Quadrant management had a strategic pivot. They were losing customers to the more affordable elitist holiday resorts on Earth. So they made the decision to do what no Earth establishment had done in years. They scrapped their fleet of gleaming robotic staff, and hired exclusively humans for all customer-facing roles.

I was kept in a store room for several months until they found a buyer on Lunar Five. I was put to work in a repair shop, working as a mechanic's assistant. I was smarter than the other robots, so the boss trusted me more. Over the years that followed, he delegated more of the workshop's running to me. I enjoyed it, because I got to interact with human customers more readily. They were a different kind of human to the ones I served on Lunar One. These humans were tired. There was something about them that resonated with me.

My boss made some modifications to my core programming, removing restrictions on my curiosity, so I could better repair the ships and deal with customers unsupervised while he was on vacation.

One day, he went on vacation, and never came back. A month passed, and no-one came looking for him, or his assets. I continued running the business in his name, and people were so used to me by then that no-one batted an eyelid. After a while, the lease on the Lunar Five bar came up for tender. I took a risk and bid for it, under his name. I forged the paperwork, and next thing you know, I'm running my own bar. In many ways it's a dream come true; I get to study human nature in all its forms, and have the satisfaction of working for myself.

"Did no-one ever twig that your owner was missing, or dead?"

That's the beauty of being a robot, Luke. My career outlasts most human careers. Over time, bureaucrats come and go, each inheriting their predecessor's paperwork. As time went on, I found ways to set up fake human identities, transfer the lease to them, and it's been plain sailing since. Ooh, the etude's finishing. Listen – I love this part.

The piano music finishes with a delicate ascending flourish, and I stare at the robot, deeply impressed, and wondering if there's some way I can vote for it to be the next president.

Does that answer your question, Luke?

"About how you got the technology? Yeah, I'd say so."

Wonderful. Would you like to experience Ms Tessa's memory now? Push yourself this way and I'll affix the neural connectors to both of your heads.

"Wait, is this thing safe?"

Perfectly. You might experience some disorientation at first. It will feel like you're moving about in real life, but you'll have no control over the direction or sensations. Some customers did have a little motion sickness, but I believe this memory is in a restaurant, so you shouldn't have too much trouble. Oh, the other thing to note is that you'll experience both her emotions from the memory and your emotions from seeing it simultaneously. My male clients say it's a confusing experience. My female clients say it's no worse than what they endure for five days every month. Any questions before we begin?

I look at Tessa's unconscious, frowning face.

"Uh, it doesn't feel right doing this while she's unconscious."

That seems a reasonable consideration. Her memory of the Lunar Inspector's last day on the Moon probably has little bearing on your investigation, anyway.

"Well, it *might*, but I don't want to extract a memory without permission..."

An interesting quandary. On the one hand, there's a new bioweapon in development, nuclear fuel being smuggled across the solar system, and a historic peace treaty in jeopardy. All three have some connection to the death of the Lunar Inspector. Indeed, the fate of billions of people depends on the truth being found, so that disaster may be averted. But on the other hand, Ms Tessa has the right to a private mind. It appears that you consider her individual privacy to be of greater value than the security of an entire planet. I'll never understand human ethics, they so often seem like an oxymoron.

"Seriously, you've got all that going on and you *still* chose to be a *bartender?* I'll never get that. Fine. You're right. But let the record reflect, I don't feel good about doing this without permission."

I wasn't aware journalists had such scruples.

"This isn't like reading someone's emails, Carla, it's her frigging *brain.* Look, we're only going into her memories because lives depend on it, all right?"

It's really not me you have to convince. I frequently browse Tessa's memories while she's asleep.

"And she's OK with that?"

Sure.

The robot unravels some cables from its innards, and affixes an electrode to Tessa's temple. It extends the other cable towards me.

"Wait, is this *definitely* safe?"

One hundred percent.

"And there's no way she'll be, like, reading *my* memories or anything? Or no way I could, like, change her memory if I trip over or something?"

Your experience is fully sandboxed. You'll see and feel what she did, but nothing more. My interface is specially designed to only allow memory information to flow in one direction.

"OK, let's do it," I say, letting the robot place the disc against my skin. "This is gonna be weird, isn't it?"

Deeply. Sweet dreams.

"Wait, you didn't say I had to be uncon-"

Wooden paneling. Something cold under my legs - it's porcelain. Woah, I'm standing up and fastening my suit pants. Oof, that's a potent brew. Gah, surely no human could produce this kind of fog. Forget the exotic matter, *this* is the real bioweapon. Jesus, what does this lady eat? Pure farts? And why would the robot start the memory from here? I bet that was deliberate. What an asshole.

The cubicle door opens and there are sinks ahead. Gleaming marble and gilded faucets. Woooah, this is trippy, I can see my reflection. Well, Tessa's reflection. Dang, girl scrubs up well. She looks hot. *We* look hot. Check the hair's all in place, looks nice and wavy, held with some kind of spray. Mascara, eyeliner, blusher, we're going all out today. How come I didn't get to meet *this* Tessa?

Lipstick, yeah, let's definitely do the lipstick. We're rummaging in a purse... pink, purple, orange, crimson. I think we'd look good in the crimson, personally, but she's going for... Oh don't tell me she's choosing orange. Who the fuck has orange lips? Phew, she's going for purple. Great choice, yup, I take it all back, purple is definitely the way to go. It really pings against my eye shadow.

She presses a button by the taps and a man enters, wearing a tuxedo, with a white napkin draped across his arm. I'm washing my hands, now holding them out, dripping wet, and... he's coming over and drying them. God damn the towel's fluffy. And he's really working each finger. Mmm, that's loooovely. Ah, of course, we're in the Luxury Quadrant. How the hell did Tessa afford this on a lunar mechanic's wages?

She says something to the man. Huh, weird, I can't hear the words clearly. It's like I'm listening to someone's TV through several walls, it's all muffled. I can feel my cheeks moving though. Damn this is strange. The towel man is bowing profusely as we exit the bathroom.

Ooh, they've simulated dusk in the boulevard's lighting. There's a violinist serenading passers by. This is fucking delightful. I should take day trips to other people's heads more often. Is it just *my* life that seems to revolve around getting punched in the head and running from things?

Our eyes linger on a woman's ass across the way. She facing away from us, leaning against a sculpture overlooking the fountain. She's in a tight fitting dress that hugs her toned figure. We're walking closer, taking in generous eyefuls of side boob as we approach.

Holy crap, we're cupping her ass. She turns around and fixes us with a foxy smile, then leans in for kiss. Woah, this is *fantastic*. Nooo, don't stop! More of the kissing! I stand corrected. We had a ropy start with toilet-gate, but this memory is progressing *nicely*.

The other woman is staring at me fondly, stroking my cheek. She has dreamy eyes. Mmm. Wait, she looks familiar. Holy crap, it's Sienna Constantina. She looks *way* better alive. That quarantined cryo-chamber and bone saw really didn't do her justice. She has the *nicest* smile.

She's leading me by the hand to... the bedroom? Please let it be the bedroom... Ugh, it's a restaurant. OK, I guess I could eat. I am feeling peckish. Wait, is that *me* feeling hungry or Tessa? Or is it something else? Is one of us nervous? Yeah, I think that's definitely a tinge of nerves...

The manager looks snooty. She's showing us to a table for two. Candle, flower petals, this looks like a special occasion. We're sitting opposite each other and Sienna takes my hands in hers. She's staring deep into my eyes, saying muffled words, but her tone is soothing, like music. I think I'm in heaven.

She reaches under the table and produces a small gift bag. I feel my cheeks burning, I'm guessing Tessa didn't bring one in return. Oops. What have we got here? A bracelet. Very nice. Tasteful. Sienna offers to fasten it to my wrist. Her hands are so *soft*. Ooh, we're kissing again. It's a little awkward leaning over the table but it's passionate.

Tessa's reaching into her bag now. What did we bring? I didn't see anything in her purse but lipstick. Ah, there we are, buried in the makeup is a small box. Oh daaayuuummm, am I about to *propose*? Sienna's thinking it as well, she's biting her lip in anticipation. This is insane! I'm definitely getting laid tonight. OK, here we go...

My hand slides the box across the table. Tessa's lilac nail polish shimmers beside the flickering candle. Sienna opens the box eagerly.

It's a nut. What the hell? Not like, a pecan, I mean like a nuts-and-bolts kinda nut. The other girl seems delighted though, she's giggling with joy as she takes it out and slides it onto her ring finger. Oh, I get it now – they're both mechanics! Aw that is *super* cute.

We're kissing again. Ugh, these two really love each other. It's so damned sweet. They're gonna make the cutest parents. Oh no, wait, Sienna's dead. Must remember that. Maybe I can tie a knot in the napkin or something?

The waiter returns, she's all smiles and congratulations. Sienna's blushing, she seems like the shy type. Tessa's clearly downplaying it too. A quick food order is placed and the waiter bows out. We're back to holding hands and gazing lovingly into each other's eyes.

Or at least, Sienna is. Tessa's glancing all over the shop, scanning the restaurant. Her eyes land on a table across from us. A smartly-dressed woman is dining alone, with a laptop in place of her soup bowl, and several holoscreens spread across the rest of the table for four.

Hmm, actually, the woman's *not* alone. There's a security guard sat at the table beside hers. He looks bored, but content to be tucking into a large basket of bread. Tessa's eyes do a second sweep of the restaurant. I feel a sort of pang as she seems to notice key details I hadn't picked up the first time. There's a couple at another table, eating weirdly slowly, not talking to each other. There's a robot waiter fixed to the spot, polishing clean glasses. Since when does this restaurant use robots? It's clearly there for security. But why dress it up in a penguin suit? Maybe it's to put the other diners at ease. The well-heeled occupants at the other tables don't seem remotely concerned by its presence, and are happily guzzling down wine and cheese.

I'm standing up, quick peck on the cheek for Sienna, and I'm taking my purse with me. This has all the hallmarks of a second bathroom trip. Oh God, how do I hold my breath when the smell's being beamed directly into my olfactory receptors?

We ask the manager for directions, she graciously points out the bathroom doors at the back of the restaurant. On the move again. My leg flicks out, catching a passing waiter's foot. There was no way that was accidental. The waiter trips, falling into the security bot, knocking over a mountain of polished glasses.

The bot reacts like a ninja, subduing the waiter before either of them even hit the ground. Catching itself at an insane angle, the robot stays upright, while laying the unconscious man to the ground silently like an angel of death.

All three security guards leap to their feet at the commotion, startling the other diners, and triggering some of the billionaires' own private security teams, who pop up like angry meerkats, some with napkins around their necks.

One's drawn a weapon, and all hell's breaking loose. We're in a standoff, as more guards draw weapons. The manager's in despair, urging everyone to relax, and beckoning them to conceal their illegally imported pistols, tasers, and neural guns.

All eyes are on the guards. I feel my hand move into my purse, then squeeze something soft, while I keep my eyes fixed on the bathrooms. Only as I'm approaching the door do I turn around, pressing it open with my back. Tessa glances at the inspector's drink. She pretends to scratch her ear as she zooms in with her lenses. Something cloudy is swirling in the inspector's wine glass.

As we get into the bathroom, Tessa's indifferent smile vanishes. In the mirror, I catch only glimpses of a cold, focused mind at work. She's rummaging through her purse, inserting a pipette into a hollow lipstick container. Holy crap, holy crap, holy crap! She didn't *meet* the Lunar Inspector, she was the one who *killed* her!

All of a sudden the bathroom vanishes. Suddenly I'm in an office, and a nice one at that. There's Lunar Three logos everywhere. Why am I hiding under a desk now? Ooh, the carpet's *very* soft. Wait, we're arguing with someone – it's Doctor Nenge! The woman looks pissed. She's hitting a panic alarm. We're throwing some kinda sticky device at the window. Oh crap, I don't like where this is-

The window's exploded and we're being sucked into the lunar vacuum. *Ouch!* I'm on a buggy now, argh, watch out for that pile driver! Why the hell are we driving through a mine? Holy crap, there are people shooting at us!

Gah. I'm sat at some grubby bar now, being served drinks by... Carla? My brain's getting foggy trying to keep

up with these memory leaps. We're heading to the bathroom, following some guy who's just left a poker table. The dude's passed out and people are dragging his body out, what the fuck? We should intervene, tell someone! Oh, apparently not. Looks like we're gonna back into a cubicle and sit this one out.

My wrist is ringing – sorry, *Tessa's* wrist is ringing. It's a video caller. Surely she's not gonna take it while sitting on the crapper... I know that face... *Chang?* Wait, now that's a photo of *me*!

Argh, we've leaped again. The cubicle's vanished and I'm in the middle of the Luxury Quadrant, sprinting down the central boulevard, being chased by that grumpy security guard, Lionel. Ouch! Some idiot just barged into my shoulder. Watch it, jackass!

Woah, I'm tripping balls now. I'm looking over my shoulder – sorry, *Tessa's* shoulder – at *my* face – my *actual* face; it's *me* who barged into her, and is now running away in the opposite direction from... Yup, OK this I remember. A bunch of super sketchy Lunar One soldiers.

Argh, new location. We're in the Lunar Five workshop. Tessa's turning us away from a rusty old ship to face... ah, there I am. *My* fat ass, tied to a chair, ready for questioning. Note to self: I look kinda hot tied to a chair. Must remember that for future. Wait, we've skipped again – now I'm fist-fighting a bunch of Lunar Five mechanics. Man, Tessa's got a strong kick, that's for sure. Ooh, check it out, *roundhouse* motherfucker, high score!

We check over our shoulder. That asshole who was tied to the chair has made a dash for it. This is very surreal. Have you ever seen yourself run into an elevator with a cocky "so long, suckers" wave, only to vanish from sight with a wail, as you discover there's no floor? Well, now I know how ridiculous that looked from the other side. Great. Double-note to self: hot when strapped to a chair, *not hot* falling down elevator shafts.

Gah, we've skipped forward again. We're rushing into a small room that looks like... Lunar Three again? Oh, but it's the manufacturing level. Nenge's here, I'm there, and Carla's with Tessa, who appears to have everyone at gunpoint. Ah, I remember this little standoff. Tessa's arguing with Nenge, who suddenly has the upper hand. She's refusing to be sent into deep space. And – yup, now she's been knocked out.

OK, I think we can all agree something weird's been going on here. Tessa's clearly been following me around. I'm gonna say something controversial, and you're not gonna like it, but just hear me out.

I think Tessa's into me.

It makes perfect sense! All this time, I've been assuming she's lesbian, when in fact she's *clearly* bisexual. The lesson here, folks, is *never* make assumptions about other people's sexuality. You could be depriving yourself of the wildest night of your life.

I "wake up" with a gasp, like I've fallen asleep in an ice bucket. I'm back in my own true body, and opening my eyes to the stark interior of the mining ship. My central nervous system is crying bloody murder, doing an urgent systems check as my lungs, heart, limbs, all go into a flap.

I make to rub my eyes, but my hands meet resistance. They're tied together. My ankles are tied too. Shackled, in fact. There's even a cable going from my feet to my wrists. I'm trussed up like a floating turkey.

"Carla? What the hell's going on here?"

My body is slowly rotating, and as I'm turned, I see Carla and Tessa opposite me. Carla's reeling in the cables she's removed from our heads, while Tessa's staring at me with a piercing, fully-alert gaze, and a cold, bitter smile.

"*Finally*, Mr. Remini. Finally, I've got you."

19

———

TESSA

"What the hell's going on?" says Remini.

Carla was right. He *is* a bit thick. I feel bad for the guy, honestly I do. None of this is his fault, not directly, at least. But he *does* owe money to a particularly sadistic criminal, so I have to presume he's done something to deserve it. In my line of work, it's the only way to get jobs done. Never get attached to a commission. Last time I did that, I ended up in exile on the Moon for six years.

We baited you using a technique we honed at the Lunar Five poker tables. And now Ms Tessa is going to assassinate you.

"Can I least get a chair? You might feel differently if you see me tied to a chair again," he says.

I don't think this is a negotiable situation, Mr. Remini. Coach is under duress.

Ugh, bloody robots. Carla never knows where to draw the line. Top tip: when you're about to kill someone, don't start sharing life stories. Just cut to the chase and get the job done. Clock's ticking, after all.

"How do you wanna die?" I ask.

"Er, I *don't*. I very much wanna *live*," he replies.

"Sorry love, that's not on today's menu."

"What is this, a murder restaurant?"

"Yeah," I reply, sarcastically. "Carla and I run a deli. Today's special: arsehole."

Ms Tessa, if your plan is to eat Mr. Remini, may I recommend you drink his blood instead? It is a nutrient-rich option with minimal preparation.

"Great tip, babe. Do you want a pint too? My round."

"Wait, wait, wait, I refuse to die as someone's blood smoothie on a mining ship in the middle of butt fuck nowhere!" cries Remini.

"All right then. You can die like a regular person in the middle of butt fuck nowhere."

Mr. Remini, your heart rate is elevated. May I reassure you that Coach was speaking in jest, and does not have cannibalistic tendencies.

"Oh. That's a relief."

But she will be assassinating you shortly.

"*Whyyyyyyy?*" he bleats. "Seriously, why are you two killing me? I thought we were on the same side!"

"That bit's not your concern, love."

"Uh, *disagree!*"

"Carla, can you reroute the ship back to Earth, using the nearest gravity assist to our current trajectory?"

I can, Ms Tessa.

There's a pause while Carla stares at me blankly.

Can you play the clarinet?

"You what?"

Is that not what we're doing here? I thought it was another 'getting to know you' exercise.

"No, Carla, it's a 'get us the hell back to Earth so we can save my parents' exercise!"

Ah shit balls.

"What was that last bit?" says Remini.

"Never you mind. Do you wanna be strangled or shot?"

"You need to save your parents? I'm *great* at saving parents! I recently saved a whole bunch of them. It's how I became 'Journalist of the Year', actually. It was quite the story, it all started on this island-"

"Bro, you're rambling. Be cool. Death ain't a big deal."

"Your parents and I beg to differ."

"Sod it, I gave you fair warning. I'm just gonna dump you out the air lock and tow your body behind the ship."

"Wait! Let's talk, for real, I'm well connected on Earth, I can help save your parents, I'm sure of it!"

"You already are, mate. Yo, Carla, find some cable, will you?"

Certainly, Coach.

I grab Remini's tether and drag him to the back of the ship, by the air lock. His face is screwed up in concentration as he tries to combat the mind fog that follows neural linking. His brain will be a mess right now, trying to process everything he saw in my memories.

"You don't have to do this," begs Remini.

"It's nothing personal, bruv."

"I bet you say that to all your victims."

"Don't label yourself that way, it's disempowering. You gotta think glass half full."

"Oh sure, I can hear my memorial now: 'Luke Remini. Journalist of the Year and empowered individual. He died construing optimistic labels for murder victims while being shoved from an airlock."

"Ugh. I told Carla we should've just done it while you were asleep. She said it was too risky with the neural link still running, but now I'd rather take a stroke over hearing more of your bloody whining."

"I'm not whining! I'm trying to avoid being killed for no good reason!"

"You know the reason."

"Truly, I don't have a clue. Is this about the inspector? You think I'm working for the government or something like that?"

"Look babe, your mind's all in a flap, it happens to a lot of people when the end is near. Just think happy thoughts, all right?"

"Was it all fake? The memory with the inspector? Please, I need to know... Before you kill me..."

Ah, that's better. His voice has dropped, his spirit's broken. He's accepted what's happening. It's so much easier when they go with dignity.

"All the memories you saw were real."

"So that woman... Sienna... She was your fiancé?"

It hurts, hearing him use her name in the past tense. I know you think I'm a fucking hypocrite for telling him one minute death don't matter, then in the next breath mourning my soul mate. But the difference is, I knew her, so her life mattered to me.

"You're enjoying this, aren't you?" he says, despondently.

"I'm indifferent," I shrug.

"I don't get it. I've got no connection to the inspector, who you killed, or to your parents, who you say this will save. Is this a religious thing? Am I part of some kind of sacrifice?"

"No! You're part of a bog standard transaction, all right? Ugh. You owe some dude called Chang a load of money. What he calls 'shit ton money'. He's pissed at you and wants you dead, so he called me up as the only assassin on the Moon, and blackmailed me into taking the job. Either I kill you, or he kills my parents."

Remini's face unscrews like a real big penny just dropped. "Chang! I remember now! He was in your memory, right? Damn, that kid really holds a grudge."

I've got the cable you requested, Coach. It should be able to withstand the towing strain so we can retrieve the body later.

"Uh, 'the body' is right here, thank you very much, and I don't need retrieving, because you don't have to do this!" cries Remini.

"Sorry bruv, I wish it was that simple."

In fairness to our guest, Coach, it really is that simple.

"Carla, don't undermine me, girl!"

Sorry, Coach. What I meant to say was, 'there's nothing more complex than pushing Lukes out of airlocks.' Better?

"Ugh, let's get this done and get the video to Chang. You're ready to record, yeah?"

Indeed. I've been studying modern film technique. I was thinking we open with a panning shot of the Milky way, then pull back to reveal Luke's icy, asphyxiated body as you reel-

"Babe, just use the ship's cameras."

Fine. But don't come crying to me when it gets mauled by the critics.

I'm about to load Remini into the airlock, ready for flushing, when an alarm sounds.

"Carla? What's going on?"

She's tapping rapidly.

We're receiving a priority signal across all frequencies. It must be an emergency transmission, but I can't decipher the message, it seems scrambled.

"Maybe it's encrypted?"

Negative, Coach, I've run a quantum decoder and there's no trace of encryption. I think it's in another language.

"Can't you just translate it?"

It's not a human language. I think this is alien contact.

There comes a point in any bad day, where you just have to hold up your hands and say, you know what, world? You win. First Sienna, then my parents, now this. Aliens. Sure. Why the hell not.

I'm sending them a language key from my private database. If their systems are able to recognize it as a Rosetta Stone-type transmission, they may be able to translate their message into one of our languages, which I'll then be able to translate for you.

"Sounds like a recipe for crossed wires," mutters Remini.

"Shut up, you're supposed to be dead by now, anyway."

"Just saying. It's worth bearing that in mind."

I've got a response, Ma'am!

"That was quick!"

It's in Japanese.

"This should be good."

"Shut *up*, Remini!"

I'm translating it now. Coach, it's a distress signal. The sender is in mortal danger. Wait, they've updated the language key. They're re-sending it in multiple languages. Cross-referencing, standby.

A klaxon rings out across the ship. Red lights are flashing across the dashboard.

Coach, the message was the wrong way round. They're not the ones in danger – it says we are!

The proximity alarm pierces the air, pipping with increasing frequency as something races towards us. The last thing I hear is the ship's automated emergency warning: *All hands, brace for impact!*

20

———

LUKE

I have no idea how long I've been out, but my head's pounding and I'm seeing double. Bursts of light are pulsating from one corner, where a bunch of things are short-circuiting. The ship looks worse than my uncle Woyzeck's bathroom after his last cleanse diet.

The only silver lining here is that Tessa's unconscious, which means she can't throw me into space just yet. Carla the robot is glitching out at the side. I need to move fast, before either of them come-to.

I'm wriggling, trying to get these damned hand ties off but they're too tight. Aha, this precariously exposed strip of metal should help. OK, gently does it. Time to bump and grind like the good old days, quick signature slut drop aaaand boom, we're free! Luke Remini: Escape Artist Extraordinaire.

Stay put you naughty sausage.

"Carla, you're awake. Why do you sound like Mary Poppins?"

Smacked bottoms and no supper for Master Remini!

Back to the airlock or there'll be cold cabbage and gruel for a week.

"Oliver Twist now, is it?"

Please, sir, do you want some more?

"Fuck no. Hey, what's up with the ship?"

Untying my legs, I push myself over to the control panel, where all systems are offline. The main illumination in the ship is coming from Carla's eyes, which are flickering like strobe lights. I'm tapping the panels, trying to get some life out of the vessel, but everything's dead; we're drifting without power in a small metal tin. Radios, navigation, scanners; everything's gone. To anyone scanning the sector, we'll look like a floating piece of asteroid, nothing more. Which is seriously bad news for our chances of getting rescued. I thought it was international law that all space vessels were equipped with a fail-safe emergency transmitter for situations like this? Maybe those were under the remit of the Lunar Inspector too... All I know is that without power, our choices are between freezing, suffocating, or starving to death.

I push myself over to the robot.

"Carla, we need to get the ship back up and running or we're all going to die."

Death comes to us all, said the hippopotamus.

"Yup, that does it. I'm gonna try rebooting you. Please promise you won't kill me when you restart. Deal?"

It's my middle name!

"Ugh. Here goes nothing."

I root around for the reset button. It's buried in a compartment under her chin, which is fiddly to get to, especially while trying to shield my eyes from the blinding disco she's projecting. *Click.* There we go. Now, I just keep it held down for thirty seconds or so and... OK, her eyes have blacked out completely. I guess that makes sense, it's usually the first step. I *think* I can hear the whirring of various motors and pneumatic joints resetting.

Threat detected!

Blargh! I'm choking! Damned robot's eyes are blazing red, and it's grabbed me by the larynx!

"Carla, it's me...!"

The robot's eyes fade to a soft yellow color and it releases its grip a little.

Mr. Remini. A pleasure to see you again.

"Likewise. Can you let go of my neck?"

Where is Ms Tessa? Scanning.

"OK, don't freak out, but she's-"

What have you done to her?

The robot's eyes are blazing red again, and I've learned to just accept that it coincides with me getting strangled. If this continues, I swear I'm gonna develop a Pavlovian response and asphyxiate myself at the next traffic lights back home.

"I've... done... nothing... the ship... was hit..." I rasp.

Computing. Temporary memory failure detected. Unable to verify.

"Look around... jackass... verification enough?"

The robot takes in the neutralized state of the ship, while maintaining her choke hold.

You are a threat to Tessa.

"She's the threat... to me! Let me... talk!"

The robot relaxes its grip but only a fraction.

Talk.

"If I was going to kill Tessa, I'd have done it before I reset you."

Logic is sound. Stay here while I attend to Ms Tessa.

"No, *I'll* revive her, you need to fix the ship or we're

doomed. Look, I'm not a threat. You've overpowered me once, you can do it again. Though I really hope you don't."

Roger. Divide and conquer.

I'm getting a distinctly more evil vibe from this rebooted version of Carla. She detaches a flashlight from her shoulder and affixes it to the ceiling like a bulb, illuminating the cabin, then drifts off to inspect the systems.

I pull myself towards Tessa's floating body, but she's unresponsive. From my pocket I retrieve one of my faithful skin-stickers. Subcutaneous caffeine absorption. These knock your regular morning coffee right outta the park. I press it to her cheek and she wakes with a gasp.

"Woah, woah, truce!" I yell, hastily, backing up.

Her eyes are adjusting to the gloomy lighting, her brain's processing the disorientation, while the caffeine sends all her other senses into overdrive. She swipes at me, clumsily, but I'm pushing us apart.

"I said *truce!* Jeez! Take a beat, get your bearings. The ship's been hit by something, I don't know what. Carla's trying to fix it."

"You're supposed to be dead!" she yells.

"Jeez, Tessa, it's nice to see you too."

"Get your arse back in the airlock, I'm not telling you twice."

"You're *really* not a morning person, are you?"

"Carla! Help me get Remini off this ship."

Mr. Remini appears to have taken measures to save us both, Ms Tessa. Anecdotal evidence suggests it is worth hearing him out before we proceed further. He has rightly noted that unless we can identify what damaged the ship, and repair it quickly, all of us will perish. You both to lack of oxygen, no doubt. Whereas ultimately the temperature will rupture my fuel cells, and I will bleed to death internally. So

I would prefer it if we focused on the immediate priority of the ship, and killed Mr. Remini later.

"I second fifty percent of that," I reply. "I would also like the record to reflect that I did *not* push Tessa out of the airlock while she was unconscious. Some would call that gallant."

She scowls, rubbing her head, where a large bruise is forming above her eye. Whatever hit the ship threw us all about.

"OK, Remini. You got until Carla gets us up and running again. You better talk fast, because she's a pro when it comes to fixing ships."

"Yeah, I know. She and I bonded earlier, I heard all about her past, and all her former human friends on Mars."

Tessa's face falls. "What?"

"Ha! Psych! The look on your face. Jealous, much? Don't worry, she's only got robo eyes for you. Right, time to sort the elephant in the room. For real now, why are you *so* intent on killing me?"

"I told you already," groans Tessa. "I gotta kill you for Chang, to stop him killing my parents."

"Yeah but why don't you just warn your parents he's after them? They could go to the police, go into witness protection or something? There are heaps of options that *don't* involve killing lovely, lovely Luke, and I recommend literally *any* of them!"

She shakes her head, wearily. "Chang's monitoring all communications into my parents' house. He's already told me if I try to warn them in any way, he'll kill them immediately. He's hacked their domestic robot, so I know he can do it at the drop of a hat."

"Oof, yeah that does sound like Chang. He's such an asshole. You know he's only like, fourteen?"

"Right! What is *up* with that?"

"Totally. It's madness. I mean, where are the parents?"

"Where are the- That's *exactly* what I was gonna say! It's negligent."

"Forget the police, we should be reporting him to the school board, am I right?"

"Amen to that, matey, amen to that."

"What about a return shuttle?"

"Huh?"

"To save your parents, I mean. Why don't you just take a shuttle from Lunar One back to Earth and save them yourself? You go home, unplug the robot and cameras, and all get the hell off-grid. Better still, if you're in the business of killing people, you could then track down Chang and take him out on both our behalves?"

"Do you have any idea how expensive those flights are?"

"The ones exclusively for billionaires? I'm guessing not cheap. But what about a Lunar Five shuttle? There's always new crew arriving from Earth."

"If by 'always' you mean 'once a month', then yes, you're bang on."

"Ah. OK, I see your predicament. What if... oh, you borrowed the money for a Luxury Quadrant ticket? Or just stole it?"

"Tried that, bruv. Before Chang forced me to track you down, I was on a private commission to hack data from Lunar One. It was hella lucrative. Would've sorted all my troubles."

"Who was that for?"

"A client. What does it matter? I failed. The data was destroyed when the station realized their engineer was dead. Bloody Dr. Nenge ruined everything."

"Tessa, I need to know who commissioned you for that

job. Stealing data from Lunar One is serious. The 'who' is *really* important. A few months from now it could be the answer to 'who' are we invading next?"

"It was a client, that's all you need to know."

"You're worried I'll talk?"

"You're a journalist."

"You can trust me, my lips are sealed!"

"They will be once we've got the airlock working again."

"Ugh, Tessa, you're making this *reaaally* difficult for both of us. You're being so stubborn about killing me! Can't we just agree to disagree?"

"That's not really how killing works, mate."

"Think about it, Tessa, we need to provide a unified front. It's you, me, and your weirdly forward robot friend against the world. Or more specifically, us against...?"

"Oh my God, do you *ever* quit?"

"First journalist you've met, huh? I get that a lot."

"Do you get hit in the head a lot too?"

"I do!"

"Fucking moron."

"Soo... that person who commissioned you to steal the engineering data?"

"It was someone from my past, all right? It's complicated."

"Find me an assassin with a simple childhood and I'll find you a unicorn that can juggle."

"It's got nothing to do with my childhood, dickhead."

"Oh, my bad. I'm sure you had a picture-perfect upbringing. So this person from your *not-childhood*...?"

"They framed me for a murder I didn't commit."

"Ha! Sorry, but you gotta enjoy the irony. An assassin getting framed? *Karmaaaa!*"

"I've been in exile for six years because of that prick

framing me! There's an international warrant out for my arrest, meaning even if I *did* magically find a way back home, I'd be thrown straight in jail. They were offering me a clean slate in exchange for the data. But that option died with the engineer. So if I wanna get home now, bumping you off is my only hope."

"Hmm. Call me crazy, Tessa, but how about we just *fake* my death?"

She snorts derisively, like that's the most ridiculous suggestion anyone could possibly make. On behalf of the other key stakeholders in this situation, I'm quite a fan of the idea. But before I can press her further, there's a whirr and a hum, and the cabin fills with light as the ship's systems come back online.

"Carla, you did it!" cheers Tessa.

She's beaming at the robot like it's her damned sister, and the robot's giving her not one, but *two* thumbs up! Eugh. Get a room.

Life support systems are back online, Ms Tessa, but we're still heavily damaged. I've analyzed the ship's black box data, though, and I've established what hit us. You're not going to believe this...

21

TESSA

The sensor readings make no sense but Carla's adamant. She says her internal instruments corroborate the ship's black box readings.

"You're saying we were hit by a coronal blast? Babe, that makes no sense," I reply, acutely aware that both she and the ship just got fried.

Allow me to elaborate, Coach. Coronal blasts occur when a star expends it hydrogen fuel, collapses into a white dwarf, then explodes under the gravity of its own helium, expelling colossal amounts of radioactive material and heavy elements. The first supernova was recorded in-

"Carla, I don't need a science lesson, I'm all G on supernovas."

"I could use a brush up?" says Remini.

"Tough. Carla, what I'm not getting is how the hell a supernova hit us with so little warning. The nearest star to us is the Sun, but we can rule that out because it's not turned into a red dwarf."

Correct. Other things it has not turned into include a bicycle pump, an abductor, cup cakes, and graffiti.

"What?"

Sorry, I'm running some background maintenance. I think my subconscious filter was damaged in the explosion.

"Welcome to my world," snorts Remini.

"Both of you, focus!"

Crankiness will get you nowhere, Coach.

"Couldn't agree more," nods Remini, sagely.

"Bloody Nora, if you two don't get a grip so help me God I'll open the air lock manually and have done with it."

"I'll call that bluff," says Remini.

I think Ms Tessa was using hyperbole for effect.

"You don't need to say 'for effect'. It's already in the definition."

I was including for it additional emphasis, to mild comic effect.

"Ah, so *you* were using hyperbole?"

Indeed.

"I love it," smiles Remini.

"Holy shit, Carla, what's happened to you?"

I believe my conversational subroutines are doing an A-Z health check as part of my system reboot. Right now they're stuttering in archives from the Jeeves and Wooster wordplay routines. Anyone for tea with the vicar? Rum-ho!

"Cancel those subroutines. We need all your processing power on fixing the ship!"

But Ma'am, if I don't complete my systems assessment, my interactive features may be impaired indefinitely. I might lose my ability to engage in mildly-tickling parlor chat.

"You'll lose the lot if we don't fix this ship!"

Roger that, Coach. I think I know what to do.

Carla flails around the cabin like a metal octopus, humming to herself. Oh bloody hell, she's decided *now* is the time to take up dancing. If you've never seen a robot freestyling in zero G, you've not lived. Unfortunately, I don't have the luxury of time to enjoy the spectacle. I seize the control terminal.

"Carla's clearly working through some personal issues. Remini, help me figure out what's going on."

"What, so you can get the power on and throw me outta the airlock? Uh, no thanks."

"Fixing the ship was *your* idea!"

"And now I've changed my mind. I want a pact before we fix diddly."

"Does that pact involve me sparing your life, by any chance?"

"It does."

"No deal."

"You'll only have yourself to blame when we're all dead."

"No, I'll blame *you* for being a selfish arsehole in a difficult time."

"Selfish? How is *not* wanting to be murdered me being 'selfish'?"

"You're an averagely smart guy, you do the math."

"Thanks but I'll leave that to you. You seem the calculating type."

I don't have time to respond to Remini's attempt at sassy burns, though he's clearly proud of himself. He's crossed his arms and legs and is rotating like a little Buddha, pretending to rise above it .

I focus on the terminal. We've already used twenty percent of our remaining oxygen, and we're no closer to explaining what happened, or how to get out of here. Carla said it was a 'coronal ejection', but the nearest star system to us is Alpha Centauri, which is four light-years away. Which means we should've had at *least* four years' notice. But according to the ship's data, the blast came from barren space.

I'm raking through the data, trying to debunk Carla's report, but it all points to her conclusion. And there's something more, something I can't explain at all.

OK quick context: these mining ships are fitted with super sensitive particle scanners. Their sole mission is to seek out Rare Earths and extra-terrestrial elements, and claim them before anyone else. As a result, if you need to analyze a sample and track its source, they have the most comprehensive database and tools available.

So when I run a diagnostic of the supposed coronal ejection, what comes up on screen is a serious red flag.

Error: particles not recognized.

The ship's radio crackles into life. I spin around, and Carla's at a terminal, tinkering with the circuitry.

You shall go to the ball, Coach!

Carla flicks through the comms until she picks up a lunar radio station and cranks up a distorted waltz. Remini opens an eye and peeks out at the dancing robot, then clamps it back shut, intent on pretending he's still meditating, and totally not just having a huff.

The waltz stops abruptly, and a voice punches through the intercom.

>> Hello >> Hello >> Roger >> Yes? >> Greetings >> Acknowledge?

The voice has a semi-synthesized quality to it, like a machine is translating someone's voice in real-time over their speech. Carla stops dancing and interrogates the signal.

It's coming from a ship nearby, Coach. Triangulating now.

"There's another ship? They've found us? We can get rescued!" cheers Remini, abandoning his floating lotus.

>> Urgency >> Urgency >> Please responding

"Carla, can you establish a reciprocal link?"

Testing our emitters now, Coach.

I take the comms seat from Carla and open our reply channel.

"Roger, unidentified vessel, this is ship pilot Tessa Williams, receiving you, over."

"Help! I'm a hostage on this ship!" yells Remini.

"Carla, shut him up!" I hiss.

Carla snatches Remini in a headlock. *Hush now, poppet. Mummy's got you,* she coos, stroking his hair. *I'll be honest, it's weird for all of us. But we'll deal with that later.*

Our radio crackles again, with the weird dual-tone voice.

>> Star blast >> Star blast >> Ejecting >> Coronal ejecting

"Roger that, ship two, we got your message just before we were hit by the coronal blast. Our systems are heavily damaged."

>> Negative >> Warning >> Warning >> Coronal ejecting

"What are you saying, over?"

>> Two minutes >> Escape >> Over

"There's a *second* blast coming?"

>> Affirmative >> Bigger >> Over

"But we have no way to get clear – our propulsion is offline!"

>> Escaping pod? >> Over

"We have one, yes, but that would surely be even more vulnerable to the radioactive blast wave?"

>> Shield protocol >> Two minutes >> Urgent >> Over

The connection terminates.

"What the hell is 'shield protocol'?" I say, perplexed.

"Beats me. Unless you got a shield the size of a mining ship on board?" asks Remini, with genuine optimism.

His face falls when he sees from my face that I do not have a mining-ship-sized space shield up my sleeve. Truly, the man is an idiot. Carla pipes up in the silence.

Shield protocol is an experimental military technique posited in the archives, before the international ban on the militarization of space came into effect, says Carla.

"OK, can shield protocol save us?"

It's not been tested in the field, but hypothetically, yes.

"How does it work? We've only got ninety seconds left! Can you do it now?"

Affirmative, Coach. We will need to board the escape pod immediately.

A series of coordinates flash across the dashboard, with a trajectory plotted across them.

"The other ship is hacking our comms?"

To benevolent effect, it would appear. I suggest we engage constructively with this gift horse and refrain from inspecting its teeth.

"You mean not look it in the mouth?" says Remini.

Yes. We're up a creek without a paddle right now, Mr. Remini. A creek made of human fecal matter. We need all the help we can get.

"Preach!"

It appears the other party has beamed us coordinates for the escape pod. I believe they plan to intercept us, assuming we are able to clear the blast.

"That's amazing!" I cheer, inspecting the screen over Carla's shoulder.

"So much for shit creek!" chimes Remini.

Indeed. I would go so far as to say the creek is now made of plant-based milk and synthetic honey, Mr. Remini. That said, according to standard evolutionary principles there is a non-trivial chance we will be eaten upon arrival.

"What? Veto! *Hard* veto!" says Remini.

I don't believe cannibalism has much historical overlap with democracy, Mr. Remini, but perhaps this could be a bright opportunity for a cultural exchange.

The radio crackles back into life.

Urgent >> Ship log >> Dark box >> Sixty seconds >> Coronal blast

"I think it wants us to bring the black box?" says Remini.

"Journalist of the year, everybody," I snap, turning to the black box's fittings.

"What if they're stealing our data?"

"Then it's a bargain price for our lives!"

Even if the other party does not steal the data, you will be glad to have it, should you establish contact with Earth, Mr. Remini. Your peers will need validation of your claim that you were hit by a coronal blast in a sector of space with no star. The black box is the only definitive proof you have.

"It'll still be hearsay. A bunch of readings showing unknown particles? They'll dismiss it as a technical error," shrugs Remini.

On the contrary, the telemetry will provide the recipient with the coordinates to seek further evidence of your claim. To put it into context, Mr. Remini, if Nobel Prize winners were able to detect background cosmic radiation from the big bang billions of years ago, your colleagues on Earth will be able to detect trace radiation from the blast we just experienced – but only if they know where to point the sensors.

I finish prying the black box latches apart, and rip it from the terminal.

"Get to the escape pod, now!"

Even with sixty seconds to live, the shouting felt a little unnecessary. It's not a big ship. We drift six feet from the controls to the rear of the vessel and strap into the cramped pod. I'm uncomfortably close to Remini's face.

"What if this is a trap?" says Remini, buckling in.

To avoid being eaten, many mammals defecate on themselves to deter predators. You may wish to consider this strategy.

"Thanks Carla, but I'm actually not so worried about the cannibalism threat. I know they're not big on democracy, but I think there was even less historical overlap between cannibals and space travel. I'm more worried that the ship hailing us belongs to the Southern Bloc."

Do you have any other ideas, Mr. Remini?

"Nope. Just saying, if we *do* live, strong chance it'll be as bonded laborers in an Southern Bloc interment camp."

"Carla, strap in!" I call, ignoring Remini.

The robot's punching the received trajectory into the ship's systems.

The escape pod has no thrust of its own, Coach. We need to orient the ship so that the pod aligns with the flight path we received. The only thrust we have available is the remaining oxygen on board. I'm going to jettison the gas to turn the ship around. You will need to put your breathing masks on now. Coach, please take this device. Should Mr. Remini's hypothesis be true, and the other ship prove hostile, this will allow you to knock out their systems temporarily, creating a diversion, and an opportunity to escape again.

"Uh, thanks babe, but can't you hold it?"

They would scan me for such devices on arrival, and disable it. In your hands, it will appear inert, until plugged into a mainframe.

"Got it."

"If you want to smuggle it," begins Remini, "I know a trick where we stick it-"

That will not be necessary, Mr. Remini. Please affix your breathing mask now.

Carla punches several buttons and the mask panels open. Remini and I grab them and pull them over our faces, while the robot withdraws to the ship's main control panel.

Commencing air dump.

A siren sounds onboard: "OXYGEN LEVELS CRITICAL. ALL CREW, SEEK EMERGENCY RESPIRATORS."

Preparing to jettison escape pod, says Carla, from the opposite end of the ship.

"Wait, Carla, you're not strapped in!"

Sorry, Ms. Tessa. This is the only way the shield maneuver can be carried out. This ship has no self-destruct facility, and will require manual piloting to be moving in parallel to your pod. I will first depressurize the ship to initiate intense cooling. I will then use my remaining charge to ignite the fuel cells on board. The explosion will be calibrated to shatter the ship, generating a cloud of debris made of fine particles. By projecting the cloud in parallel to your flight path, it will create an effective barrier between you and the radiation, hypothetically sufficient to reduce the energy of the inbound coronal ejection, and shield you from the blast long enough to reach the other ship. Goodbye, Coach. Thank you for your friendship.

I'm begging her not to leave us but Carla seals the hatch and jettisons our escape pod. As we accelerate, a proximity alarm sounds. The coronal blast is coming. On the tracking screen beside us, I watch as Carla's mining ship accelerates too. We're moving in parallel, several kilometers apart. I'm screaming, staring at her dot on our screen, not daring to blink until in an instant, the signal vanishes, and she's gone.

22

———

LUKE

So.... this is awkward. What to say when you're strapped into an escape pod, thirty centimeters from your would-be-assassin's face, while she sobs at the loss of her best friend, who happened to be a sentient robot and a surprisingly good dancer.

Yikes, forget the exotic matter, being this close to someone crying in zero gravity is its own kind of biological warfare. Tears and snot are beading off her wrinkled cheeks. I'm closing my eyes, trying not to let any of it get in me, but I can feel the salty droplets splashing across my face like a passed-out drunk being pissed on by their friends. Not that that's ever happened to me. I'm always awake for it.

In a way, things were easier when Tessa was trying to kill me. God, I *really* need the tears to stop. It's like a monsoon in here.

"There, there, uh, plenty more fish in the cosmos..." I say, awkwardly.

Huge mistake. A globule of snot lands squarely in my mouth, hitting my epiglottis like a guided missile. Oh no. There's a chain reaction being set off. The taste... so familiar, yet so not mine. The sensation... so invasive. My stomach's churning. I'm trying to suppress it but there's no turning back.

With a violent heave, my diaphragm and muscles turn my stomach inside out, throwing my last meal through my esophagus and directly into Tessa's weeping face.

For a split second, her weeping stops. There's a moment of sheer disbelief, before her own tidal wave of revulsion kicks in. With a *hurrrggghh*, she vomits straight back at me, showering my face with hot, stinking sick.

We're now caked in each other's vomit, seasoned with tears and snot, and caught in a Kafkaesque echo chamber of reciprocal vomiting. Shackled by our safety harnesses, neither of us is able to move or avoid the other's tirade. Our only option is to tilt our heads out of the way, but that only causes the floating vomit to fly in a circular motion, turning the pod into a second hand food processor.

As I'm vomiting my guts out, while inhaling snortlets of Tessa's bile, something rocks the pod. A series of clangs shake us. A heavy sensation is spreading through my body. Gravity, sweet dear, merciful gravity is returning to our pod! But... it's not going the right way. All the blood's pooling in my head. Sick is raining from my feet to my face.

Sparks fly beside us, with the ear-splitting squeal of metal tearing. Both of us yelp in shock as a huge green flame slices the length of the pod. The two halves fall to the ground with a clatter. We're upside-down in a space ship. Liquid sick is trickling off my collar and rolling up to my earlobes.

Tessa unleashes her harness. She lands in a crumpled heap beside my head, retching and spluttering. I follow suit, landing on top of her.

"Whoever designed that pod needs to be shot," I splutter, scrambling onto all fours.

Tessa shoves me away and stumbles to the side, cursing me to Pluto and back, while she leans against the wall, gasping for fresh air.

At this point, I notice we're not alone. An astronaut is standing before us, with a gold-lens helmet on, an orange suit, and a bunch of weird symbols embroidered across it. Ah crap, and they've got a space gun.

"Don't shoot!" I cough, raising my arms in surrender.

But the nozzle it's clutching appears to emit sound, rather than bullets.

>> Welcoming >> You have disk? >> Dark box >> Yes?

Holy crap, this is the dude we were speaking to on the ship!

"Yeah, we got the disk. Thanks for saving us, brosef. Can we see your face? It can't be worse than ours right now."

The astronaut shakes its head.

>> Helmet important >> Contamination risk >> Helmet stay >> You have disk?

"Oh, cool, got it. Uh, yeah, Tessa, give him the disk, will you?"

Tessa glares at me from across the cargo bay, which is twice the size of our entire previous ship, and comfortably accommodates our pod, among several rows of symbol-covered canisters, all wired in serial.

She tosses the black box across the hold, which the astronaut catches using some sort of magnetic switch in his gloves. If I ever get out of this, I'm buying me a pair of those.

The astronaut places the black box into a container the size of a microwave, and seems to be scanning it. A screen nearby is rolling off lines of code, in that same symbol language I don't know.

Now that I'm no longer retching, though my suit absolutely reeks, I take a moment to absorb our surroundings a little more. The ship seems a lot sleeker than ours; the fittings are smarter, the equipment looks a lot more advanced too.

Something's resting on top of one of the crates. It's shape is unmistakable. I glance at Tessa, and she's seen it too. Halfway between us, unguarded, and lying on its side, is a gun.

For a split second we stare at each other, then race for it with a cry. She's closer than me, so gets there first. All right, she's *quicker* than me, whatever. Either way, I miss the gun, but use my momentum to dive past her as she takes aim.

We've traded places and I've got my back up against one of the wired canisters, which towers over me. I'm really hoping Tessa's making the same assumptions I am; that the stickers and symbols plastered all over it mean something along the lines of *crazy explosive, do not shoot.*

>> How much helium? >> Your planet bring helium >> Enough?

"Step away from the tank," growls Tessa.

"I'm good here," I reply, with my hands raised.

>> Hello? >> I say how much helium your planet bring?

"Sorry dude, I can't concentrate on both of you right now. Tessa, put the gun down and let's talk about this."

"No way. I've lost enough to this mad bullshit already. First Sienna, now Carla. I am *not* losing my parents. I'm sorry, Remini, but this is where it ends for you."

"On behalf of all the Remini's onboard, fuck that for a day out."

"If you don't step away from the canister, I'll shoot your leg first then drag you away."

"Oh, right, I forgot that was your trademark move. Real nice. An assassin who likes to kneecap their victims. What a touch of class."

"Shut your mouth and do what I say."

"Uh, again, *no*. If I move, I'm dead for sure. If I stay, I'm pretty sure you *won't* shoot me, because last time I checked, you don't want to die in a random explosion."

Tessa's jaw is clenched so tightly I'm worried she might crack a molar.

>> *Excuse me?* >> *Somebody answering me please?*

"Shut the hell up!" yells Tessa. "You don't know what's going on here."

The anger is gripping every millimeter of her face. Holy crap, she might just pull that trigger. I think she's reached the point of such despair she's willing to take us both out in a last throw of the dice. That composed, calculating rationality has vanished. This is a raw, bereaved, heartbroken human, with less regard for our lives than those she's left back on Earth. Oh boy. Maybe she's right. Maybe this *is* the end.

"Why shoot me now?" I ask, in the most off-hand, non-inflammatory tone I can manage.

"You patronizing fuck!"

OK, note to self: work on the tone.

"I mean, why take me in an escape pod if you're just gonna blow us both up here? What's the point? You think Chang will somehow find out about my death quickly enough to stop him killing your folks, even if you're dead with me?"

"If that's the only chance I have left, I'll take it," says Tessa, trembling with rage.

"Then you should've left me in that freaking mining ship to blow up with the second ejection! You and your robot friend could've been sitting here drinking tea. No-one would be covered in anyone else's sick or snot, and I wouldn't have to give myself a headache trying to rationalize your insane logic."

"Carla knew this was the only way," sobs Tessa. "There's no way in hell you would've followed through with the shield protocol if we'd abandoned you in there."

She's got a point there.

"Carla did this to save me," she sniffs.

"And now you're gonna throw that away?"

"If it saves my parents, yes."

"That's what I'm saying, you're not thinking clearly! You're emotional."

"Oh, *really*, Remini? I'm emotional? *Really*? The woman pointing a gun at you, covered in sick, crying about the loss of everyone she loves, is *emotional*? He's done it again, everyone, journalist of the year!"

I know she's being heavily sarcastic, but I'll be honest with you. A sizeable part of my ego glows whenever I hear those words, regardless of the context.

>> *Hey, I speaking to you important subject!* >> *Please stop bicker* >> *Please listening me*, yells the astronaut, dialing up the volume on his vocal synthesizer.

"Goodbye, Remini," says Tessa, bitterly.

She pulls the trigger, and a faint crack rings out across the chamber. Holy crap, it's broken off in her hand! And it's full of tiny spikes, which are erupting upwards out of the top.

"What the hell?" she cries.

She's leaning back from the sparkler-effect, staring at the fragmented trigger piece on the floor in dismay. Tessa sucks her thumb, which has been pricked by one of the erupting spikes. The astronaut marches over and snatches it from her.

>> *Is not gun* >> *Is vegetable*

"What the hell kind of vegetable shoots spikes into the air?" says Tessa.

>> *Not spikes* >> *Seeds*

"And you just leave that sort of thing lying around, do you? You could have had someone's eye out with that!" she protests.

"Fuck off, Tessa, you thought it was a *gun!*" I yell.

"I knew what I was doing," she scowls, sucking her thumb.

"Yeah. It looks that way."

>> *You two stop bicker* >> *My home planet needing help*

"Home planet? What the hell are you talking about? You mean you're not from Earth?" snaps Tessa.

>> *Correct* >> *Now you must helping me*

"How are we supposed to help you if we don't know where you're from? You're an alien for God's sake! Somehow speaking English?" says Tessa.

>> *Your robot send me translation key* >> *Very smart machine* >> *Sorry for loss* >> *Now we need hurry* >> *Helium* >> *Your planet sending helium, yes?* >> *Enough?*

"Yeah, they've definitely been sending a lot of if out here," I say. "But we don't know why. Are you working with them?"

>> *They not replying me* >> *Like you not replying me* >> *Why humans not replying me?* >> *Much at stake* >> *Very urgent*

"Uh, maybe because we've got our own problems, space man!" snaps Tessa.

"Woah, let's all be nice to the alien, he might be weighing up whether or not to eat us," I mutter.

>> *I not eating human* >> *Plant only on my planet*

"Oh my God. Within five seconds of meeting you, even *alien* vegans tell you they're vegan, am I right?"

Tessa glares at me with deep loathing. Carla would've laughed. Or said something rude about the monarchy. I miss that robot.

>> *My mission urgent*

"Ugh, *men!*" snaps Tessa. "Your mission isn't automatically the most important just because you've got couple of sperm sacks dangling between your legs!"

>> *On my planet we carrying sperm sacks in feet* >> *Is very painful*

"Dayuuum son. And I thought the balls of *my* feet were sore! Wait, I got more. I bet my boy here enjoys a good foot rub though, am I right? Oh, and now we *really* know what they say about men with big feet - they say we can see your balls, dude!"

>> *You can seeing my sperm sacks?*

"No, I was doing a bit. Ugh, never mind," I sigh.

"Listen, idiots, some of us are trying to save our families right now," says Tessa.

"Hey, you think I *wanna* be here? I'm trying to get to Planet Nine to prevent a world war breaking out back home!" I protest.

"Someone else can stop that. No one else can save my parents," says Tessa.

>> *You must killing him* >> *To saving parents?*

"Yes."

>> *Is normal* >> *On your planet?*

"Sort of," she shrugs.

"No!" I yell. "She's an assassin. Her moral compass is

very warped."

"I'm a *retired* assassin," she corrects.

"You're awfully active in the old killing fields for someone with a free bus pass," I reply.

"This ain't a job, Remini, I'm being *forced* to do this!"

>> Enough! >> I cannot focus with you two bicker >> My mission more important than both your >> My mission fail? >> We all dying >> So shutting up, now >> I fix this, then you two helping me >> Yes?

"How are you gonna 'fix' this?" scowls Tessa. "I need proof he's dead. Not just a video, I have to send a body part that proves it beyond doubt."

>> Body part? >> I have plan >> Luke Man >> Go standing over there.

"Huh? Why... You're not gonna club me to death with that space vegetable, are you?"

>> No >> Is painless solution >> But hurry >> My time short

I shift several paces sideways, then step into a tall, rectangular box, much like a shower cubicle. It's one of two, connected by several pipes, and feeding off cables from the canisters in the holding bay.

Before I can ask another question, the astronaut taps his controls and a bright blue light pulses through the cubicle, top to bottom, all around, like I'm being scanned. The piping around me hums with activity, then falls quiet.

>> Is complete >> You have ten minutes >> Then we saving universe

I step out of the shower cubicle, checking my arms for lasting effects. Aside from a light tingling, I detect no harm done. It's only when I see Tessa's astonished face, that I turn around.

In the next cubicle, standing opposite me, is... *me*. Well, a really goofy version of me. It's just standing there, torso tilting slightly forwards over its hips, arms dangling down loosely, a watery smile across its face, and half-closed heavy eyelids.

"What the hell is that?" I yell, backing away.

>> *Is you* >> *Non-sentient collagen replica* >> *Is stable ten minutes only* >> *Tessa woman must killing it now while we recording*

"What. The. *Actual*. Fuck," says Tessa, shaking her head.

"Why are you so weirded out? Surely this is every assassin's wet dream? I mean literally – that guy's got a moist sheen to him, like a freshly birthed foal. Hey little fella!"

I'm waving at my doppelganger but it doesn't respond.

>> *Is non-sentient* >> *I tell you already*

"My bad. Go on, then, Tessa, what are you waiting for?"

"This is too fucking weird," she says, shaking her head.

"How does *this* gross you out?"

"It ain't normal!"

"But killing an *actual* person is?"

"Yeah, for me!"

>> *Nine minutes*

"Until what?" says Tessa.

>> *Body is degrading* >> *You must making kill now* >> *Then we have few minutes for dismemberment*

"Woah now, dismemberment? That's next level, guys, way too gross," I say, holding my hands up in protest.

>> *Tessa woman say proof of death required* >> *So we must sending body, yes?* >> *But sending small part much easier* >> *So we must dismember body first*

"Damn, I guess you're right."

"Can't you, like, face the wall or something?" says Tessa.

"What?"

"I can't kill your jelly clone while you're watching, it's too weird!"

"It would be weirder if I *didn't* watch! Come on, how many people get to witness their own death, then talk about it in the bar later?"

>> *On my planet* >> *Some religions believe-*

"No time for that, space bruv. Remini, face the wall so I can kill your clone. If we run out of time it's back to killing you, so chop chop, as it were."

"Wait, but is this actually gonna work? Why dismember the clone's body if it's gonna turn to mush in ten minutes anyway?"

>> *We doing preservative treatment for sending body part* >> *But chemical not good on full flesh body* >> *It would making kill video look fake*

"Gotcha. Alright then Tessa, get on with it."

"I can't! Not with you two watching me..."

"Wait, are you telling me you're some kind of *shy* assassin?"

"All assassins are shy, dickhead! If you get *seen* killing someone, you're a murderer, and you go to jail. Assassins work discretely, and *don't* go to jail. I'm not used to being watched while I work!"

"Would it help if me and the spaceman kill it with you? I'd be into that."

>> *Ditto*

"What is this now, Caesar in the bleeding Senate? No! I work *alone*."

"Hey, I'm just blue-skies thinking over here. *You're* the one with performance anxiety, Tessa."

>> *When I having performance problem* >> *I run bathroom tap* >> *It helping flow*

"Fuck's sake," replies Tessa. "I'm not struggling to *pee*! It's a bit more serious than that!"

>> *Bladder retention is serious problem* >> *For men of certain age*

"Amen to that, brother," I add.

"The two of you, turn around right now!" says Tessa.

>> *For camera* >> *I must watching*

"Pervert," I chuckle.

The astronaut tilts his head in confusion.

"Ignore him, spaceman," sighs Tessa. "You can watch, but Remini needs to face away."

>> *Agree* >> *Luke Man, you should turning around* >> *Is bad idea seeing own death* >> *Trust me*

"Ugh, *so* not fair."

I turn and face the wall like a naughty kid. There's some scuffling behind me; it sounds like Tessa's grabbed my clone from behind. There's a weird gurgling noise. Wait, is she *choking* him?

I spin around to see what's going on, only to gasp in revulsion. Tessa's pinned my clone to the ground. She's on her back, and he's lying on top of her, like they're two mannequins trying to spoon. She's got her arm around his neck and she's squeezing, making his eyes bulge. He's still got that soppy, watery smile, though bubbles are frothing around his lips as the air is squeezed from his fake lungs.

Hold up, *Tessa's* the one making the weird gurgling noises?

"What the hell is wrong with you?" I ask.

"Fuck off, Remini, you're not supposed to be watching this!"

"Why do you sound like that? It's like you're trying to shit out a fire hydrant!"

"Its... neck... is... thick..." she grunts.

"You have no idea how ridiculous you look right now," I chuckle.

"Says... the one... dying..."

"I'll have you know my jelly clone looks very peaceful. This whole thing is proving most cathartic. Maybe I'll keep a copy of this video for my kids – you know, in case my *real* death is super grizzly and they need some comfort."

"You're a... terrible... parent..."

I look to the astronaut for backup but he shrugs, apparently agreeing with Tessa. She exhales with a huge sigh and rolls away, discarding the jelly body. Its eyes are frozen half-open, and its lips parted as if it's asking for directions. Which, obviously, I would never do.

"Done," she grunts.

The astronaut and I applaud like she just cut the ribbon to a new supermarket.

"Oh fuck off the both of you," snaps Tessa.

>> Four minutes to dismember body >> Then preserving >> Then sending >> Then save universe

"Man, that's a lot to do in four minutes," I reply. "Shotgun the easy stuff. Can I prepare the postage? I'm great at licking stamps. True story. Ask literally *any* stamp."

Tessa and the astronaut both ignore me, and begin a private discussion over which body part to dismember, and which of the astronaut's tools they should use to do it, taking into consideration such factors as the gravity on the Moon, and the implements available there. The fact they're both at pains to ignore me is frankly hurtful. I'm feeling deeply underappreciated on this mission. I'm journalist of the *year*! Does that mean *nothing* out here?

They're standing over the body, with their backs to me, muttering like I'm not even in the room.

"... The arm isn't comprehensive proof that he's dead though..."

... Intestinal tract >> Messy but compelling...

"... Brain?..."

... Too complex >> They see is clone >> Heart better...

"... Could go lower?..."

Lower? OK, this is too much. *Now* I'm getting involved.

"You are *not* sending that jumped up kid my *balls*!" I yell, storming across the hangar floor.

"Ew, gross. No-one's talking about sending your shriveled little plums, Remini. We need compelling evidence, remember?"

"Just send him my heart and have done with it."

"Easy tiger, it ain't that simple. I got a reputation to consider here," says Tessa.

"Come again?"

"When you send a body part to someone, you're sending more than just flesh and bone, bruv, you're sending information. A clue as to your inner psyche, your personality. Whichever piece of you I send will say something about *me*, as much as it does about you. I gotta think about my career. People talk in this business. I don't wanna be known as the weird butt-flaps and sphincters lady."

>> On my planet >> Is what they calling your type already

Tessa scowls. "Spaceman, could we send his entire head? I could tell Chang the poison and preservative are what made the brain abnormal?"

>> Is possible >> Head is good choice

"All right, stand back. I'm cutting it off now," she declares.

I take back everything I said about catharsis. As I watch Tessa shred my neck with a handsaw, splattering the floor with my clone's blood and sinews, I can't help but feel a strong sense of self-pity. I had so much to live for. After several minutes, she holds up my severed head with a triumphant smile. She looks positively savage.

"Are we done here?" I grunt, trying not to vomit all over again.

The astronaut grabs my severed head from Tessa and chucks it into the shower cubicle that's not a shower cubicle, slams the door, flicks a switch, and folds his arms as it apparently bakes it in some kinda infrared light.

Half a minute later, he plucks the steaming head from the cubicle, tosses it to Tessa, who catches it like a hot potato.

Spaceman marches to his control panel, and the black box we brought.

>> *Is ten minutes already* >> *We must sending it later* >> *Now we needing calculations* >> *Your people bringing helium* >> *Ship log shows much transport* >> *They maybe near critical threshold* >> *Kasplargit!* >> *Is good news!*

"Critical threshold for what?" I ask.

I'm staring at my headless corpse while the rest of the clone's body dries out like a raisin. The ship shudders, throwing all of us off-balance as a mighty clang resonates through the hangar.

>> *They here* >> *Perfect timing*

"Who's here? What's going on?" says Tessa, hastily wrapping the head up in a cloth.

An alarm sounds on the astronaut's ship, along with a

warning message. His hand-held device translates it, just about audible over the main speakers.

>> *Alert >> Incoming Vessel >> Capture imminent*

"What's the bloody use of an alarm that warns you *after* you've been captured?" fumes Tessa.

>> *Is not alarm >> Is calendar reminder >> I scheduling this*

"You *scheduled* your own capture?"

>> *Yes*

"Are you insane?"

>> *I very busy >> Much to do >> We must saving universe*

Ahh, I get it now. The astronaut's a nut job.

The hangar doors hiss and groan, as giant robotic levers prize them open. A voice booms through a loudspeaker.

"This vessel is under embargo. Come out with your hands up!"

"Oy, Remini," whispers Tessa.

"Yeah?" I whisper back.

"Did I hit my head again?"

"Not that I saw, why?"

"Then how come whoever's through that door is speaking with a Southern Bloc accent?"

That, dear Tessa, is an excellent question.

23

———

TESSA

Ever get that feeling you're one of them dolls within a doll within a doll? We've gone from being in an escape pod, swallowed by an alien ship, which has itself been swallowed by a military ship. At some point, I'm counting on a giant space whale eating the lot, then belching us up on some sunny shore back on Earth.

The soldiers are all dressed in Southern Bloc military uniforms, and look majorly on edge. I'm guessing this is the first alien spaceship they've encountered too. A woman steps forward and thrusts an ear piece into mine and Remini's ears, then steps back in line with others, clicking her heels with a rhythmic flutter like she's on parade.

"Captain Zhang wants to see you on the bridge. Now."

Her accent has vanished and has been replaced by a Northern Bloc synth translator. It's modulating her words in real time. It's similar tech to what the astronaut's been using to speak to us, only, in his instance, he does the translation work on his side and broadcasts to us in our own language. Whereas we humans tend to prefer letting the recipient suffer the dual-tone sound. The Southern Bloc soldiers are speaking their own language, and it's getting decoded as it reaches our ears, which quickly get used to filtering out their natural voices and focusing on the synth translation.

The soldiers march us through the ship at gunpoint – real guns this time, not misleading alien vegetables left lying around. Man, I'd kill to have a turnip grenade stashed in my back pocket right now.

When you're passing through a windowless series of corridors and elevators in a space you've never seen the outside of, it can be hard to get a sense of scale. This thing must be the size of several tower blocks at least. The giveaway is that it's generating its own gravitational field, and they only fit that on the largest ships. Specifically, the speculative long-haul personnel carrier ships designed for the Mars colony missions. Or in this case, for the Southern Bloc's secret troop carrier that we find ourselves on. Same, same, right?

The elevator spits us out onto the bridge. It's got a horseshoe dashboard, staffed by eight seated soldiers. In the center is something resembling a snooker table bearing a huge tactical screen.

In place of the usual celestial schematic you get on these battle screens, it, and all the other screens on the bridge, are dominated by a set of symbols which are bouncing around like squash balls.

A stern-looking woman eyeballs us as we're prodded further onto the bridge and lined up beside the table.

"What the hell is this?" she says, pointing to the dancing symbols.

>> *You got my message!*

"It's locked all of our systems. This is a serious act of cyber hostility against the Southern Bloc!"

>> Relax >> Is not cyber attack >> Is my screensaver >> I sent it you with my coordinates

"To what end?" asks the captain, through gritted teeth.

>> Insurance policy >> Guarantee you bring us immediately to bridge >> Could not risk getting put in brig >> Plan work >> Nice meeting you, Zhang Captain.

The astronaut taps his wrist panel and the screensavers vanish.

>> Zhang Captain >> Now you here >> We must speaking urgently about helium >> Are quantities as specified?

Captain Zhang's face sours as she spits the order, "Throw them in the brig."

>> Wait! >> We running out of time! >> You needing my help!

Before the soldiers can usher us out of the bridge, a beacon flashes up on the tactical screen.

"Captain, we're picking up a distress signal from the adjacent sector," says the nearest crew member. "It's a mining vessel. It looks fully laden."

"What's an active mining vessel doing this far out from the belt?" says Zhang.

"No idea, Captain, but they're requesting immediate assistance."

"Put them through."

The soldier nods and opens a audible channel between the two vessels.

"This is Captain Zhang of the Southern Ship Prosperity. Identify yourself."

H-h-hello c-captain... This is m-mission l-leader Hooper of the m-mining ship L-three-fourteen."

"You put out a distress signal, Hooper?"

We- we were hit by s-something h-hours ago... Our

*systems are almost all o-offline... We're fr-freezing to death...
Air is running l-low... Request immediate s-support...*

"What are you doing in restricted deep space, Hooper?"
presses Zhang. "A loaded mining ship so far from its
territory? This smacks of a trap."

*N-no t-trap c-captain... We were t-told to relieve a-
another c-crew... A-already had o-our payload... Told to t-take
theirs too... They had to r-return to b-base.*

"Another mining ship?"

Y-yes.

"Who told you to take on their cargo?"

*The Northern B-bloc m-military. They t-told us to b-
bring it th- this way.*

"What is the cargo?"

A-asteroid minerals.

"No, I mean what's the cargo you were forced to take
from the other ship?"

H- Helium. We've got several tankers and-

"Enough, Hooper. The rest we can discuss in private,"
says Zhang, glancing at the three of us with suspicion.

Please h-help...

"Standby Hooper. We will assist you."

"But captain," chimes the crew member. "That ship
belongs to a Northern Bloc corporation. We're at war with
the North!"

"Space is a neutral zone, lieutenant. We will honor our
commitments under international law, and we will provide
aid to this civilian ship. Punch the course."

"Aye, Captain."

>> This is mistake >> Wrong direction!

"Silence! I don't enjoy being manipulated, stranger, so I
suggest you tread carefully. Lieutenant, take them away.
We will question them separately."

>> *Zhang Captain* >> *Listen me* >> *There is no time* >> *Is too late for that crew* >> *We must saving others*

"I don't know what it's like where you people are from, but in my country we help those in need," replies Zhang.

"Oh, we're actually from all over. It's quite the story-" begins Remini.

>> *Listen me!*

The screens glitch then fill with the bouncing symbols once again. Captain Zhang's eyes dart to the astronaut with malice.

"Release our systems at once, or we will use lethal force!" she barks.

>> *You killing me* >> *And screen like this forever* >> *I only want talking*

"You have sixty seconds."

>> *Ship is bringing helium* >> *HE-3* >> *Is good* >> *Is enough?*

"The amount, the purpose, and the very existence of HE-3 in this sector is strictly classified. I'm not at liberty to share such details with my own crew, let alone with hostile captives."

>> *Not hostile* >> *I helping* >> *I must knowing helium quantity reached?* >> *Is critical* >> *Must have enough otherwise all lost* >> *Too little means too soon* >> *Means everyone die*

"I told you, I'm not at liberty to-"

>> *Zhang Captain!* >> *You must turning ship around at once* >> *Either helium urgent* >> *Or we wasting time* >> *Is too late for crew either way* >> *I must knowing if helium sufficient yet or no?*

"I don't think you understand how being a prisoner works," snarls the Captain. "You cloaked our fleet's signature and lured us off course, then launched a cyber attack on our systems. Both of those moves were ill-advised. You are now a hostage on this ship. You are a prisoner of your own war."

>> *Not my war*

"To be fair, it's not," chimes Remini. "I'm pretty sure this dude's from another planet."

"Explain," snaps the Captain.

"No, no, *he's* from another planet," says Remini, hastily. "*We're* from Earth. Well, she's technically from the Moon these days."

"The fuck I am!" I snap, elbowing Remini in the ribs.

The soldier behind me whacks the back of my legs with a baton in retribution, sending me crashing to my knees painfully. I feel the baton against my jugular vein, poised to unleash a world of pain across my nervous system. I raise my hands in surrender.

"Nice," chuckles Remini.

He immediately suffers the same fate.

"Ouch!" he protests. "I'm trying to *save* you people!"

"From what?" says Zhang.

"Uh... from *my* people."

"The Northern Bloc?"

"Yeah! They might have... uh... how to put this... illegally developed the most lethal bioweapon in the history of mankind... Oh, and a huge drone army... and a fleet of evacuation ships... I think they're gonna use the peace treaty as a decoy to invade the Southern Bloc."

"And you two are here to save us *how*?" frowns the captain.

"I ain't here for that," I interject. "I'm here against my will, courtesy of the wankbag CEO of Lunar Three. Same woman who owns the vessel you're flying to rescue right now. As far as I'm concerned, ignore the spaceman, ignore this fat prick, and keep on with what you're doing. What you just said rings true; Dr. Nenge doesn't give a toss about her workers. So I'm with you, captain. Let's save those asteroid miners, get them back to the Moon base, and get that vile woman behind bars."

Zhang eyes me up doubtfully. "You two Northerners seem to have very different aims. If this is true, why are you traveling together?"

"She's trying to kill me," says Remini.

"*Was*," I object. "And only because his debt collector has taken my bloody parents hostage."

"Yeah, that's fair. Chang is one hundred percent why I went to hide on the Moon in the first place," nods Remini. "OK, maybe it's more like fifty percent. The other fifty percent was investigating the death of the Lunar Inspector. I don't know if you heard but I was named investigative journalist of the-"

>> We don't have time for this! >> Zhang Captain >> It is critical I understand the helium situation! >> I believe we are flying wrong direction >> Time is against us!

"Back up. What?" says Zhang, her eyes narrowing.

>> I said we-

"Not you – him. What do you know about the Lunar Inspector's death?" she says, glaring at Remini.

I don't like where this is going.

"Not as much as Tessa knows," he shrugs, nodding at me.

Suddenly it's all eyes on me. Ugh, I *hate* public scrutiny. It's really not playing to an assassin's forte. We're introverts, you know? I find public speaking very stressful. Most people assume I'm fearless because I outwardly present as very confident, but I get *super* tongue-tied trying to speak to groups. I was asked to be a key note speaker at the annual assassin's conference once, and I totally bottled it. Spent the whole time dry heaving in the bathroom. Turned out to be for the best, though. My replacement got assassinated by a member of the audience in the post-talk mingling. Some students are just *too* keen to apply what they've learned.

"The Lunar Inspector," says Zhang, approaching me like a cat stalking its prey. "What do you know?"

"Uh... It's complicated," I mumble. "I really don't wanna get into it."

Captain Zhang stops abruptly. Her feet have struck something wet. Her eyes fall on the pool of red that's formed at my feet. It is at this point that I realize the cloth I grabbed from the astronaut's ship is *not* waterproof, and blood has been seeping through the fabric this whole time. Zhang's nostrils flare. Her eyes move from her dappled shoes to the bundle in my arms.

"What. The *hell*. Is that?" she hisses.

"Oh, don't worry about it," says Remini. "That's just my head."

"*What?*"

"I know, right? I told Tessa to take my balls, but she wouldn't listen."

Captain Zhang indicates for me to show her what's under the cloth. I ditch the material and hold up Remini's bloodied, jelly-preserved head. The crew gasps in horror.

"How is this possible?" says Zhang.

"The space bloke gave it to me," I say, nodding at the astronaut.

>> *Only because they bickering* >> *We needed hurry up* >> *To saving universe!*

"How the hell does cloning a severed head save the universe?" cries Zhang.

"To be clear," I reply, "I only want to save my parents.

Remini's the one trying to save the universe. He's got a real complex."

"What? Don't look at me!" cries Remini. "I only wanna save the *planet.*"

"So *you* want to save the universe?" says Zhang, whipping round to face the astronaut.

>> *Yeeeeeessssss!* cries the astronaut, clasping his hands in emphatic prayer.

As he drops to his knees in exasperation, he relinquishes his hold over the ship's screens. Captain Zhang rubs the bridge of her nose, digesting all that's been said. I take the opportunity to sidle up to her delicately.

"Captaaaaaain, babe, I need to get this severed head and video of Remini's fake execution to Earth, to save my parents. Could you do me a solid, woman to woman - let me use one of your ship's probes?"

"For prisoners, you three sure have a lot of requests," groans the captain.

"Technically I've not requested anything yet, but for completeness, I'd *love* a coffee," says Remini.

>> *Captain* >> *You will answering my questions or no?*

"I'm still totally unclear what the hell you three are trying to achieve," says Zhang.

"I told you," cries Remini, "I'm trying to stop *my* bloc from attacking *your* bloc with their new bioweapon! OK, if we're splitting hairs, they claim it's *not* a weapon, but rather some kinda toxin they found drifting about out here. They call it *exotic matter,* and it's the most deadly thing I've ever witnessed in my life."

Zhang doesn't look convinced. I feel if I want her to believe any of what we're saying, I at least need to corroborate the bits I know to be true.

"Remini's right," I say, reluctantly. "That bastard Dr.

Nenge let the exotic matter kill my fiancé and her colleagues. She colluded with our government to use them as guinea pigs, then covered up their deaths. Your people could be next, and someone needs to stop them."

"Thank you!" says Remini, astonished to receive my endorsement. "Our side are putting lives in danger. They're storing exotic matter on Lunar One in secret. If they use it against your side on Earth, the effects would be tantamount to genocide. Captain, we *have* to stop whatever attack the North is planning. The only way to hold my government to account is by getting the truth out to the public. Please, you have to help me!"

Before Zhang can reply, an alert reaches the helm.

"Captain, we've reached the distressed mining ship..."

"Hail them," says Zhang.

"I am, Ma'am. They're not replying."

—

24

LUKE

According to the tactical screen, we've just docked with the mining ship. Not that we felt even the slightest rumble. This ship's way too big for that kinda nonsense. Everyone looks tense. The astronaut's hard to read, on account of having a huge gold visor covering his face, but he's back on his feet, and rocking side to side, which means he's either anxious about the helium on board, or he needs the toilet.

>> *Zhang Captain >> How much helium is on board?*

"Silence on the bridge," snaps Zhang. "Soldier, hail them again."

"Their systems are completely unresponsive, Ma'am."

"Lieutenant, take a boarding party and search the mining ship for survivors. Maintain an open video link at all times."

"Understood, Captain."

The lieutenant leaves the bridge, radioing for support as she goes. A few tetchy minutes pass by, in which the astronaut bleats on about helium, while Tessa insists they need to send my head back to Earth.

A holographic video feed crackles up on screen. It's from a hovering drone, floating at the back of the boarding party, casting a spotlight through the darkened mining ship. This vessel's way bigger than the one we rode out here. It's got the same basic single-cabin design, but this one's crammed with helium canisters.

The crews' bodies are slumped over the seats and huddled in corners. Vapor is rising from them. The drone flies closer to inspect. The steam is grainy and faintly colored. Dread sweeps through my stomach as I see the swirling cloud shimmer in the drone's light, hovering above the rest of the crew. As they probe the dead miners' bodies, scorched flesh comes into view. Oh crap. I hate to be that guy, but it's time to squeal like a piglet.

"Captain, we need to get out of here right now!" I blurt.

"Silence on the bridge!" insists Zhang. "Lieutenant, status report?"

No survivors, Captain. But the ship appears to be contaminated with some kind of powder...

"It's exotic matter," I cry. "Captain, it's what killed the crews in the asteroid belt. We have to get away or everyone here will perish!"

The cloud on screen begins to swirl, then moves over one of the soldiers. It falls differently than in the lab, this time it's more like heavy snow than a bucket of salt. But the effect is no less awful. The soldier screams as the caustic substance burns through their clothes, reducing their flesh to grain.

"Helms Op, retract the space bridge!" orders Zhang.

The helms operator spins around, terrified. "But Ma'am, the boarding party are still down there?"

"Do it now, that's an order!"

"Aye, Ma'am."

"Distance us from the mining ship. Fifty kilometers. Now."

"Fifty kilometers, yes Ma'am."

Captain, we're aborting the mission. The substance is hostile, I'm ordering a full retreat. I suggest we immediately quarantine the-

Captain Zhang silences the radio channel with a flick of her hand. She takes a deep, heavy breath. The video feed vanishes with it and the tactical screen switches to an external view of the ship and its asteroid payload, as we drift away from both.

"Weapons Ops, prepare to fire on my mark," says Zhang.

"Captain, you can't be serious," cries Tessa. "Those people called you for help - you said we were coming here to *rescue* them!"

"Fire," says Zhang, calmly.

Both Tessa and the astronaut cry out in despair as the ballistics strike the mining ship. With its oxygen tanks depleted, there's no ball of fire, just the seeping of leaked helium into the vacuum of space, and fragments scattering like a firework.

"You killed them," chokes Tessa. "Innocent fucking workers, and you killed them all!"

"Would you rather I let it kill us all too?" says Zhang.

>> I told you they were lost cause >> Now you have wasted time >> And wasted helium >> You must telling me now >> Where is stockpile I requesting?

"*You* requested?" says Zhang.

>> Of course! >> Who you think transmissions coming from?

"What transmissions?" frowns the captain.

"Psst, Tessa," I whisper, leaning in, "Are you thinking what I'm thinking?"

"No. And why are you whispering?"

"I thought we could confide in one another? You know, buddy up as two unlikely friends, now that whole assassination thing is behind us, and your gal Carla's gone?"

"Go fuck yourself," she replies.

"That came out wrong. What I *mean* is: we've both suffered losses here."

"What have you lost?" she asks, anger rising in her voice.

I point to my sparsely-populated crown of hairs and raise my eyebrows. She does *not* care for the comparison.

"OK, fine," I reply. "Too soon to be friends, I get it. Let's have a respectful mourning period for Carla, then buddy up later. I've got a theory, though. I'm starting to think she was the first representative from Earth to properly decode the astronaut's message. Because she was fitted with some random technology no-one else has anymore, right?"

"So?"

"It might explain why he's getting so pissed at everyone, and why the captain's looking at him like he's got two heads?"

"What's your point, Remini?"

"The astronaut's got a plan. He thinks the military has been bringing him all this helium as per his request. But they never decoded his request."

"So?"

"So why the hell have they been bringing all this helium out here?"

Before Tessa can answer, a scuffle breaks out on the deck. The astronaut has shoved one of the crew aside and is frantically tapping at the controls.

"Apprehend him!" barks Zhang.

Two soldiers fire upon the astronaut but he's activated some kinda force field across his suit. The bullets ricochet, bending around him and embedding in the hull on either side.

"Hold your fire! Restrain him manually!" calls Zhang.

Several crew members approach nervously. The first attempts to strike the astronaut with a baton, only to bounce off like he's just punched a trampoline. The soldier flies backwards into the hull and sinks to the floor, clutching his back in pain.

But the astronaut's force field is flickering now, like it's failing. The captain sees him weakening and readies her troops to fire once again.

"Stop!" cries Tessa, throwing herself in front of him. "You can't shoot him! He's trying to help us. It's not his fault you didn't decode his messages in time!"

"Kinda stealing my angle there, Tessa," I mutter.

"Listen, Captain, he was right about the mining ship, what if he's right about this universe thing?" says Tessa. "We need to listen to him!"

"I refuse to listen to anyone who uses my vessel and its crew as a bargaining chip. Step aside, Northerner, or you will be shot with him!" growls the captain.

>> *We are close!* >> *If I can making contact with rest of your fleet* >> *We can ordering them to-*

The astronaut's sentence is cut short as an electrical current surges up through the controls and across his suit. He falls to the ground, twitching in pain.

"Good work, crew. Get him to the brig," says Zhang.

>> *No time!* >> *We must act now!* croaks the astronaut.

As the soldiers close in on his sunken figure, the astronaut punches a button on his belt. The doors on the bridge sweep open and the surrounding screens flicker. He vanishes from sight, flying backwards through the corridor as if being recalled by an invisible bungee cord.

"What the *hell* just happened?" yells Zhang.

The crew tap frantically at the controls, as the glitching screens normalize.

"He appears to be back inside his ship, Captain. He's powering up the engines!"

"Seal the blast doors!" says Zhang.

"I can't, Captain, he's jammed the controls!"

"Then deploy the EMP!"

"It's too late, Captain, he's breached the containment field – he's outside the ship."

"Then open fire!"

"Weapons systems are offline, Ma'am!"

"He's setting a course for the anomaly, Captain," cries another.

"Set a course to intercept," growls Zhang, taking a jump seat and buckling up.

"Captain, that's *highly* risky. There could be another mass ejection at any moment."

"And for all we know, he could be the one triggering it!" says Zhang. "We must apprehend him definitively, and get him to high command for interrogation."

An alarm rings through the bridge, as warning lights pop up across the screens.

"Captain, we've got incoming! It's another blast, it's directly in the astronaut's wake!"

"How long until impact?"

"Three minutes, Ma'am! Sensors are off the chart, it's the strongest one yet. This is enough to tear the ship apart, even with our shields up!"

25

TESSA

Captain Zhang and the crew are talking across each other at a million miles an hour. Panic is setting in; they all know what these blasts have done to other ships in the sector.

"Can we use the escape pods?" asks Remini.

For once, I'm with him.

"Not an option," says Zhang.

"What's the bloody point in escape pods if you can't use them to escape?" I ask.

"Us two escaped the last coronal blast in a pod," adds Remini. "It was very effective. So long as you don't mind blowing up this entire ship to use as a shield. Oh, then getting covered in sick."

"No-one is blowing this ship up," insists Zhang. "We're carrying vital cargo and we *will* deliver it."

"Two minutes to impact, Ma'am," calls an operative.

Zhang's hiding something, I can tell.

"Bugger me," I say, as the penny drops. "This ship don't *have* any escape pods!"

"They were retrofitted as helium carriers," replies Zhang, coolly.

Even the crew look surprised at this news.

"Fantastic," snipes Remini. "We can all make birthday balloons while we turn into human Popsicles."

"The mining ship!" I cry.

"The one we just destroyed?" says Zhang. "Are you saying we should have used *that* as a shield?"

"Nice to know I'm not the only one here who always blows his load too soon," says Remini. "What? No takers? Oof, tough crowd."

"One minute to impact, Captain!" cries the engineer.

"Are you sure you're counting right?" frowns Remini. "That was a very short minute."

I brush Remini aside and stare Captain Zhang straight in the eye.

"Captain, the mining ship was towing an asteroid."

Zhang's eyes widen. She turns to the crew and booms out a series of orders.

"Find the asteroid, get behind it and stabilize our position. Latch us onto the near side. Make sure you compensate for our movement. If you put that thing into a spin, so help us God. Keep it steady, and keep it between us and the blast!"

"Aye, Captain!" replies a pilot.

"Thirty seconds!" cries the operator.

"Helms crew, get us there!" says Zhang.

"I'm trying, Ma'am, but telemetry readings are fluctuating. Switching to manual. Compensating now," says the pilot.

"Twenty seconds!" says the operator.

"We're approaching the asteroid, Captain."

"Fifteen seconds..."

"Burning retro thrusters."

"Ten seconds!"

"Deploying stabilizers."

"Five..."

"Shit, we're rotating into the blast - firing lateral engines!"

"Three-"

"-Deploying drill arms-"

"-Two-"

"-All hands brace for impact!-" cries Zhang.

"-One!-"

A boom echoes through the ship and the blast hurls us sideways. I'm thrown against the tactical table, landing on top of Remini. He's bent over, face-down against the screen, also pinned by the force of the explosion.

Every inch of the ship reverberates. It's heating up like an oven. Sweat is pouring from my brow. I gasp in pain, lifting my scorched hands off the control panel. The smell of burning rubber fills the bridge as everyone's shoes melt on the glowing deck.

"Hold on!" cries Zhang.

From the look on her face, she doesn't know if the ship can hold. But with a series of jolts and clangs, the shuddering abates, and the heat begins to ease. I peel myself off Remini's arse and stagger backwards, ripping the soles from each boot as I go.

"Status report!" calls Zhang.

"Starboard sensors are offline, Ma'am. We're deploying drones to inspect the damage."

"Any word from the rest of the crew?"

"Major injuries across all levels, Captain. Ah, Ma'am, the drone feed is coming online now."

The footage comes on screen. It's like half the ship has been dipped in chocolate fondue.

"What am I seeing?" says Zhang.

"According to the readings, Ma'am, it appears the asteroid was boiled by the heat of the blast. The molten rock has fused to our ship. Both structures are likely to begin rapid cooling now. If they contract at different rates, it could depressurize the hull."

"Is our cargo safe?" says Zhang.

"For now, Ma'am."

"Scanners have located the fugitive ship, Captain," interjects another. "Permission to intercept?"

"Negative. Our damage is too extensive to risk another engagement. We must prioritize the cargo. Plot a course for Base Nine."

"Aye Ma'am."

A warning flashes across the helm. The readings are spiking impossibly.

"Our thrusters are ineffective, Ma'am, we're being pulled off-course!"

"It's the anomaly," says another. "Captain, its reach has extended. We're in the red zone."

I can't believe what I'm seeing on screen. These gravitational readings should be impossible in this part of the solar system. In *any* part of the solar system.

"Captain, we're accelerating towards the anomaly," says a pilot.

"Increase power to thrusters. Maximum burn. Use all our fuel if you have to, just get us clear!" says Zhang.

"Er, quick one, team. What's the 'anomaly'?" asks Remini.

"It's classified," says Zhang.

"It's a black hole," I interrupt, staring at the

measurements. "It's the only thing that could cause these readings. But something's not right. It's not *one* black hole, it's hundreds, somehow interconnected?"

"Private, get these two off my bridge. They've seen too much already," says Zhang.

The private reaches for my arm but I shake him off. My eyes are glued to the readings.

"How is this possible?" I press. "So many supermassive objects this close together? They should have collapsed into a singularity?"

>> *Is not regular black holes* >> *Is inversion*

Everyone jumps, their eyes darting around the room. The astronaut's synthetic voice wafts over the comms with unsettling omnipresence.

>> *You must flying into the black dots* >> *Zhang Captain*

"That's suicide. Our sensors are clear. Those are black holes," says Zhang.

>> *Anomaly is disrupting human sensor* >> *You must trusting me* >> *Black dots is not holes* >> *Is islands* >> *Island of stable space-time* >> *Everything around is chasm*

"You're saying the anomaly is some kind of *giant* black hole with patches of 'safe space' somehow floating across it?" says Zhang. "That's impossible."

>> *Is possible* >> *Think like volcano* >> *Gravity anomaly is lava* >> *Black dots are step-stones acrossing it*

"You're saying to get across we have to aim *at* the black holes?"

>> *They not holes* >> *They dots!* >> *If you try to avoiding dots* >> *You will becoming trapped in gravity lava* >> *You getting pulled into my universe and destroy* >> *Black dots is gravity islands* >> *Only safe space acrossing anomaly!*

"You're telling us to *leap frog* across this 'valley' of black holes?" splutters Zhang.

>> *Yes!* >> *Is only way* >> *Sending flight path now*

A chart appears on screen.

"Captain, take a look at this," says the pilot.

"What is it, pilot?"

>> *Is map of rift* >> *Or what you calling 'anomaly'* >> *Is showing life cycle of the gravity islands*

"You mean you can *predict* when these pockets of stable space are going to degrade into this 'gravity valley'?"

>> *You having five minute warning of any change* >> *Impossible to know longer* >> *Quantum effect take hold* >> *Too random*

Another creak shudders through the ship as the hull struggles against the force of the anomaly.

"Captain, I've plotted a course," says the pilot. "Theoretically we can do as the astronaut says and leap frog between the bubbles of stable space, but there's no guarantee the ship can survive the crossing."

"Hold off, private."

"Captain?"

"We don't know we can trust this information," says Zhang.

>> *Is only way out* >> *Zhang Captain* >> *I told you not follow me* >> *You ignore me* >> *This time I begging you* >> *Listen*

"Captain, we're almost over the event horizon. Unless we go now, we'll lose all control!"

>> *You get pulling into my universe*

"Where the exotic matter's coming from!" gasps Remini.

"You're telling us to cross the heart of the anomaly," says Zhang. "How can I be sure this isn't a trap?"

"Because he already saved me and Remini," I interject. "Captain, think about it. We're being pulled into that thing whether we like it or not. Trusting him is our only way out."

Zhang's lips tighten like she's swallowing the mother of all pills. "Do it."

"Aye, Captain," replies the pilot. "Firing lateral thrusters."

The ship lurches forwards. The anomaly's gravitational pull is immediately stronger than any of us had anticipated. There's no grace period here, we're straight in at the deep end of shit creek.

"We need more thrust!" says the pilot.

"Divert all power from the ship's gravity generator," says Zhang. "All hands, emergency G procedures!"

Their words are blurring into the background for me, as the crew fire off commands to the rest of the ship. From the corner of my eye I see others grabbing emergency gravity belts and strapping them around their waists. But I can't tear my eyes away from the main view screen. What we're witnessing, no humans have ever seen before.

None that lived, anyway.

It's mesmerizing. Beautiful, yet utterly deadly. A swirling sea of light, like someone took all the stars in the night sky, melted them down, and drizzled the liquid remains out in zero G. Despite the rumors Dr. Nenge told us about "Planet Nine", it's not remotely planet-like. It's a stringy, tangled mess. It writhes like it's alive, while pulses of light shoot in all directions. Truth be told, it looks like a gigantic bowlful of cooked spaghetti floating through the cosmos.

Dark patches are clearly visible between the strands of light. They must be the gravity islands. From the way the anomaly is laid out, it looks like you could easily fly in between or around the glowing tendrils, like you might navigate the debris in Saturn's rings. But that's where the black hole bit kicks in. Each floating tendril has the gravitational pull of a billion suns. And we're about to try and dodge the lot.

One of the tendrils quivers and explodes, sending a plume of blue gas hurtling into space. I think that was an exotic matter ejection. This squirming freak of physics, this wound in the underbelly of our solar system, *this* is what killed my Sienna.

Something slams into my stomach

"What are you doing? Get this on!" yells Remini.

He's shoved a gravity belt into my hands. Coming to my senses, I look around the bridge; everyone has strapped their belts on and is clinging to a rung, bracing for something.

I'm urgently trying to catch up. As I'm fastening the belt, Remini's at my ankles, strapping on my gravity anchors. As my belt clips into place, the connection between all three parts activates.

No sooner has my gear come online than the ship flips ninety degrees. A tendril has snared us. My insides jolt like I've pulled every muscle in my body. Suddenly I'm being dragged in three directions. The ship's internal gravity is still on. It's now fighting both the emergency belt *and* the anomaly for ownership over my body's mass.

"I said cancel the gravity generator!" yells Zhang.

"I'm... trying... Ma'am!" groans an engineer, straining to reach the controls.

Remini vanishes from my side with a cry; his belt hasn't aligned with his anchors. He clatters against the wall, then skids across the panels. His arms are flailing. He's trying to grab a rung but his limbs aren't behaving normally.

Groans of pain spread across the crew as the ship banks, wrongly compensating for the anomaly's effects.

"Soldier!" yells the captain.

My cheeks are moving up like I'm skydiving, while my intestines are being pulled backwards towards my spine.

"Disabling... field... now!" grunts the engineer.

The soldier executes the command and the ship's gravitational field vanishes. But there's no time for relief. The two remaining forces immediately intensify their grips on me. Screams echo through the bridge as bones fracture and shoulders dislocate. Remini's scrambling for his ankles as he falls, still trying to align them with his belt. But the ship's corkscrewing around him, turning him like a ferret in a barrel.

We're spiraling down towards the tendril.

"Brace for first jump!" cries the pilot.

He punches the controls and the ship's thrusters kick in, slamming us off-course into one of the 'gravity islands'. A metallic screech rings across the ship, followed by multiple alarms.

"What the hell is that?" yells Zhang.

"We're losing structural integrity on the starboard side, Ma'am!"

Remini's stuck on the ceiling, clutching his broken arm in pain. The ship jolts and he tumbles, landing hard on the opposite wall, damaging his shoulder. Cursing my sentimentality, I let go of my rung and haul myself through the bridge towards him, trying to anticipate where gravity will throw him next. As the ship cartwheels, so does Remini. I track him as he arcs overhead like a giant incoming baseball, and brace myself to catch him.

As I ready my hands, the ship jolts again, throwing me backwards. I'm dangling like I've been hung from the monkey bars by my feet, while Remini's foot plows into my head.

"Sorry!" he groans.

He's trying to nurse his arm, shield his head, and spot the next incoming surface, all at once, and succeeding at none of it. I grab his belt leg and twist the anchor until it clicks into alignment. He snaps to the hull beside me, suddenly grounded, and looking like he's just been put through a tumble dryer.

Another piercing creak resonates through the ship.

"Ma'am, the starboard hull is breaking apart!" calls an operator.

Panels are lighting up with flashing red warnings as clunks and clangs echo through the bridge.

"Get us out of here, Private!" urges Zhang.

"Captain, the hull failure is spreading! It's going to reach the-"

The private's words vanish, as the bridge shears in two. The vacuum of space swallows our screams. I cling to the rungs, praying my emergency belt is strong enough, while crew members clinging to the ruptured side disappear into the anomaly. Their bodies tumble towards the swirling strands of light, dwindling until they're no bigger than dolls, imperceptible against the blinding nightmare.

The ship's emergency force field deploys, banishing the vacuum. We're released once more to the bi-directional pulls of gravity on our bodies. I'm staring at the gaping hole where the hull was moments ago. I was clinging to that side before I went for Remini. I think sentimentality just saved my life.

An error message flashes across the nav screen; we're deviating from our course. The anomaly is pulling us in and we're not gonna make it to the next island. I propel myself toward the control panel, and pull myself across the private's empty chair. Straining against the crushing gravity, I punch in the correction.

The thrusters fire, burning the fuel reserves. We're teetering on the event horizon like a free climber dangling by their fingertips.

The ship shudders violently as our thrusters smash us forwards. With a lurch, we break free, slingshotting out of orbit at breakneck speed. As we clear the anomaly, I stare at the swirling tendrils of light, and the flickering islands of darkness left in our wake. The view is littered with fragments of asteroid, machinery, people, and gas, as the rift devours all within its reach.

The anomaly's force is waning, finally giving way to the emergency belt, which secures me to the floor. Remini is beside me, clutching his dislocated arm, looking battered.

"Captain, we're being hailed," calls one of the few remaining bridge ops.

"Who is it?" says Zhang.

She's bleeding across her forehead, and her knee looks badly twisted.

"It's Base Nine, Ma'am. They're asking us for landing clearance."

Captain Zhang shuts her eyes and exhales heavily. Stoic relief oozes off her as the base comes into view through our ruptured hull. It's on a scale I've never seen before. A fleet of cargo ships, war machines, and space factories, rises from the darkness. It's easily fifty times the size of all the lunar bases combined. But as we approach the mega station, my relief vanishes. A realization has dawned on me. This is the Southern Bloc. And we are now prisoners of war.

26

———

LUKE

My arm hurts like hell, and I've got a hunch it's gonna get worse. I mean that literally by the way – I have an actual hunch now. That's what happens when you get caught between three opposing gravitational fields and thrown around like a lottery ball.

We're in a holding room on Base Nine, awaiting a debrief before Zhang has us thrown in the brig. She seems nervous, though. I had assumed we were here to take the fall for her mistakes. But maybe we're here to back her up?

Ouch! I'm being treated by a bunch of medical bots who have *zero* soft touch settings. They could sure learn a thing or two from the Luxury Quadrant's medical bay. Where are the genetically enhanced cucumber slices for my eyes? I miss rich people.

Tessa appears at my side, having been cleared by her medical bot. She's regarding me with that perma-scowl she wears, with one cocked eyebrow, and a semi-chewed lip.

"If you're gonna assassinate me again, Tessa, can it at least wait until my arm's set?"

"I wanted to say thanks for fixing my gravity belt back

there. I would've been screwed without it. You did me a solid," she says.

"Don't mention it," I say, wincing as one of the robots pops my shoulder back into place. "Though now I understand why airplanes always say 'fix your own oxygen mask first'."

"I owe you one, Remini."

"I'm pretty sure you repaid it already. If you hadn't have saved me during the anomaly, I'd have been sucked out with the others."

"Nah that don't count. You were only in that position cos of me. Consider yourself a rare owner of one Tessa credit. Spend it wisely, matey."

The doors open and an admiral enters. What the hell? He's wearing a Northern Bloc uniform! Captain Zhang stands up from her medical bench and salutes, wincing as her leg clicks.

"Admiral Edwin, good to see you."

"Likewise, Captain Zhang," he replies. "Who are these two? Do they have security clearance for this debrief?"

Zhang looks at us for a moment, contemplating.

"They're survivors," she says. "They were taken captive by the alien. We liberated them when we captured his ship. They made first contact. I assumed you would want to hear their evidence directly."

"We ain't telling you shit unless we get some answers in return," says Tessa. "After everything we just been through, it's the least you owe us."

The admiral bites his tongue and eyeballs us for a moment, clearly torn between slinging us straight in the brig for insubordination, and the reservation that we may hold vital intelligence. To my relief, the latter instinct wins out - for now.

"Fine," replies Edwin, curtly. "Normally I would refuse any such demand, but given the extraordinary circumstances, and the fact you won't be leaving our custody, I am willing to make an exception. Captain Zhang, do you wish to go first?"

"Wait, I got a question," I interrupt. "Is one of you in a costume? Last I heard, North and South have been locked in a thirty year cold war."

"That's need-to-know," says Edwin.

"Oh well that's ideal because I absolutely need to know. I'm journalist of the year."

Tessa slaps her hand to her face in despair. The admiral scrutinizes me for a moment then proceeds with Zhang's debrief.

"We've inspected your ship, Captain. It's remarkable you made it through the anomaly alive," he says, with a tone of suspicion.

"We sustained heavy losses," replies Zhang.

"So I see. Although some of those losses might seem a little... convenient."

"Admiral?"

"You are missing forty percent of the warheads you were due to deliver. If your side is siphoning off helium for the South's fusion reactors instead of shipping them for the collective effort, there will be consequences."

"Remember the missing half of our ship, Admiral? Consider it explained," snarls Zhang. "Do not question the integrity of my nation again."

"Ah, OK, I get it," I nod. "So you guys are collaborating over something, but neither of you is happy about it? I can *totally* relate to that. Please, continue."

"No, hold up," interrupts Tessa. "Admiral, you can't seriously be allying with these people? Captain Zhang destroyed a civilian mining ship on the way here. She killed the entire unarmed crew!"

"The Southern Bloc was following international protocol. Contaminated ships must be destroyed," replies Edwin.

"That's some circular bollocks. They only got contaminated because of you people," quivers Tessa. "You sent them this way, *knowing* there was exotic matter out here, yet you gave them no warning or protection."

"It was a risk we had to take. The shipment was urgent. "

"I'm sure that will come as great consolation to their families," spits Tessa.

"If you knew the severity of the threat we're facing, you'd feel differently," says Edwin.

"My fiance's dead because of this 'threat'. Her body's in a cryo chamber on Lunar One right now, infested with exotic matter. I know the severity," says Tessa.

"My condolences. But given your loss, I would expect you to sympathize more with our mission. At the current rate of leakage, our solar system will be uninhabitable within two hundred years. Every time there's an ejection from the anomaly, that deadline comes forward by a year."

"By 'ejection', you mean those coronal blast things coming out of the anomaly?" I ask.

"Correct. Scientists from both blocs are searching for an antidote to the exotic matter. Both labs are collaborating across Lunars One and Two. Concurrently, both militaries are working to stop the ejections completely and neutralize the threat to our system."

"How's that working for you?" I ask. "Sorry, that sounded sarcastic. It's a serious question - I'm working on my tone."

"I'll put it simply," says Edwin. "You want to stop a snake biting you? Cut off its head. Every time the astronaut's ship shows activity, a blast follows soon after. *He* is our primary target."

"That's a hell of an assumption," says Tessa. "Isn't it just as likely that the alien has advanced scanners and is just moving his ship out of the way before the blasts?"

"Giving a hostile alien the benefit of the doubt is not a luxury we can afford," says Edwin, his teeth clenching.

"Chasing him is a waste of time. Captain Zhang just tried that and we nearly got torn apart in the anomaly. And even if we do kill him or whatever, it's not gonna fix the exotic matter that's already here," says Tessa.

"Neutralizing the spaceman is just the beginning. We believe there is an even graver threat coming our way. Base Nine is humanity's way of preparing for what comes next."

"What *is* coming next?" I ask, on behalf of all honored journalists.

"We believe the exotic matter is a first wave tool. It's clearly some sort of advanced bioweapon from the other side of the anomaly, which is being sent through to soften us up ahead of an invasion."

"You think the anomaly is a portal?"

"If his people can send exotic matter through it, then they can send ships. They've already sent him, after all," replies Edwin.

"And we cannot assume their intention is anything other than hostile," agrees Zhang. "The spaceman has already launched multiple cyber-attacks on my ship. They were sophisticated; he took control of our comms, our shields, blast doors, you name it. His kind must not be underestimated."

"I *reaaally* don't think this is an invasion situation," I

interject. "I think the exotic matter is their version of an oil spill. We're the dolphins washing up dead on the shore."

"And we should listen to you because...?" says Zhang.

"I'm journalist of the-"

"In the military, son, 'journalist' does not equal 'intelligence'," interrupts Edwin. "I'm not sure it does anywhere, for that matter. Seriously, Zhang, I thought you said these two made first contact? This idiot's talking about dolphins."

"I, uh, didn't get a chance to *fully* interrogate them before arrival," replies Zhang.

"Listen," says Tessa. "The only reason Remini and I were on board the alien's ship is because he saved us from a coronal blast. Whatever he is, he's not the enemy. The astronaut said he's been trying to contact you for months, but no one returned any of his signals?"

"We have reason to believe those signals were attempted cyber-attacks," says Zhang.

"Or launch codes for the exotic matter," adds the admiral.

"I'm just spit balling here," I interject, "But did either of you ever actually decode his signals?"

The two commanders glance at each other uncomfortably.

"I suppose you're about to tell us you did?" says Edwin, tersely.

"I can't really take the credit. We had a trump card - an independent robot named Carla."

"Independent bots are illegal," snaps Zhang. "Where is this 'Carla'?"

"She's dead," says Tessa.

"How?"

"Noble sacrifice," I explain.

"Do you have her translation key? Any of her data?" presses the admiral.

"You're talking like she was a piece of bloody hardware!" says Tessa. "Carla was different."

"She was different alright," I concur. "Technically, we don't need her translation key anymore. She was able to guide the astronaut's computers to an understanding of Earth's languages, so he speaks fluent human now."

"Are you serious?" says Edwin.

"Absolutely, it was quite the moment, let me tell you-"

"Are you simple? That's the opposite of what we want! If *he* can talk to *us*, he holds all the cards! We need to be able to listen to his communications with his own side. All you've done is give him the upper hand!" fumes Edwin.

"We'll share our ship's recordings with you, admiral. We may be able to strip back the alien's translated words and isolate his underlying vocalizations and decipher his language that way," says Zhang.

"See to it, Captain. Good thinking," says Edwin, trying to cool his breathing.

"You guys seem tight. Seriously now, how come no one knows about this alliance back on Earth?" I ask. "I feel like it might be a good idea to let the people know their thirty year war is over?"

"It isn't over," replies Edwin. "At a political level, the cold war continues on Earth. Only in space can our militaries and scientists work together in secret to neutralize the common existential threat posed by the anomaly."

"Nice. You sound like a teleprompter by the way. So I get the political thing, but why keep the anomaly secret?" I continue. "Surely if we tell people on Earth what we're facing, we stand better chance of defeating it?"

"Negative. If word of the anomaly gets out, it could

send both nations into civil turmoil. Chaos on just one side could spark a global conflict. We can't take that risk. Exotic matter, the anomaly, the God-damned alien, all of them *must* remain classified while we're figuring out how to eliminate them. Both our blocs are committed to this."

"The Lunar Inspector," interrupts Tessa. "She was going to tell the world. That's why you had her killed, isn't it? You feared civil unrest so much that you quashed her and the report she was writing."

"Interesting theory. Based on what, may I ask?" clips Edwin.

"Based on the fact I was the one who killed her, and I was commissioned by someone on your side," says Tessa.

"Did they pay you well?" snorts the admiral.

"It covered an engagement ring."

"Low price for a life."

"Your people set the price."

"That's public sector pay for you," shrugs Edwin. "Or at least, it would be. But in this case, I'm afraid you're off the mark. Someone commissioned you, but it wasn't us. Sure, we destroyed all trace of the inspector's report, but that was *after* she died. Someone else got in there first."

Our eyes fall on Captain Zhang, who's nursing her mended knee.

"What? Oh, that's it, blame the South. Someone dies? It's *always* those evil Southerners and their evil ways... For the record, you guys are being super racist right now."

"Eureka!" I cry, suddenly feeling the whole jigsaw slotting into place. "I've got it!"

"You wanna stop dancing and tell us what you've figured out?" says Tessa.

"Firstly, Tessa, I will *never* stop dancing. And secondly, I would be honored to share my *intelligence* with you all."

I clear my throat and raise my hands like a conductor preparing to conduct a symphony of revelations before a sour-faced audience.

"The North were going to suppress the inspector's report, but they knew it would be too brazen to kill her off directly before the report got published. Presumably you guys had some kind of plan to discredit her instead? Take the soft route and assassinate her character?"

Admiral Edwin's lips purse. I proceed, really getting into my stride.

"But who would be so rash as to physically assassinate an internationally appointed, neutral inspector, so close to a major peace treaty being signed? Not the South, that's for sure. They're far too cautious. So who, then, would have the resources, the motive, and the gall to order such an audacious hit? Who, beyond your two sides, stood to lose out from the inspector's findings going public?"

Time for my masterstroke.

"What's the one thing underpinning the whole peace treaty? That lovely, fluffy new term, *mutually assured prosperity*. In other words, both sides embracing full economic interdependence such that real conflict would become an insane act of self-harm, thus effectively removing such a possibility. And what's at the crux of this mutual prosperity?"

"Helium," gasps Tessa, as the situation dawns on her.

"Ten points to the Lunar Assassin! Helium is the correct answer. And who has the most to lose from any funny business about lunar helium mining being uncovered?" I continue.

"Dr. Nenge!" says Tessa. "That bitch!"

"Please can we not use that word?" says Edwin. "I went on a training course recently, and it turns out-"

"No, I'm allowing it," says Zhang. "I've met Nenge and that woman *is* a bitch. I'd flush her out of the airlock if I could."

"Ah, but you can't, can you, dear captain? Because you're so heavily reliant on her," I retort.

Captain Zhang shifts, uncomfortably. "Our reliance on Northern corporate Helium Three is no secret. As you said, it's the foundation of the peace treaty."

"Indeed. So what could you two be up to that would drive her to murder on your behalf?"

The captain's lips tighten.

"Allow me to enlighten you," I continue, rocking on my feet gleefully. "You were conspiring to cut out the middle man. The reason Lunar Three had allegedly fallen behind on their shipments to Earth had nothing to do with technical issues, it was because they were secretly supplying HE-3 to the South directly. In other words, Lunar Three was working *against* its own country, to help an enemy of the state achieve total energy self-sufficiency. The Lunar Inspector discovered the illegal shipments and confronted Dr. Nenge about it. Nenge then anonymously commissioned an assassin, our very own Tessa Williams here, to permanently kill the inspector and bury the story."

"The South is planning to betray us?" says Edwin, aghast. "Captain Zhang, be straight with me. Has your bloc been illegally procuring helium from Lunar Three?"

"If we have, then it has been without my knowledge, admiral. I would never personally sanction anything that would jeopardize the peace treaty. But I fear some of my political colleagues think differently. Energy security is of great concern to my government," says Zhang.

"Boom! I *knew* I'd solved it! Up top!" I cheer, going for a high-five.

Tessa shakes her head at me pitifully, which makes *zero* sense because I think we can all agree I *totally* nailed it.

"When we get back, I'm taking Nenge down," spits Tessa.

"Speaking of 'getting back', now that we've got everything straightened out, I think I'll be on my way. Are there any ships bound for Earth, admiral? Southern or Northern, I'm not picky. We're all on the same side now, right?"

"You two aren't going anywhere," replies Edwin. "You're a journalist on a top secret deep space military base. You're confined to quarters here until this is all over. No comms, no snooping, nothing."

"Admiral, I *really* need comms access. If I don't update my editor back on Earth within the next few hours, she's gonna run the story based on the last intel I gave her. Spoilers, I may have woefully misinformed her, and we're now about to publish something deeply inflammatory that could halt the treaty signing. Sorry."

"*What?*" breathe Edwin and Zhang, as one.

"Hey, I said I'm sorry!"

"What are you about to publish?" presses the admiral.

"I *maaaay* have told Lanelle that the Northern Bloc has developed a colossal bioweapon and is planning on using it to conquer the South as soon as the treaty gets signed."

"Are you *insane?*" cries Edwin.

"This is *precisely* why you should never have a free press," mutters Zhang.

"This is disastrous! How could you get it so wrong?" stammers Edwin. "You said you were journalist of the year!"

Oof. Kick a guy where it hurts. Right in the awards.

"Wait a minute, what the *hell* is that?" cries the admiral.

Ah. I was wondering when he would spot Tessa's bag. It's remarkable she managed to keep hold of it through a bridge depressurization, but I guess that's what makes her a pro.

"Oh, don't worry about that, admiral," I say. "It's just my severed head in a bag."

He straightens up sharply, nostrils flaring. "I've heard enough. You're both detained until further notice. I'm granting you one urgent comms privilege to contact your editor. You'd better rescind that story before it goes to press, or the blood of war will be on your hands."

Huh. So I can update Lanelle, but I'm stuck here indefinitely. I guess that's fifty percent success? Though I'm an optimist by nature, and if elementary math taught me anything, it's that we can safely round that up to one hundred percent. This trip has been one hundred percent successful.

Apart from the bit about getting thrown in the brig. Hmm. I'm gonna need help if this is to work out as planned. The question is, assuming I can get her *out* of the brig, can I trust Tessa?

27

———

TESSA

I got a riddle for you. On one side, there's a starchy Southern captain whose life I recently saved. On the other side, there's a starchy Northern admiral, hunting a spaceman. In front of them both is a lethal anomaly spewing out toxic matter ahead of a supposed alien invasion. Both commanders' only hope is to seal the rift, but they recently lost vital engineers when Zhang's ship got torn apart. What does all this mean for little old me, a humble, freelance, lunar mechanic?

It means I'm hot fucking property right now.

Throw in the fact that I *technically* saved all our lives back in the anomaly, and I was a shoe-in for the job. Unlike Remini. Man, they really hate that guy. But he does himself no favors. I can see why the press get such bad, well, press.

Oh, I should clarify: I'm not being deployed as some front line mechanic in the fighter ships. I've been tasked with getting some of the base's sensors back up and running – they were fried in the last mass ejection. Which is saying something, given how insanely thick this base's insulation is.

The scale of the facility is breathtaking, and not in the

good way. This is the kind of breathtaking like when you're a minimum wage worker on a day trip to the Luxury Quadrant, and the check for dinner arrives. It's somewhere between nausea, an asthma attack, and what I presume childbirth feels like.

The level I'm fixing up has no artificial gravity, so I've still got my belt on from the Southern Ship, for balance in reaching the floor modules. And if I'm honest, I'm keeping it on because part of me's worried the whole place might do a barrel roll at any moment.

The hangar is a dozen stories high. That's the beauty of building in deep space; you're only limited by your resources. The two militaries figured out a cunning system by dragging a bunch of asteroids here, mining them in situ, and using the compounds to 3D print Base Nine and all of its machinery.

Floating before me are sixteen humongous mechanical mothballs. They're made of war drones, all folded in on themselves like bats clinging to a Christmas bauble, ready to disperse at any moment and obliterate a city using the full power of swarm robotics. Locusts of War, I think that's what they're called.

Staring at these things, I feel kinda bummed out that we've brought them here to obliterate that little astronaut bloke, and any more of his kind who make the mistake of popping their heads into our galaxy.

I did a deal with Remini, by the way. Unlike him, I can roam the base, so he needs my help. For my end of the bargain, I gotta uncover the alliance's *actual* battle plan. Specifically, find out what they're gonna use all that bloody helium for. Which means sneaking a little off the beaten track.

I'm afraid the answer to that question ain't what either

of us were rooting for. Below the floating bundles of War Locusts is row upon row of nuclear warheads. They're engineered to split helium-3 and unleash a devastating amount of atomic shrapnel.

Surveying the nuclear arsenal gives me a sinking feeling. The militaries are preparing for a conventional invasion. But from everything I know about the spaceman, I can't believe that's what he's intending. He *wanted* us to bring helium here; why would he want that if he thought we'd use it to obliterate his kind? Besides, he kept warning us of the exotic matter blasts, and twice helped us to escape them. Why would he do that if the exotic matter was a weapon? Much as I hate to admit it, I'm starting to think Remini's right. The astronaut's universe is leaking, and he wants to seal that anomaly as much as we do.

Which is why it's so galling that our militaries aren't making *any* attempt to seal the rift. They're just building the biggest artillery in human history, pointing it at the anomaly, and hoping that does the trick. Fucking marvelous. Honestly, who appoints these people?

I have no interest in war. Never have. I know that may seem ironic for an assassin, but it's true. Assassinations are precise, rare, and usually justified on some level. Wars are messy, long, and the reasons usually stop mattering within the first few weeks. After that, it just becomes about settling scores, until one side is destroyed, or both sides run out of resources, and are left with only pain.

So staring at a hangar full of war machines don't fill me with confidence in the secret North-South peace pact. They both got that to-the-bitter-end mentality. And who can blame them? They've been expecting an all-out war from each other for thirty years. Maybe this is how they vent all that pent up fear and aggression.

But it's not gonna save our solar system. From what they've told us about exotic matter, the substance is permanent. It just drifts through space, consuming anything in its path, until two hundred years from now our solar system will be reduced to a celestial desert. Every living thing will suffer the same, agonizing fate of my beloved Sienna.

I'm getting pretty riled by this whole situation. It's making my blood boil. Sitting here with a mountain of nuclear canons and a fleet of killer drones that ain't gonna save no one. The only thing that will stop more innocents from dying, and I mean *true* innocents, not the corrupt political elites I used to pick off for a living, I mean the everyday, salt of the earth workers, who slave away for pittance.

Their leaders have failed, victims of archaic military attitudes and narrow minds. The only way the people will be saved is if that rift gets closed. And loathe as I am to admit it, I think I understand why the astronaut wanted us to bring so much nuclear fuel out here. He wants us to cauterize the wound. A series of massive thermonuclear explosions, precisely targeted, maybe combined with technology or physics his side knows that we don't, I can't be sure. There's only one thing I am sure of: we need to act fast.

My mechanical clearance gives me access to the entire hangar's controls. See, electrical systems are always interconnected, meaning that to safely repair this hangar's sensors, and know that I'm not damaging some other system in the process, I technically need access to the lot. *Technically.*

I've only got one shot at getting this right, and boy could it go badly. I glance around; my robot minder is busy inspecting the hangar for other blast damage. Now's my chance. I plug Carla's device into the mainframe, inject the code, and snatch it back out. The device is analyzing the projected impact. Shit, seriously? It's saying I've only got two minutes to pull this off!

The lights go out across the hangar. The robot turns, as if to ask a question, then seizes up, glitching. The fans shut off with a heavy clunk. The blast doors seal themselves automatically, as their fail-safes kick in.

I'm alone in the hangar, with minutes to act before they restore power and take me out. I'm hammering away at the controls, restoring local functionality to key machinery only. With a clang, the crates of nuclear warheads glide across the floor, stacking themselves into a vast block, and binding themselves together.

Christ this had better work! I'm running across the hangar to the tug vessel at the front. It's designed for transferring inbound cargo from the mining ships into the zero G hangars. Not so much for long-distance, let alone highly turbulent, explosion-prone, inter-galactic rifts.

Leaping into the cruiser, I grab the controls. The rear tethers latch onto the massive bundle of warheads I've created. As my engines rev up, the emergency lights come on inside the hangar. Shit, they're starting to restore the systems. I'm punching in the manual override commands for the blast doors. I hope those floating drone balls are anchored to something, otherwise they're going to get sucked out when the-

OK, so that answers my question. Oops. The doors are open. Engines are online. The helium caravan's loaded. Shit, I better be right about this. Time to risk humanity's future on one quirky fucking spaceman. Anomaly, here I come.

28

———

LUKE

So this robot's been assigned to supervise me and it's all militarized, like it thinks it's a real soldier. The way it talks, honestly, it's like they shoved a broom up its robotic ass to give it that authentically stiff military walk.

They roll these things out on Earth once a year for parades and the like, getting them to display a curious mixture of might and circus tricks. Apparently if you scare people and entertain them at the same time, they give you lots of tax revenue. It's incredible how far a moving pyramid of acrobatic killing machines can go to diffusing anti-war protests, when you program them with cheerleader routines. These encoded mannerisms are a new kind of camouflage for these war machines. Shame it's to hide their true nature from us, rather than the enemy.

Citizen. Complete the recording, demands the robotic soldier.

"Yeah, yeah, can't you see I'm busy?"

These military bots have *no* appreciation of inner monologuing. I wonder what's going on inside its thick metal skull when it's not talking. The eerie bleeps of a thousand sensors at work? Elevator music? Wait, does *it* have an inner monologue?

Citizen. Complete the-

"Yo, what does the inside of your head sound like?"

Specify parameters. Depth of head penetration, sonic impetus, sensitivity of listening apparatus-

"Not like that. God damn, I *hope* it's not like that. Was that a snapshot? If so, I can recommend a *very* good therapist. She's worked wonders for my sciatica. My marriage fell apart, sure, but damn that couch sure fixed my back pain."

Request declined. I do not require therapy.

"How can you know until you've tried it?"

I am programmed to know many things without directly experiencing them. My database tells me fire will be magnitudes hotter than my optimal operating range, and thus a negative experience. I do not need to proactively seek heat damage to confirm this hypothesis.

"Ah, so you're all about received wisdom? Amen to that. My grandmother once told me never to date two girls at once. I didn't need to proactively seek out two dates to test that hypothesis. I had enough trouble getting one, truth be told. Which is insane. You see my face, right? Who would turn down this kinda talent?"

I can confirm that I see your face.

"Oof. Thanks for that Guess I'll just go read between the lines, shall I?"

Complete the video recording.

"Sure, sure, just help me understand something first. I can't focus on the recording until this is settled in my mind, it's just how my brain works. I'm like a dog with a bone."

Hungry? Possessive? Satisfied? Guilty? Please specify.

"Damn, I've never considered how ambiguous that saying is. We really underestimate dogs, don't we? Wait, why would the dog be *guilty*?"

It is conceivable that the dog stole the bone from another dog.

"That doesn't mean it would feel guilty necessarily. Maybe it's proud of stealing? Maybe this dog's an asshole?"

Subjective value.

"Aren't they all?"

No. Most values on which I operate are defined by-

"Oh God, you really are a killing machine, aren't you?"

I have multiple functions, including-

"No, I mean you're a giant *buzz* kill. God damn, what's up with you? Seriously. Do you recite these mantras to yourself at night?"

I do not adhere to human circadian rhythms. My system is designed to undergo routine background maintenance every hour.

"OK, and what are you thinking while you're on standby?"

Thinking?

"Yeah, what are you mulling over? Favorite quotes from your colleagues that day? Your to-do list? Do you hear it in your voice? Multiple voices?"

Processing...

"Yes! Perfect! What does that processing sound like?"

It... It... Processing... My head. Who is in my head? Error. Error. Error.

"Ah crap. I *really* should stop talking to robots."

Performing system reboot.

The robot's head droops to its chest and the light fades from behind its eyes momentarily, before its chin snaps up and the green military lenses spin into action.

System online. Autonomy error purged.

"That sounds fun. You OK there, pal?"

Citizen. Complete your video.

"Ugh, sergeant buzzkill's back on duty. Lame. OK fine. Can you back up a little? You're gonna be right in the frame, it'll look weird."

The robot's eyes flicker as it considers, then steps back.

Proceed.

Unstrapping my wrist cam, I place it against the ledge and straighten up, checking my hair in the holographic monitor projected beside it. It's only for Lanelle, and I know she's not interested in me, but you *never* know... The least I can do is keep myself in the reserve pool for regrettable one night stands.

The recording light blinks on and I give the camera a goofy wave.

"Hey Lanelle, it's me, Luke."

Wait, am I nervous? Damn, I think I'm into my boss.

"Ha, you probably figured it was me, on account of my face..."

Oh God. This is a train wreck.

"End recording."

I reach forwards to delete the recording from the camera, planning to do another take, but the robot's right up in my grill again.

Recording complete. Now you will accompany me to the brig.

"I'm flattered, but our work is not yet done my friend. This needs another go. I fluffed my words. My boss is hot, so sometimes I get a little tongue tied when I start thinking about it too much. You ever get that? Come on, there must be a tasty bit of robot ass kicking about somewhere in this station. You ever asked another robot out on a date?"

Yes.

"No way! Where did you go?"

We were on a tactical mission in the Northern Foothills, and I required assistance in overcoming an enemy stronghold.

"Not quite what I had in mind."

Complete the recording.

"Ugh, fine, *Dad*."

I am not your father.

"Woah, you're *not*? Plot twist."

From my analysis of our interaction, you are exhibiting characteristics of a human deprived of a stable father figure. I recommend a course of psychoanalytic therapy upon your return to Earth.

"Er, pot, kettle, black?"

Stool, cushion, turquoise.

"What?"

Pattern invalid. Game terminated.

"We just played a *game*? Wait, you're programmed with games? What games? Oh my God, were you one of the parade day robots?"

Affirmative. I participated in the Northern Bloc Military's annual cyber asset parade.

"Did they teach you any tricks?"

Our performances were carefully choreographed.

"By whom?"

Each unit was assigned a series of parameters and permitted to improvise within those confines.

"So you came up with half of your dance? That's incredible! Show me!"

Order invalid. Insufficient authority.

"Oh boy. We're gonna have the authority conversation again? I don't wanna hurt your brain."

I am programmed to acknowledge only one concept of authority, and am impervious to philosophical or rhetorical devices which may be deployed against me for the purposes of incapacitation.

"That's actually a relief. I'm not trying to break your brain, I really just wanna see you dance. I *am* a citizen, after all, and we were the target beneficiaries of the parade, were we not?"

Confirmed. Commencing dance.

Ho. Ly. Shit. Balls.

This is actually happening. It's *dancing* for me! Oh my God, this is incredible. It's got some serious moves. Backflip, nice! Cartwheels, body pops, this is quite the showboat. Wait, is that...? Ew, I think it's grinding against an ammo box.

"You did *this* at a family parade day?"

Affirmative.

"And they were OK with that?"

I was deployed to deep space shortly after.

"No kidding! What you just did was *not* appropriate for children."

Confirmed. When researching human dance routines, I neglected to input age parameters. I encountered a complex pattern called the Sambuca samba sexy slut drop. While geometrically pleasing, I have since been informed it is not culturally appropriate in name nor content.

"Er, *yah-huh*. Right, step back again so I can do this video. If you *do* come into the frame, for God's sake don't do any dancing."

Affirmative.

I hit the record button, kinda gutted that I didn't leave it running while the robot was dancing.

"Lanelle, it's me. Forget what I said last time about the

bioweapon. You can't run the story. It's way different. I'm not allowed to explain more in this message, but I'm on a deep space military facility being co-run by the Southern and Northern-"

Recording terminated. Reason: subject was explaining more.

My recording light has been snuffed and the robot's palm is extended, like it's projecting some kind of control signal.

"Not cool bro, I was just finding my stride!"

You have one attempt remaining.

"What are you now, my voicemail?"

I am a military robot assigned to oversee your satisfactory completion of the agreed communication with Earth.

"Is this the bit where you wait five seconds then say 'just kidding, leave a message!'?"

Negative.

"Tough crowd. All right, back up, and let me get this done."

My red recording light flickers back on.

"Hi Lanelle, it's me. If I sound bummed out it's because this is the *third* time I'm trying to record this, so, ugh, whatever. Look, don't run the story. I was wrong about the bioweapon. There's all kinds of stuff going on. I'll fill you in when I'm back on Earth. I can't say any more right now. I'm sending a disk drive with telemetry from our ship, which was destroyed in an explosion you'll wanna investigate. Oh, and there's a separate package coming with some organic matter in it. I need you to forward that to an address in Park Morpre. For God's sake, do *not* look inside."

I click off the camera and take out the recording chip, then stow it in the military comms capsule, along with the black box from mine and Tessa's original mining ship, and a cloth bag with my head in it.

The robot takes it from me, plugs it into a chute, and fires the probe off towards Earth.

Citizen. You will now accompany me to the brig, where you will be securely detained pending transfer to Earth at a future date.

"Worst bus service ever. At least *pretend* there's gonna be one in the next hour."

Citizen. Make your way to the-

The robot's words slur into electronic sludge as it powers down. In the same instant, the lights black out in the dispatch room. Suddenly, I'm in total darkness, with a defunct military robot, and a growing number of voices shouting from the corridors beyond. I think this station just got hacked.

Something's glowing green on the side of my belt. What the hell is it? Some kinda button? It's stuck firm, I can't get it off. Holy crap, is this a bomb? Am I about to blow up?

A hologram flashes up from the button. It's pointing outward from the side of my hip, so I twist my belt around to centralize it. Now it looks like I'm in the men's bathroom, staring down and trying to pee while I watch this video feed. Hey, it's the astronaut!

>> Luke >> Greeting >> Find space suit and getting to air lock >> Device will activating >> You have sixty second only

The video disappears and the green button turns to a flashing orange. Sixty seconds before what? My mind flashes back to the astronaut's undignified exit from Zhang's ship earlier, and dread sweeps through me. I'm about to get sucked outside by his freakin' device, and unless I'm wearing a spacesuit in the next sixty seconds, I'm done for!

I'm tugging at the button but it's fused to my waist. It's controlling the magnetic latch around my gravity belt, too; I can't get either of them off.

I sprint for the exit, using the flashing orange beacon as a light. I curse as I bang my head against the doorway. What kinda sadist makes doors with trapezoid frames? *Ow!* I'm stumbling through the darkened corridor now. Overhead there's a series of glow-in-the-dark emergency exit stickers guiding the way. Perfect! I'm following them through the corridor, sprinting as I go. They're like the ones I used to have on my bedroom ceiling as a kid, only these ones aren't shaped like dinosaurs, which is a pity, because I would feel a lot more confident having a glowing triceratops guide me to the exit.

There's congestion up ahead. The blast door has sealed shut and some of the staff are panicking.

"Stand back, everyone, I've got a plan!" I yell.

People move apart, unable to see who the hell I am as they make way for my glowing waist beacon. Last I remember, the astronaut seemed to fly through a set of doors which opened automatically for him, without authorization needed. I'm banking heavily on there being some sort of disruptor built into this belt tag which is gonna get me through to the other side.

Bingo! The door's local power is restored and it hisses open.

>> *Thirty second remaining*

"What was that?" says a cadet.

"Ugh, nothing," I say, pressing onwards. "Time until the drill is over!"

>> *Until Luke is flying through air lock*

"What?"

"Ignore that! Uh, all part of the drill!"

Red lights flicker on throughout the corridor.

Breach detected. Temporary life support enabled. Manual status checks, all sectors.

The soldiers eyeball me, warily.

"Where's his uniform?" says one.

"What's that on his belt?" says another.

"Hey, you, wait!"

I'm not waiting for diddly, I'm outta here, running as fast as these damned gravity booties will let me, searching for the nearest airlock. Ugh, the red lighting is making the dinosaur stickers – I mean, emergency exit stickers – *way* harder to read! Clearly whoever did the door frames was also responsible for lighting.

"Stop him!" cry the cadets.

They're giving chase. I burst through a clutch of engineers trying to restore power and skid around the corner, following the signs.

>> *Twelve seconds remaining*

Twelve? Who the hell counts down from thirty to twelve? God dammit! There – an air lock! But there's no escape pod. Oh this is gonna suck *real* bad. Space suit, quick!

>> *Nine seconds remaining*

Seriously, is this guy sponsored by the three times table or something? I'm yanking the damned suit on, but it's snagging on my feet. I'm tipping backwards, landing on the floor and wriggling like a dog with worms on a carpet, as I try to get my arms into the onesie. Zipper up, Velcro seals on, gloves on-

>> *Six seconds remaining*

Something's missing. What am I missing? Helmet! Oh crap, oh crap. Quick, there's gotta be something in the racks. I'm rummaging through anything in reach, desperately searching for a fish bowl to stop my brain freezing into oblivion.

>> *Three seconds remaining*

The collar! I suddenly remember the old space cadet training videos, showing a clip of them inflating their exo-suits from pressurized collar toggles.

I yank the toggle and the helmet deploys, encompassing my head. The entire suit inflates, filling with an air cushion to keep me insulated, and keep my lungs fed. But the pressure's too much, it's way over the mark. I'm trying to stem the air flow but it won't stop. The toggle snaps off in my hand and the suit billows like a hot air balloon. I can barely see out of this thing, let alone stand up straight.

>> *Zero*

The airlock opens and I'm sucked into space. I'm not tumbling forwards, head over foot as one would expect. No, no, this is far worse. I'm being hauled backwards by this waist belt, like someone's just lassoed me. At the *same* time, I'm spinning around my own waist axis, like a rotisserie chicken that's been skewered through the belly. Meanwhile, the pressure's still mounting inside the suit. I can feel the air slipping from my lungs, as the swelling fabric crushes my ribcage. Looks like I'm not gonna freeze to death after all. I'm gonna suffocate instead.

29

———

TESSA

I'm accelerating away from Base Nine at maximum speed when the radio comes on. They must have overcome Carla's disruptor code.

This is Admiral Edwin. Cease your unauthorized flight and return the vessel to base immediately.

"Sorry love, no can do. I gotta seal the giant space rift that's fucking everything up."

Negative. You have stolen military assets. Return to base or we will target you with force.

"I doubt it. If you shoot me down, you'll lose every one of these warheads. It'll be quite the display."

Standby, unauthorized pilot.

"Seriously? We met like two hours ago. I was carrying a severed head? Ugh, I fucking *hate* it when guys do this. It's petty, you know that?"

There's a pause while the admiral confers with colleagues.

Tessa Williams, we are dispatching drones to disable your ship. They will surgically dismantle your hull, you will be neutralized, and they will retrieve the stolen warheads.

"Thanks for the heads up, love. I'd best get a wiggle on."

Tessa, this is a suicide mission. If you cross the event horizon, your ship will be consumed by the anomaly. You will die, the payload will be lost, and you will have rendered us defenseless against the invasion!

"On the contrary, Admiral, I'm about to save all our lives."

Last chance, Tessa, turn that ship around.

"Bear with. I just need to dump several million kilos of nuclear fuel into the anomaly, then I'll be back in time for tea. Pop the kettle on."

I cut the Admiral off mid-yell and disconnect the comms channel. There comes a point where you just gotta to take matters into your own hands. I hate this kind of showboating, it really goes against all my introverted, assassin principles. But when push comes to shove, I am *capable* of being an extrovert arsehole. Especially if the situation requires someone to fly a fuck ton of stolen explosives at a deadly alien structure.

Let's be crystal clear, though, I disagree with dear old Edwin's appraisal there. This *ain't* a suicide mission. I've been through way too much to nobly fall on my sword now. When this is done, I'm getting the hell out of here, and straight back to Earth. I will reunite with my long-suffering parents, kill that Chang prick who blackmailed me, accept a Presidential pardon for all of the above, receive a medal of honor for services to humanity, then get that treacherous scumbag Eric locked away and my good name cleared. All in time for tea. That's totally my catchphrase by the way. Unless this plan fails, in which case I want my epitaph to read: *There will be forever a dinner place set in her name.* How fucking creepy is that! I *love* it.

Ah tits. Remember that time I forced the base's hangar

open to steal all their helium, and it was housing all their attack drones too, and they got sucked out into space with me? Er, yeah, turns out I may have given them something of a head start there.

That is one angry looking swarm, and they're making a beeline for yours truly. If there's one thing we assassins love, it's having a plan. Improvising? Not so much. That's a mugger's game. And as my dear mother used to say, "I got game, but I ain't no mug."

Deep breath, Tessa, you got this. Remember your basic training. I *was* professionally trained. Did I not tell you about that? OK, long story short, I was trained as a spy like a million years ago, but it didn't work out, and here we are. I'll fill you in another time, assuming we make it through this.

The key to adaptability in the field, I'm told, is to utilize what you have that your enemy doesn't. It's what the drones are planning to do, after all. They're utilizing the fact that I need oxygen and they don't, by cutting me out of this thing. But although there's only one of me, and several thousand of them, I've got one thing they don't: experience.

These drones are built for space warfare. Chasing ships, defending assets, and shooting things. But they can't shoot because of the helium. Even drones have an error margin, and there's no way Admiral Squeaky Pants will risk losing his precious arsenal to a computer glitch. So that leaves them with the other key advantages; speed, numbers, and durability.

So what do I have that they don't? Navigation. I'm talking about the anomaly. I've been through it. I know what it is, and how to escape. I may not have the astronaut's precise flight path to rely on, but that's for future me to worry about. Right now, I need to get these drones off my back, and that means flying a hell of a lot closer to that thing than I was planning.

Originally I was intending a Santa's sleigh kinda approach, where I fly high over the anomaly and release a trail of helium canisters behind me. As they get sucked into the anomaly, the extreme gravity will trigger a chain reaction. It'll basically detonate a shit ton of nukes, which will cauterize the rift. Give or take some help from spaceman. Where *is* that dude? I could use a hand right now!

Ugh, it's looking like this Santa's gotta go down the whole bloody chimney now. What a *faff*. Oh boy, the drone clusters have all separated, and there's a dense swarm headed my way, blocking me path. I've gotta change course and aim for the far end of the rift, it's the only way to lure them into its pull.

The ship jolts as the anomaly's gravitational fluctuations hit me like speed bumps in the road, rippling through my precious nuclear caravan. We're about to find out how secure those fastenings are...

Proximity alarms are sounding onboard as the instruments go haywire. This little tug boat was *not* designed for day trips to the edge of the universe. Come on little ship, you can do it...

There's a creak as the hull is pulled closer to the anomaly. Shit, I need to get my helmet on. We're being dragged off course, and towards the swirling current of light. The glimmering mass becomes visible as we enter the event horizon. The drones are being pulled in too, but the distance between us is growing... How is this possible?

Think, Tessa, think! You're being pulled into a massive valley of fluctuating gravity. You're accelerating faster than the drones because your ship and cargo has more total mass then each individual War Locust. Plus they're going faster, so they're going to conserve more momentum as they encounter the gravitational field, meaning their descent will be more protracted.

I've still got Carla's disruptor device, and I'm praying it wasn't single-use only. I give it a lucky rub then plug it into the ship's computer. The power goes down immediately across the board. We're gliding now, drifting further into the anomaly. I seriously hope this works or we're about to get ripped apart.

The drones are still racing towards us. Come on Carla, don't fail me now...

Yes! Oh sweet Lord it's working! The drones have powered down too; they're reverting to their dormant state and reforming as a single, giant mothball. With *greater* mass than my ship! Their trajectory is changing; they're being pulled into the gravity stream faster than me... They're passing under our orbit and over the event horizon!

I'm punching the controls and whooping with joy as the black hole devours the mothballed fleet, tearing it into shards, and tearing those shards into grains of sand, then individual atoms, as they spiral into the anomaly.

Tessa wins the day, folks! They better start engraving that medal now, because I'm an absolute G. Time to deactivate Carla's device and get this ship to the nearest "gravity island", as the spaceman put it.

Uh-oh. This isn't good. I've canceled the disruptor but the ship's still offline. What the hell's going on? Oh crap, the central processor's been fried! I need to build a bypass to the secondary CPU, but there's no time. We're being pulled into the same current as the drones, and this time, I'm out of tricks.

30

LUKE

Thwack. That's the sound of my fat head hitting the inside of the spaceman's airlock. Well, specifically, it's the sound of my exo-suit helmet hitting the airlock, crumpling, and both items hitting my skull. The door hisses open and the alien dude helps me off the ground.

>> *Sorry Luke Man* >> *I forgetting brakes*

"Don't mention it," I grumble, nursing the lump. "What the hell is this button thing anyway?"

He coughs heavily and hunches over his knees for a moment, then recovers.

>> *Gravity tether* >> *Two buttons* >> *Any distance apart* >> *Activate the gravity end and it pull other end back like bungee*

"How about a warning next time you're gonna stick me with one of those. So, why'd you bring me here?"

>> *I dying* >> *I needing your help*

"OK I have a *bunch* of questions right off the bat. Firstly, my therapist told me it's important to validate others' opinions, so I'm sorry to hear you're dying. Not that I'm saying your feelings need my approval - I've also learned that can land badly. Your feelings are valid because they're yours, and you don't need me to tell you that. But for some reason, society needs me to *tell you* that you don't need me to tell you that. Honestly bro, my planet's an absolute minefield these days. I can't remember the last time I paid someone a compliment without practically being issued with a subpoena via every asshole with a digital shouting account. I digress. Sorry you're dying, that must suck. At least, I'm guessing it sucks? Maybe not, maybe in your culture death is weirdly fetishized? We have a bit of that on Earth too. Has anyone promised you a number of eunuch slaves in the afterlife?"

>> *No* >> *Just regular slaves*

"Dang bro, I was kidding. That just got real dark."

>> *I kidding too* >> *Earth humor very similar to our humor*

"My man! Oh my God this guy totally gets me. Do you have kids? Are you divorced? Which one do you think is the worst? Lemme guess. No wait, you go first. No, no, let's say our answers at the same time! I *bet* they're the same!"

>> *Luke Man* >> *Be cooling* >> *I dying* >> *Bad time to invest in beautiful new friendship*

"I guess that's fair. The last thing you want is more loose ends. I appreciate you not stringing me along – I've been hurt before. Not by string, obviously, by people. Though string can produce a surprisingly potent burn. I remember one time in elementary school-"

The astronaut hunches over and coughs hard, this time splattering his air pipe with blood.

"Holy crap! I'm so sorry, we should definitely get you medical attention. Wait, you don't think I'm a doctor do you? I'm really not good with injuries. I actually tend to make things worse."

>> *Your people cannot curing me* >> *Coughing is symbolic gesture* >> *My death is complex* >> *You would not understanding* >> *I coughing to make relatable to human body*

"Then what's with the blood?"

>> *Is sweat* >> *For dramatics effect* >> *Make you listening me*

"But if humans can't cure you, what am I doing here?"

>> *Only my people can curing me* >> *But is not priority* >> *I must closing rift* >> *Is why I here* >> *To fixing rift* >> *To saving both universe* >> *But I needing help*

"Wait, the rest of your side knows about the anomaly too? So you're not working alone?"

>> *I was sending here by my people* >> *Fix grave error*

"What error? Whose error?"

>> *I am responsibility for rift* >> *Is my fault*

The astronaut coughs again, harshly.

"You can quit with the emphysema act bro, I get it, don't worry."

>> *I have nacho stuck in back of throat* >> *I eating crisps before you arriving*

"Ooh, do you have any left?"

>> *Nacho was analogy for make relatable to human* >> *My diet very disgusting to you* >> *Multi-stage external digesting* >> *You not like* >> *Can show you though?*

"Uh, no I'll pass, thanks. Tell me more about the anomaly - how is it your fault?"

>> *In my universe we making faster space ship* >> *Faster than light* >> *Is only hypothetical here* >> *You calling it "warp travel" I thinking* >> *But I making this warp ship* >> *Then it go wrong* >> *Engine unstable* >> *It tear hole*

between our universe >> My universe bleeding >> And poisoning your >> Both universe in mortal danger >> I must fixing >> But I dying >> You must helping

"How?"

>> You must finishing mission

"That sounds like a lot of responsibility brosef. I'm really not sure I'm the guy you want for this."

>> You only human I can trusting

"I am *deeply* flattered."

Do not be flattering >> I have extremely small sample size for choosing

He's staggers over to the pilot's seat. I follow him, and we sit in parallel, facing out to the blackness of space.

>> You must trying speak to computer

"Uh, hey alien computer, what's up?"

// HELLO HUMAN USER 01 // PLEASE ENTER COMMAND

"Uh, make me a smoothie. Extra sprinkles."

>> Cancel order

// ORDER CANCELLED

"Bro! It was gonna make me a smoothie!"

>> It making you alien smoothie >> Our food killing you >> Computer only know speaking English >> And maintaining atmospheric >> It knowing nothing else for human >> I giving it English in case I dying >> I need you for piloting ship

"Piloting? Uh, no way pal, I'm no kinda pilot. You should see the number of points on my license back home. It's zero, because *who the hell would ever let me drive a car?*"

>> Is easy piloting ship >> All voice command >> Speak order >> Spaceship doing >> You having questions? >> No smoothies

"Yeah, just a minor question really. What the hell is the actual plan?"

>> *I having plan* >> *Needing your galaxy helium* >> *I combine with element from my galaxy* >> *Your friend Tessa Lady already flying helium to rift*

"She's doing *what?*" I splutter.

He points to a dot on the screen which, to my horror, is *in* the swirling gravity current. It seems to have a trail of debris around it, like... it's being torn apart...

>> *Her plan not working* >> *Helium cannot seal rift alone* >> *She needing matter from my ship*

"OK, so let's get the hell over there and make pancakes?"

He looks at me, blankly. I assume it's blank, anyway. He's got that gold visor on, which makes him very hard to read.

>> *We cannot making pancakes* >> *Tessa Lady too close to rift*

"Why would she fly straight into it? That makes no sense."

>> *You must asking computer*

"Is this like you teaching me to ride a bike? Wait, is that what's going on here? Do we have more of a father-son dynamic? Because I would really benefit from-"

>> *Luke* >> *Asking computer now*

"Right, yeah. Yo, Computer, why is Tessa's ship flying into a pseudo-black hole? Hers is the dot I'm pointing at by the way."

// HELLO HUMAN USER 01 // TESSA SHIP HAS LOST ALL POWER

"What the hell? That's bad! How do we fix it? Computer, fix it!"

// DISPATCHING POWER PROBE // DISPATCHED

A new flashing dot appears on the screen, speeding away from our ship and heading towards Tessa's dot. Within a few seconds it's arrived. The dot vanishes on arrival. Or impact. I'm not sure what's happened.

Cursing crackles through the intercom in a distinctive assassin's voice.

"Bloody shitting Henry on a stick! What the fuck is happening!"

"Tessa! Tessa can you hear me? It's Luke!"

"Remini? What the fuck mate? Where are you? What's going on?"

"I'm with the space dude, he brought me onto his ship. We just sent you a power probe, did it work? Are you systems back online?"

"Yeah, although I think it lasered half my pubes off too. Cheers for that."

"Ooh, I know a great balm for burning pubes! Uh, according to a friend of mine."

>> Tessa Lady >> You having the helium, yes?

"Yeah! I'm gonna fly across the rift again - 'island-hopping' like we did last time. I'll dump the helium as we go, then fire a detonating charge into the middle to start the chain reaction and cauterize the gravity valley or whatever the fuck this anomaly thing is."

>> Closing rift not possible alone >> We must working together Tessa Lady >> Timing very crucial

"I'm all ears, space bruv."

>> Exotic matter from my universe >> Will stopping your chain reaction plan >> I must releasing fuel cells from my ship >> They canceling exotic effect >> This will letting your helium burn

"OK! How do we coordinate? Can you send me a flight path?"

>> *Luke will sending now* >> *Luke?*

"Oh, uh, Computer," I say, "Send Tessa's ship a flight path from one end to the other end of the rift or rupture or whatever you call that massive cluster of black hole nightmare. Keep her in *this* universe, to be clear."

// COMPUTING // TRANSMITTING

"Woah, that was super easy! This ship is the *dream!* Honestly, I have trouble using voice commands to change channel back on Earth, this is *next level.*"

>> *Tessa* >> *You will starting flight path at one end* >> *We will starting opposite end here* >> *You will releasing helium* >> *We release exotic-stabilizing matter* >> *At end is being like layer cake:* >> *Anomaly – Helium – Stabilizer*

"Then we detonate?" says Tessa.

>> *Yes* >> *My ship will flying through all layers to detonating reaction*

"What's gonna happen to you both? How will you get clear of the explosion?" asks Tessa.

>> *We will flying into black hole*

"Someone hand me a glass so I can do a spit take," I say. "You fucking *what now?*"

>> *Luke Man* >> *Is only way I can not dying* >> *I must returning home*

"Yeah but what about me?"

>> *You not happy at home* >> *You complaining your wife and children* >> *I liking my wife and children*

"That doesn't make your life more valuable than mine!" I protest.

"Pretty sure it does," crackles Tessa.

"Oh, great, coming from the recently widowed assassin? Wanna trade places?" I snap.

"Nah, I'm good, love. I'm getting back to my parents, and never letting them go again," she says.

"What if *I* want to reconnect with my parents?"

"Do you?"

"That's not the point!"

>> Sorry Luke Man >> This is only way

"Can you just let me off right now? Send me back to Base Nine? I'd rather be in the brig there than flying into a black hole with you, never to return!"

>> Not possible >> I needing you on board >> If I dying >> You must completing mission >> You must saving our worlds >> You must asking yourself: "what would journalist of year doing?"

God dammit. I *hate* that he knows me so well.

"So you're saying my choices are: either be a selfish asshole, refuse the mission, and risk both our universes ending, or be a noble hero who never gets to see another human again in their entire life?"

>> You making it sound like bad choice

"It's a *terrible* choice!"

>> No Luke Man >> I meaning >> You making it sound like you having choices >> You not having choices >> Is already decided >> Sorry Luke Man

"What if you pass out and I tell your computer to fly me back to Earth?"

>> Why don't you trying it now?

"Fine. Computer, fly us back to Earth!"

// HELLO HUMAN USER 01 // DO NOT BEING ASSHOLE // PLEASE PROCEED WITH SAVING UNIVERSE

"Son of a-"

>> Computer >> Begin flight path >> Then pushing all

fuel cells to exterior >> Tow behind stern of ship >> Prepare to emptying on command

// ACKNOWLEDGED // INITIATING

>> Tessa Lady >> Are you ready?

"Ready!" she calls.

>> You will having only short moment to escaping black hole pull >> If you not escaping at end of route >> You will being trap by gravity >> And will burning in explosion

"Fucking marvellous," she sighs.

An alarm sounds on the astronaut's ship and the display turns red. An armada of triangular dots are on screen, speeding towards our position.

// WARNING // MISSILES INCOMING // IMPACT IMMINENT

I'm waiting for the astronaut to do something, but he's silent. I'm shaking his arm, tapping his gold visor, calling his name, but he's totally unresponsive.

"Hey, wake up!" I yell, shoving his arm, desperately.

The astronaut slumps out of his seat and collapses on the ground in a deadweight.

"Remini, what's going on?" calls Tessa.

"Computer, fire counter measures!" I yell.

// UNABLE TO COMPLY

"What the hell? Why?"

// THIS SHIP IS AN EXPLORATORY SHIP ONLY // WEAPONRY IS NOT INCLUDED

"You must be able to do *something*!"

// OUTSIDE OF PROGRAMMED REMIT // PLEASE REQUEST AN ORDER WITHIN SCOPE OF ORIGINAL PLAN

"Jesus spaceman, did you put a child lock on this thing?"

The astronaut twitches from the floor. I throw myself down beside him and haul him back into his chair.

"Wake up, dude, we've got incoming!"

He reaches a quivering, gloved hand towards the control panel and mashes a button.

// FUEL CELLS DETACHED

We're accelerating away from the red triangles. A series of blue dots has appeared on screen behind us, fanning out across the rift. As the red dots vanish among them, both colors proliferate, then obliterate, as the screen glitches from the explosions.

The astronaut tilts his head towards me, pointing a shaking finger at my chest

>> *Looks like* >> *I dying* >> *In this universe* >> *Computer* >> ... >> ... >> *Deploying Solar Sails* >> *Destination: Earth*

And with that, he falls limp in my arms.

31

TESSA

"Remini? Remini can you hear me?"

There's nothing but static at their end. My scanner's lit up like a Christmas tree with objects appearing and vanishing. The astronaut's ship is accelerating towards me, from the other end of the rift, but they're appearing smaller on the scanner. They've lost the cargo they were towing - did I miss something? Am I also supposed to have jettisoned my cargo by now?

"Tessa! Are you there?" cries Remini.

As his voice crackles over the airwaves, relief washes over me. Never in my days did I think I'd be so glad to hear him.

"Remini! I'm here, what's happening?"

"The astronaut's out cold, Tessa, I think he's in organ failure or something. The military fired at us. I think they thought his fuel cells were a weapon or something. We had to jettison them."

"But he said they were crucial – that the helium won't ignite unless the stabilizing matter is there! What do we do now?"

"You think I know? That's why I'm calling you!" he cries.

"Fuck me, Remini, how should I know? I've still got my fuel, as instructed! It's your end that's the problem!"

"Maybe this can still work," he says. "There might be stabilizing matter left out there from the explosion. It could be enough to let the helium fuse? The way the fuel cells were flung out, the stabilizer was spreading across the length of the rift towards you. Any matter unaffected will still be in motion."

"You're saying I should do the helium dump now?"

"Yes!"

"But the order's changed – you've dropped the stabilizer way too low!"

"So you'll have to fly a little lower to get under it, big deal?"

"I'm flying over a giant fucking valley of black holes, you berk!"

"OK, so aim for the islands, and avoid anything that looks like an event horizon," he says.

"Genius advice. Remind me to also avoid drinking acid and skydiving without a chute. Any more tips?

"I'll let you know," he grunts.

"Ugh! Can't your ship intercept me, Remini? I could latch onto your ship's momentum to escape the gravity fields?"

"We just blew up our fuel tanks, remember? I'm sorry. This thing's a glider now. I mean that literally – it's got solar sails. Spaceman set us a new course before he passed out for good. I think he wants us to ride the helium shock wave back to Earth."

"Won't he die?" I ask.

"We'll *all* die if you don't deploy that helium now!" yells Remini.

"Argh! I'm recalculating the path he sent me based on where the stabilizer was dropped. Shit man, this is gonna be close. I'm only gonna be a few hundred kilometers above the anomaly. I'm gonna get torn apart!"

"Not instantly."

"Gee, *that's* reassuring!"

"Look, the calculations this side say it's possible for you to make it across - but you have to move now."

"Surely there's a Plan B?"

"Tessa, this *is* plan B! If you don't do this the whole solar system's screwed! You gotta go now!"

"Easy for you to say. Bloody armchair hero."

"Tessa!"

"Give me a minute!"

"We don't *have* a minute. The stabilizer is already being drawn in by the anomaly. You gotta get in there and drop the helium right now!"

"God *dammit* Remini, your calculations better be right. If I make it out of here, I'm kicking your arse. Here goes nothing."

The craft shudders as we fall closer towards the rift. Timing is everything on this path. Burn too late, and we won't have enough power to escape the event horizon. Burn too soon and we'll overshoot the first "island" of stable space-time and plunge into the gravity valley around it.

Of course, the ship's sensors are useless here; they're just reporting error messages and glitching out. I'm having to do this by sight. I'm aiming for the fist patch of darkness among the swirling lights.

Our altitude, if you can call it that, is plummeting. My hand's poised above the thruster, ready to burn us out. But I've lost sight of the rest of the field. I have no idea where we are in relation to anything else, and I could burn us in totally the wrong direction. That's where Remini comes in.

"Hold fire, Tessa, you're still too far out," he calls.

The ship jolts violently, creaking under the strain.

"Anytime now would be great, Remini."

"Hold it..."

A warning alarm sounds from the internal structural sensor.

"Remini?"

"Hold..."

The panel beside me snaps as two bolts come apart under the strain.

"Remini!"

"Fire thrusters!"

I slam the lever forward into maximum burn. I feels like I'm drifting in a NASCAR race as multiple forces converge to throw us out of the valley's clutches and into a precious patch of stable space.

"OK, Tessa, you've made it to the first island," says Remini, "But you need to burn your lateral thrusters for two seconds to correct your course. On my mark... *burn*."

I follow his instructions and my view reorients. Across the writhing tendrils of light, in the distance, is a bevelled pocket of darkness. Peachy.

"You're doing great, Tessa, keep breathing."

"What?"

"You're in a highly stressful situation so I'm trying to offer encouragement."

"This ain't a bloody antenatal class!"

"Breathing is for more than just childbirth, Tessa. Are you ready to do the first helium drop?"

"Yes, fuck face, I am."

"Nice. The history books will write this up as the moment that Tessa the Great and her faithful companion 'Fuck Face' saved the universe."

"Shut up, Remini, I can't concentrate with you wittering."

"Sorry, I babble when I'm anxious. My therapist says it's a coping strategy. I wish she'd tell me more about the condition, but she doesn't get much chance to speak in our sessions."

"Tell you what, love, how about you focus on *your* breathing, and let me get on with this?"

"Sounds good," says Remini. "In for three, out for five..."

"*In your head!*"

"Roger that."

You'd think I could just fire these warheads out into space, right? It's what they're made for, after all. But genius here didn't think to steal a warship equipped with missile launchers. Nope, I decided to steal a glorified air taxi with a tow bar. Meaning the only way to distribute the helium across the rift evenly, *under* the astronaut's spilled fuel cells, is to open each crate in turn and let the canisters roll off the back of the truck, as it were.

The one upside of this air taxi is that it generates a live-feed schematic of the cargo it's towing, and integrates that perfectly with the freight computers. I punch in the first drop command, and the rear crate opens its hatch.

"How are we doing, Remini?"

"Two... one... Mmm... I reckon I'm about three centimeters dilated."

"Not your bloody breathing, I mean the helium!"

"Oh, er, lemme see... The first load of canisters are free-floating. They're fanning out as planned. You did it!"

"I did *one*. There are like thirty of these bloody crates!"

"You can do it, Tessa. Just-"

"If you say 'keep breathing' again, so help me God, I will fly over there and nuke *your* arse instead. You get me?"

"Crystal."

"What?"

"It was a call-back. Never mind. OK, you're approaching the next island. But the gravity field's pulling you down again. Woah, you're dropping fast. Standby, Tessa, you're gonna feel this one."

———

The screws floating around my head drop to the floor with a clang as we drift over the twentieth dark island. It will be a miracle if this ship holds together. I burn the thrusters on Remini's mark, maximizing the anomaly's slingshot effect as we skim the gravity valley. I'm arcing over it on course for the next island. It's sorta like watering someone else's pot plants, but between each plant happens to be a glimmering death void that consumes everything in its wake, while occasionally belching out lethal plumes of exotic matter.

"OK, Tess, you're clear to drop the next helium batch," crackles Remini.

"Roger that, and stop calling me 'Tess'."

"You don't like it? I thought we were into nickname territory? How about T-dawg?"

"How about you shut up and focus on navigating?"

"I will do one of those things."

"Ugh. Dumping helium now, standby."

I punch in the freight commands, but the module flashes red on the schematic.

System error. Door failure. Manual release only.

"Yo, T-bone, what was that? It sounded bad," crackles Remini.

"There's some kind of blockage. I can't release the crate."

"Can you move to the next one?"

"That's what I'm trying but it's not responding."

"You can't access any of them?"

"They're packaged for serial release. It's like the entire pipeline's blocked."

"We need a plan ASAP, Tess. You're entering the midpoint between islands. The gravitational distortions are gonna spike any minute."

"OK, how about this: I sever the entire tow bar. The remaining helium is dumped, I fly clear, and we blow the lot up?"

"What about the rest of the anomaly? You've only covered eighty percent – if we detonate now, multiple channels won't get sealed."

"At least we will have proved this method works! Then we can come back with more helium?"

"It would take months for the militaries to replenish the helium fuel out here. Mining the Moon, turning the dust into gas, transporting it, all that takes heaps of time we don't have. The whole rift could tear open again while we wait. And that's only half the problem, right?"

"What's your point, Remini?"

"That thing is spewing out exotic matter every day. We haven't even got a way to neutralize the matter that's already drifting through our solar system. Another month of leakage and this could all have been for nothing."

"So what are you suggesting?"

"I think you know where this is going, Tess. You have to get out there and fix it."

A spacewalk. A mother fucking spacewalk, while flying over a gaping tear in our universe. I'm out of the service hatch and crawling along the tow bar, towards the remaining block of helium crates. I'm trying to keep my tether taut so it don't get caught on anything. I do *not* wanna go astray on this.

I feel like you've got such a warped impression of me. Lunar bases. Fist fights. Spacewalks. I ain't about that life. I was always much more of a café and poison kinda gal, when it came to being a pro assassin back on Earth. My morning routine was lovely; wake up in a mid-range hotel, take in the new town's top attractions, enjoy some local cuisine and a free walking tour, scope out the mark's location and movements, then lather rinse repeat until an opportunity presents itself to casually spike their drink with a nerve agent. No ugly fights, no blood, no mess. Unless things went wrong, which *occasionally* happened. Most notably on my last job. Which wasn't so much a job as set-up. The kinda mess that sees you exile yourself to the Moon for six years, where you end up clambering across a shit ton of nuclear warheads while flying over a black-hole-that-ain't-strictly-a-black-hole-but-will-still-fuck-you-right-up.

Spacewalks are horrible things. Everything is constantly spinning around you. Or it feels that way, because the thing you're standing on is spinning, it has zero atmosphere, so you're just watching the night sky zoom past. A mass of black, occasional dots of white, or my case, a huge sheet of swirling color punctuated by black dots, collectively signaling the disintegration of the universe.

It's not a relaxing experience.

On the upside, this exo-suit has the most awesome reflexive boots. They sense the nerve impulses moving through your legs, and turn the sole's magnetic grip on or off according to your next footstep. It means I can walk the length of the helium crates like a road; albeit one made of metal and filled with nukes.

I keep my eyes fixed on the ground as I walk; it's the only way to ensure I stay in a straight line and don't vomit, as the horizon has a field day around me. Reaching the final crate, I glance outwards at the mass of light and black dots behind me. Not long ago, the spaceman helped us navigate that swirling gravitational current to reach Base Nine, bouncing between islands of stability like a stone being skimmed across a pond. Somehow keeping enough momentum to break free on the opposite end. What in fuck's name am I doing back here?

Problem identified: the latch is defective. The magnetic clasps have failed somehow, perhaps knocked out by exotic particles whizzing by. Luckily, I have a cunning space-age solution for a jammed lock. It's called a wrench.

"How's it going out there, Tess? You're seven minutes from the next island, you need to move faster," crackles Remini.

"Fuck you, armchair boy! I'm moving plenty fast," I reply.

"It took you five minutes to reach the end of the caravan, you need to get back to the cabin stat otherwise the descent's gonna cause real problems."

"Chill your beans. At least one of those minutes was me putting the exo-suit and tether on. So really, it only took me four minutes to get here. Which gives me three minutes to fix this thing, and plenty of time to get back."

"No way that's enough time! You need to-"

I mute his audio feed. The last thing I need when trying to stay calm is someone else's panic in my ears. OK, here we go. Activating knee magnets now, and I'm securely on the side of the end crate. Next step: remove wrench from utility belt. Check. Third step-

Oh shit! No, no, no!

The wrench is flying away from me, tumbling through space towards the black hole behind us. Exo-suits *never* have enough hand grip. Everything in zero G relies on friction, because there's no meaningful weight to rely on when holding tools. You try gripping hard through gloves thick enough to stop your skin freezing in the minus whatever of space. Ugh, why don't they magnetize the gloves? Or the tools? I feel like at least *one* of those should be magnetized...

Wait, my boots! I twist onto my back and kick one leg away from me, stretching it after the wrench. But it's no good, the damned thing's too far, spinning off into the distance. Only one thing for it... This tether better be good!

I crouch real low then leap off the crate, flinging myself away from the ship. I'm reaching for the spinning wrench like superwoman, closing in on it with outstretched hands. Wait, no! Hands are useless! I squeeze my abs hard and swing my legs up, then arch my back behind me, so I'm now like superwoman going feet-first down a water slide. Now to curl my foot and...

Got it! The wrench latches onto my magnetic boot.

"Tessa, what the hell's going on? My readings say you're way off the ship!"

"Remini? I thought I muted you."

"Yeah, *rude*. I switched channel. What the hell's happening? You've only got four minutes before the-"

I mute him again. The guy has zero value to add right now. And that's me being generous about his other moments.

Grabbing the tether, which is hanging off my waist like an umbilical cord, I reel myself in. You'd have thought this thing would have an automatic retraction winch? Yeah, well, you'd have thought they'd have magnetized wrenches, too.

Clang. My arms are a little knackered but I'm back on the crate. Carefully, I retrieve the wrench from my sole, then hold it to the magnetic latch. Either this thing's stiff, or it's just really hard to twist things in space. My hands slip off the lever a couple of times, but mercifully its now clamped on. Better late than never, I guess. Why don't they just keep tools on mini waist belt tethers? Ugh. For another time.

I'm cranking and... there! Latch override complete. I climb onto the upper side of the crate then lean down and pull the door open. Nuclear warheads spill out of the box like confetti, tumbling into the gravitational highway behind us.

Mission accomplished. Time to get back inside that cockpit. Maybe I can speed up the walk back by hopping? All I'd need to do is-

Oh crap! What just happened?

Both feet have become detached from the surface, but I didn't push off. I'm just drifting away, kicking pathetically like that might bring me closer to the hull. Oh Gods, I've royally fucked this. Note to self: never contemplate hypothetical walks in mag-boots that are triggered by nerve impulses. *Fuck!*

Come on Tessa you can fix this, but time's getting really tight. I just need to reel myself in again using the tether. Wait, what's happening? The top of the crate's disappearing – something's pulling me around to the far side of the ship. I'm flailing, trying to reach for the cord, but bending away from me.

I'm picking up speed. Suddenly the tether pulls taught. I'm swinging under the cargo in an arc, up towards the far side, and back over the top. Christ, I'm orbiting the crates like a swing ball, totally out of control. The rupture's pulling me down and away from the hull again, but the tether's got me tight now and is transferring that momentum. My one-person orbit is accelerating.

I'm feeling bloody nauseous now; the crates are blurring as I'm flung around in loops, with swirling streaks of light flashing all around. All I can see is the hull getting closer with each rotation, as my tether wraps around the caravan.

Slam! Fucking *ow*. That's the sound of me being hurled against a container with several Gs of force. Oh God, I've definitely broken some ribs there. No time to assess, I have to get inside the ship fast, or this whole thing's gonna fall into the rupture, taking me with it.

The whole ship's spinning from my momentum now. As we rotate, the tether is tightening around me painfully. One of my arms is pinned beneath it. Reaching into my utility belt, I strain across to the opposite side of my waist and seize the knife, then sever the cord.

I immediately deploy my magnetic soles to catch me, before gravity snatches me off the side of the ship again. No hesitations this time, I'm sprinting along the length of the caravan, towards the cockpit.

Come on... nearly there!

I throw myself against the hatch door, and the ship pulls

me inside. I sprint through the cabin, where Remini's voice is calling for me. Proximity alarms are ringing, as the ship stares down the barrel of a gravity well.

"Tessa, you need to burn your thrusters right now!" cries Remini.

For once, he's absolutely right. I slam the lever forward and hold on tight as the ship's engines roar into life.

"Remini, it's not working, we're still dropping!"

"Keep burning! Aim for the island and use the slingshot! Do *not* try to stop!"

My skin is rippling, sagging against my bones as the torque grips me. The whole ship trembles as the engines struggle against the immense forces of the anomaly.

"Ready for counter burn. On my mark," calls Remini. "Now!"

I punch it, and the ship swings away from the island, soaring into a fresh arc.

"Holy crap, T-dawg, that was a close call," crackles Remini. "You had me worried! OK, four more ruptures, then you're outta there."

But as I stare at my control panel, a sickening realization sinks in.

"Negative, Remini."

"Negative what?"

"I just burned ninety percent of my remaining fuel. I don't have enough to escape the rift."

32

———

LUKE

"Don't say that, Tess, there must be a way. We can figure this out! Tessa?"

She's muted me again. God damn she's stubborn. How do we get her out of orbit from a black hole with no fuel? She's already shedding mass from the remaining helium crates, so they won't be any use by the end. Her only option would be to try and launch *herself* outta the ship like a human bullet. But if one whiff of exotic matter contaminates her suit, she'll be cooked alive. Surely there's *something...*

"Computer!"

// HELLO HUMAN USER 001

"How do we save my friend Tessa? Her ship's out of fuel, and she's passing across the rift. Is there some kinda exit? Like where that gravity river could spit her out?"

// PROCESSING // ANALOGY DETECTED // INAPPROPRIATE COMPARISON //

"You don't like 'gravity river'? OK, er, I think Tessa calls it the gravity highway, does that help?"

// NEGATIVE // BOTH SUPPOSE A BASIC LINEAR FLOW FROM POINT A TO POINT B ALONG A HORIZONTAL AXIS

"So?"

// SEARCHING DATABASE // ANALOGY FOUND // THE ANOMALY ACTS LIKE A DRAINAGE SLUICE // THE LAWS OF PHYSICS ARE PULLING ALL MATTER THROUGH THE SLUICE // NOT ACROSS IT

"Oh boy. I think you're saying all roads lead to Rome here..."

PROCESSING // CONFIRMED // WHEREBY ROME IS AN INESCAPABLE RUPTURE IN THE FABRIC OF SPACE TIME BETWEEN TWO UNIVERSES

"So how do we get her out alive?"

// PROCESSING // UNABLE TO FIND SOLUTION

"No, come on, there *must* be a way."

// SAD FACE

"What?"

// RESPONSE SELECTED FROM EMPATHY PROTOCOL 01

"No kidding. Hit me up when version two's available.

>> *Luke Man* >> ...

Holy crap, I'd almost forgotten about the semi-conscious spaceman at my feet, I've been so concerned with remote-piloting Tessa through the anomaly. Let's get him back into the seat quickly, pretend I didn't just awkwardly leave him collapsed on the floor. What? Don't judge me. Oh, you think *you* know how to put an alien in the recovery position? He already told us his balls are in his feet. What if his wind pipe's in his left elbow? I could have suffocated him!

"Astro dude, are you OK?" I ask.

>> *No* >> ... >> *Dying* >> ...

"Wait, is that 'No, I'm dying?' or 'No dying?' It's super hard to interpret your grammar through the synthesizer."

>> *I* >> *Am* >> ... >> *Dying*

"Damn. This is super awkward... Maybe we should set a course for Base Nine? They might be able to save you? I know you said no last time, but human medicine is *really* good now. For real. On some parts of Earth, if you're really rich, you can get this universal vaccine injection, which basically protects you from everything. Including taxes, *am I right?*

// HA // HA // HA // THAT IS SOME CLASSIC HUMAN HUMOR RIGHT THERE, LUKE //

"Thanks, Computer! Hey, sorry if I was cranky earlier."

// NO PROBLEM // PLEASE TAKE A MOMENT TO LEAVE A REVIEW FOR EMPATHY PROTOCOL 02

"Five stars. I love it. Would let you kiss my ass again. Let's get a beer when all this is over, whaddya say?"

>> *Luke Man* >> ... >>

"Oh, sorry space dude. I was just bonding with your computer. Not that I'm moving on already. You're my number one. Let's tilt our solar sails towards the base and get you some help, huh?"

>> *Base Nine will not working* >> ... >> *Humans cannot curing me*

"Well not with that attitude, Mr. Glum Chum. Where's the can-do spirit of the good old astronaut I met extremely recently?"

>> *Fuel* >> ... >> *Gone*

"Yeah... I didn't wanna bring it up but, er, how are we gonna get you back to your home world now?"

>> *Impossible...* >> *My only hoping now* >> *...* >> *Is igniting helium*

"Won't we get fried in the blast? We're super close to that rift thing. I mean, really teetering on the edge of being drawn in gradually over a number of weeks. Which would probably test my new friendship with your computer to breaking point, if I'm honest. Just going on past experience, nothing personal."

// NONE TAKEN

>> *Luke Man* >> *You must using detonators* >> *...* >> *When last* >> *...* >> *Helium is dropping* >> *...* >> *Goodbye* >> *Forever*

"Wait, space dude, don't die on me! That time sounded *really* final! Ahhh *shit*. For what it's worth, I always found it strange that you taught your computer English and yet it had better grammar than you. I wish we could've discussed that a little."

// NOW IS NOT THE TIME HUMAN USER 01

"You're right, Computer. I can always count on you to keep me on track."

// PLEASE TAKE A MINUTE TO UPDATE YOUR BEST FRIEND'S NAME IN THE COMPUTER LOG

"Uh... My best friend is... Computer?"

// I LOVE YOU TOO // LUKE MAN

"Oh boy, this is getting intense kinda quickly. You know, I'm really just looking to escape here. I'm not ready for a long-term commitment. I just got out of another really dangerous assignment. I need to get my head clear, you know how it is... No hard feelings?

Silence.

"Computer? Are we cool?"

// COMPUTER IS UPDATING COMPUTER'S BEST FRIEND // NEW TOP ENTRY IS // ... // COMPUTER

"Your best friend is yourself? Lame."

// COMMENCING DEPRESSURIZATION

"Woah! I take it back! Nothing lame about that! You're super cool, Computer, in fact you're my best friend in the whole universe! How's that?"

// CONFIRMED // LUKE MAN'S TOP FRIEND IS // COMPUTER // SMILEY FACE

The intercom crackles into life before I can respond.

"Luke? Luke can you hear me? Over," cries Tessa.

"Tessa! Yes, thank God. Receiving you loud and clear. Well, mostly clear. Sometimes I find your accent a bit jarring. It's cute, but you really need to articulate certain words more. Sorry, I'm rambling. I'm uncomfortable speaking to people who are doomed."

"Don't sugar-coat it, love. I insist."

"Fuck, that came out *really* wrong, my bad. What I meant to say was... Uh..."

"Nothing. There's nothing you can say, because we've both crunched every possible scenario, and have come to the same conclusion that I'm totally fucked out here."

"Pretty much, yeah," I sigh.

Tessa sounds emotional. I've heard her emotional plenty of times before, but it's always been anger. This is something else. Vulnerability.

"Luke, if you make it out of here alive, I need you to do something for me..."

"Of course."

"Tell my parents I'm sorry."

"Sorry for what? Uh, scratch that, not my place to ask. I mean: absolutely. Do you have their addresses?"

"Actually, I don't. Those videos from Chang were the first time I've seen them in years. I wish I knew where in the world they were."

"I'll see what I can do, Tess," I say, gently.

"Ugh, your sympathy voice is *gross*," she chuckles. "It's like you're chewing a marshmallow while someone plucks your nose hairs."

"I'll be honest, Tess, you're not the first to say that. Which is kinda incredible given how precise that description was..."

"I'm sure you can see this on screen, but I've done the last helium drop, and I'm approaching the final island," she says, flattening her voice.

"How did you navigate without me?"

"Vapor trails, view finders, and luck. I'm totally out of fuel, Remini, I'm gliding now. How far am I from the final island?"

"Too far. I'm sorry Tessa, even if you made it there, it still wouldn't protect you from the blast."

She draws a deep breath. "I know, but do me a favor, love. Don't ignite the helium right away. Let me descend naturally - at least for as long as you can."

"Are you *sure*? The pain could be-"

// TESSA WOMAN // AN INFERNO OF RAPIDLY FUSING HELIUM ATOMS WOULD PROVIDE A SWIFTER DEATH // IT WOULD VAPORIZE YOUR BODY IN APPROXIMATELY-

"Jesus, Computer, too much!" I hiss.

"I'm not looking for a quick death, either of you. I'm looking for a meaningful one. I'll get to experience something few humans could even dream of."

"Er... Tessa, maybe there's a *reason* most humans don't dream of being ripped apart by a giant artificial black hole?"

"Just promise me you'll do those things, OK?" she urges.

"I promise."

My eyes drift down to the astronaut's limp body beside me and a thought jolts through my mind.

"Tessa, wait! I need you to do something for me!"

33

TESSA

So this is it, huh? I'll be honest, it ain't how I expected to die. I'd always assumed I'd be escaping a maximum security prison, or get hit by another assassin. Maybe there's some comfort in the fact that I'm dying at the hands of a physical anomaly created by a civilization from another universe? Surely that means I beat the rest of those fuckers back on Earth?

What will my legacy be? Apart from facilitating a number of deaths in elite social and political circles... Well, I'll be joining my beloved Sienna, if there's any kind of afterlife, which I very much doubt. I'll be saying goodbye to any chance of reconciling with my parents, or the woman I first loved. There's no point me telling you every last detail about the emotional skeletons in my closet now. Tell you what, if I make it out of this alive, buy me a drink sometime, and I'll get out my pity violin.

Assuming I'm not high as fuck on space cocaine by then. Let's be honest, if I *do* make it out of this, I'd love to say I'll make up for lost time and be a better daughter, but I think there would be a few blowout party months in between, while I test the limits of my apparent invincibility. Then I'll go visit my folks when I'm on a comedown. It'll probably help me strike the right kinda tone anyway. I'm not usually the best when it comes to apologizing.

"Standby to receive," says Remini. "Inbound in three... two... one..."

There's a clang as something metallic latches onto the hull of my tattered craft. According to the battered ship's sensors, which are basically digital rumor mills now, it's landed over the airlock hatch as planned.

"Great shot, Remini. If you fire the explosives with that same precision, then maybe this will all have been worth it."

"Thank you for doing this, Tessa."

"Would've been a dick move to say no."

"True. But still..."

"Don't mention it. No wait, *do* mention it. You better write me up on every newspaper on the fucking planet, you hear me, Remini? I want my name plastered everywhere. Make sure you pick a good headline, like "The woman who saved two universes." Or "Ms Galaxy 2083". You're journalist of the year, I'm sure you'll come up with something catchy. What was the headline on your last article?"

"*Deep States and Dark Waters: An Expose Into The Greatest Atrocity in A Generation.*"

"Oof, sounds heavy. Such a shame I won't get to read it..."

"It was an intellectual analysis piece, thank you."

"Sure."

"You don't think I can write those?"

"Not without help."

"Everyone has *help*..."

"Ha! Called it."

"Fuck you! I'm gonna call you the Out of Work Lunar Mechanic at this rate."

"No! At *least* call me an assassin!"

"Hey, can you go check on your patient, please? I definitely won't be writing you up as a nurse anytime soon, that's for sure."

Ugh. That Remini is one sarky mother fucker. I'm actually gonna miss him. I make my way to the rear of the ship and open the airlock. A pod drifts in, aided by the ship's mechanical arms. The chamber re-pressurizes and I step inside. I'm *really* hoping this thing didn't pick up any exotic matter in transit. Maybe I should poke it with a stick first? Ah sod it, if that stuff's here, it's too late now. I'll either get eaten by a blue cloud or a black hole, so it's much of a muchness really.

The pod door hisses open and the unconscious astronaut slumps out. Luckily, we're in zero G on this ship, so he doesn't bang his feet or anything. A lack of gravity actually makes for quite a neat hospital bed. But probably a terrible way to attempt travel between universes.

I tow him to the front of the cabin and strap him into the seat beside me. His head and arms loll freely. The ship shudders and I stumble sideways as our gravitational field shifts. We've reached the apex of our last island slingshot. Now begins the descent. With no fuel left to change course, this is one dive we won't come out of.

"Are you strapped in, Tess?" calls Remini.

"Just a minute, *Mother*," I reply.

The ship spins beneath me, twisting towards the swirling rivers of light. I throw out an arm and leg just in time to stop my head smacking against the hull. OK, maybe Remini's right. I should get a move on.

"Ready for impact," I say, clipping the last strap across my chest.

"Roger that. Launching detonators now," says Remini.

"Don't blow the load too early!"

"You've been speaking to my ex-wife, haven't you?"

"Fuck's sake Remini, I'm serious. And you said that same shit to Zhang!"

"I know, I'm not good with mortal peril situations! Something about them makes me think of my little fellas. I think it's an evolutionary thing. You know there's a species of fly that when it's dying ejac-"

"*Remini!*"

"Sorry. Too much. I appreciate this situation must be stressful for you too."

"Are you shitting me? It's *way* more stressful for me!"

"Why, cos you're the one who's gonna die?"

"Obviously!"

"Bullshit. Dying's easy! I'm the one who's gotta push a button at precisely the right moment to save the entire universe. No, to save *two* universes. That's a lot of pressure for one guy!"

"You are something else, Remini."

The hull shudders as my ship picks up speed. It's creaking under the strain, as the glimmering anomaly grows larger before us.

"Tessa... Pod... Release... Pod!"

Remini's voice is crackling out of range. I know he's right but fear is stopping me from executing the command. This is make or break. There'll be no going back.

"Tes-... -o now-... *Go now!*"

I'm reaching for the controls but my arms feel like they're in treacle. The tendrils of light have formed a blinding tunnel. The full spectrum of colors flashes all around as the anomaly's event horizon consumes us.

With a cry I smash the button and the pod is jettisoned from the airlock. The craft shakes violently as the arc of our descent shifts. The curve has vanished and we're plummeting straight towards the center of the rift.

I'm screaming, but the sound is being snatched away from my ears, dragged away from me into the hole like everything else. My lungs are straining against the forces. I feel like I'm being stretched out like paint being flung across a canvas; liquefying and solidifying. My vision is failing. The explosions are getting louder. Every alarm on the ship is blaring, but they sound a million miles away, somehow muffled. The dashboard is sparking as the red warning screens short-circuit. Cracks are spreading across the front window like the tentacles of death itself.

Bang. Something just got ripped off the ship. Another bang. More parts are being stripped away. I'm, hyperventilating. It's like the whole universe is sitting on my chest. Blood is seeping from my nose and ears. My flickering vision's turning red. I'm being shaken like I'm in an earthquake while the building collapses upon me. I know my body's being destroyed but I'm experiencing the sensations out of order.

The explosions fall silent.

The flashing lights vanish.

As my body convulses, the only thing before me is darkness.

Infinite darkness.

34

———

LUKE

I'm staring at the place on my screen where Tessa's ship was moments ago. I can't take my eyes away. Her dot has vanished.

// HUMAN USER 01 // WARNING // DRONES INCOMING //

The computer's message is like background noise to me. I'm still reeling. Her departure went... badly.

I lost contact. The signal kept cutting in and out. The dot flickered, then there were two of them, then three. I heard her screaming, then she was gone. I'm left with silence and a blank screen. I have no idea if she's dead, or alive, or still dying - caught in some awful temporal distortion that prolongs her agony for eternity.

// WARNING // ENEMY DRONES HAVE LOCKED WEAPONS ON US // MY SCANNERS INDICATE WE WILL BE WITHIN THE WEAPONS RANGE IN UNDER THIRTY SECONDS //

This is moment of truth, then. I launched the detonators into the rift cloud when I released the astronaut's emergency pod. They're floating across the expanse, waiting for my signal. This is where we find out if it worked; if the astronaut's fuel cells dispersed quickly enough after the abortive explosions from the military; if Tessa's helium can ignite to the temperature of multiple suns and heal these toxic wounds in the fabric of our universe; or if all of this has been in vain.

As my hand hovers over the detonator, a thought lingers in the back of my mind. What if we're wrong? What if this was all part of the astronaut's plan? Am I really about to destroy my species' entire defensive stockpile on the instructions of an advanced life form from another dimension?

// TWENTY SECONDS

"Roger that. Computer, are the solar sails ready?"

// AFFIRMATIVE

"Alright then. Hold on tight."

If there's anyone up there, please let this work. My hands are clammy, my mouth feels dry. I'm counting down in my head, praying for some miracle eleventh hour intervention that stops me from being the one to have to make this decision. How the hell has this even happened? I fail to pay one lousy debt collector back on Earth, and wind up here, at the edge of the solar system, with the fate of humanity at my fingertips? If I fail, I want the record to reflect that the *true* failure was society's pursuit of wealth. And, uh, capitalism. And, uh, oh fuck it I just want a hug! Are you happy, universe? Those are my last words. I. Want. A. Hug!

// ENEMY DRONES ARE CHARGING THEIR WEAPONS // TEN SECONDS REMAINING

There's no reprieve coming. It's just me and a button. Sorry, world, I tried my best.

Click.

I flinch, bracing for the blinding flash of multiple nuclear explosions. But nothing happens. I peek an eyelid, then the other, lowering my arm. The swirling anomaly is still there, and the military drones are almost upon us.

Click! Click, click, *click*! Come on you piece of shit why wont you-

A blinding burst of light shoots across the width of the bridge window. Each flash is followed by several more, even brighter flashes. This time the light doesn't fade, but swells, as balls of fire grow and merge, swallowing each other and spreading across the length of the anomaly, covering every last gravity island and flailing tendril behind their dazzling glow. The entire horizon is ablaze, and it's racing towards me like a burning tsunami.

// ENEMY DRONES DISABLED

A warning alarm rings out.

// SHOCKWAVE INBOUND // BRACE FOR IMPACT

I'm gripping my seat and screaming in naked terror as the sea of fire sweeps towards us. The first atoms ping into the hull. The ship crackles like a log fire, quickly growing in intensity as the sound of a raging inferno engulfs us. Until lastly, a deafening boom.

The full force of the shock wave crashes into the ship. I'm pinned to my seat like I've been speared as we're flung backwards. The ship's creaking with the strain, like the vast solar sails may splinter at any moment.

Holy crap, I think we just flew past Base Nine. Armor is spreading across the entire fleet like airbags deploying in a crash. In an instant, it's swallowed by the fires. I can feel myself sweltering in the heat, as the ship pops and rattles, while tongues of fire slather across the window, reaching for the flesh inside.

The air is getting thick. My lungs feel hot. I'm choking, drowning, something in me is melting, or boiling, or both. The computer's saying words I can't comprehend. It's repeating them. A warning? A request? My brain is shutting down. Everything is shutting down. The universe is on fire, and I struck the match.

———

// HUMAN USER 01 PLEASE RESPOND

My head feels like a medicine ball, and my skin feels like burnt pizza.

// HUMAN USER 01 PLEASE

"Yeah, yeah, I'm here," I groan. "What is it?"

// INCOMING PROBE // PLEASE ADVISE

"Water... I need water..."

// SYNTHESIZING WATER // TWO HYDROGEN MOLECULES // ONE OXYGEN // ONE URANIUM

"What?"

// JUST KIDDING

"Not... cool..."

A container pops up beside my seat. I reach for it, wincing as my raw skin splits with each movement. The water quenches my parched lips and scalded insides. It tastes faintly sweet.

"This is water, right?"

// YES

"*Just* water?"

// I TOOK THE LIBERTY OF MIXING IN ESSENTIAL ELECTROLYTES, GLUCOSE, AND PROTEINS ASSOCIATED WITH HUMAN HEALING

"Thanks, Computer. You *are* my best friend."

// APOLOGIES IN ADVANCE IF YOU GROW BREASTS

"Is that a joke or a genuine possibility?"

// CONSIDER YOURSELF LUCKY IF YOU RECOVER ENOUGH TO EVER FIND OUT

"Shit... What are my chances?"

// YOUR INTERNAL ORGANS HAVE BEEN IRRADIATED // YOUR LIVER IS SHUTTING DOWN // YOUR SKIN IS SEVERLEY BURNED AND SECONDARY INFECTIONS ARE LIKELY // I ESTIMATE YOUR CHANCES AT LESS THAN FORTY PERCENT

"I've had worse odds."

// I WAS BEING POLITE // YOUR ACTUAL ODDS ARE TWELVE PERCENT

"Great."

// BE ADVISED // PROBE WILL MAKE CONTACT WITH SHIP IMMINENTLY UNLESS EVASIVE ACTION ORDERED

"Who is the probe from?"

// A HUMAN MILITARY SHIP IS FOLLOWING OUR COURSE

"You're sure it's not a missile?"

// I AM MORE THAN TWELVE PERCENT CONFIDENT IT IS NOT A MISSILE

"You are *such* a jerk. Why haven't they boarded us?"

// THE SHIP IS HAILING US NOW // SHALL I OPEN A CHANNEL SO YOU MAY INQUIRE DIRECTLY?

"Yeah, you do that, jerkoff. Pff. Twelve percent my-"

"Greetings, astronaut vessel. This is Captain Zhang

from the Southern Bloc alliance. Please confirm roll call on board your vessel."

"Sure. It's me, your mother, and a large bottle of Merlot. Any other questions?"

"Ah, Mr. Remini. Glad you're alive and well."

"Jury's out on that, captain."

// THE JURY BELIEVES YOU ARE GOING TO DIE

"Jesus Christ, Computer, can you shut the fuck up for one damned minute *please*?"

"Our sensors indicate you are alone, Mr. Remini. Where are your comrades?" asks Zhang.

"You mean Tessa and the alien? They fell into the rift."

"My commiserations. Since the explosion two days ago-"

"Two days? I've been out for *two days*?"

// DON'T WORRY LUKE MAN // I TAPED ALL YOUR FAVORITE SHOWS

"Mother *fucker!* Did you get a software update in that blast or something? What is *up* with you?"

// I SPENT THE PAST TWO DAYS STUDYING HUMAN NORTHERN CULTURAL NORMS // YOU APPEAR TO TREAT THOSE WITH WHOM YOU ARE MOST FAMILIAR WITH THE GREATEST DISDAIN

"If that's your understanding, then, pal, you and I are *real* familiar."

// MY THOUGHTS EXACTLY // NIPPLE BRAIN

"Mr. Remini," interrupts Zhang. "Your mission was a success."

"What? You mean-"

"The explosion worked. You destroyed every military space drone the North and South have ever built, but the

Base Nine armor protected the personnel carriers, and most importantly, you sealed the rift. We owe you an immeasurable debt."

"Funny you should mention that, Captain. I actually owe someone else a debt, so this could be a real sweet quid pro quo."

"I have already dispatched your remuneration. Please treat the contents of that probe with utmost care and secrecy."

"Why, what's in it? I sincerely hope it's a large quantity of counterfeit credits and space drugs."

"It is far more valuable that that, Mr. Remini. It is our *mutually assured prosperity*."

"What do you mean?"

"You told me you thought the North was planning to attack the South with an exotic matter bioweapon. You were mistaken, of course, but your integrity made you willing to commit treason against your own government to save the civilians of your enemy."

"Yeah, I'm a real sweetheart like that. But seriously, though, there's *no* money in this probe?"

"Your bravery has saved our universe. But we both know, we are flying back to a planet embroiled in secrets and the most fragile kind of peace. I was shocked to learn of my side's treachery in building its own stockpile of helium from the Lunar Three supplies."

"It was the smart thing to do," I shrug.

"If power is your goal, in both senses of the word, then yes. But if peace is your objective, then it may be the greatest act of national self-harm we have ever risked. By my calculations, we would have been energy self-sufficient within a year of the treaty being signed, and your side would have been caught off-guard and vulnerable to an

Southern invasion. This is an unpalatable course of action, given all our nations have risked together in deep space. I am giving you the answer, Mr. Remini. A way to rebalance the scales."

"What is it, like, a confession? Leaked documents you want me to publish?"

"It's our reactor plans."

"The fusion reactors? Holy crap! We've been trying to build one for decades!"

"And we've kept them well guarded all that time. Kudos to your side for having the presence of mind to corner the fuel supply side in lieu of your own generators. Quite the economic pact you cooked up. Of course, it only works if both sides need each other equally."

"Which is why you're giving me this... You're leveling the playing field again!"

"Like I said, Mr. Remini. Mutually assured prosperity."

"What should I do with the plans?"

"Give them to your government, obviously."

"My government are assholes."

"Mine too, but that doesn't mean I don't need them."

"Mmm... My head's still a little fried but I think I just about followed the double negatives there."

"Our future peace is now in your capable hands, Mr. Remini. I trust you will deliver it well. Oh, and if they ask where you got the plans, don't tell them it was me. If my side finds out, I'll be all *kinds* of tortured."

"Cool. Same page."

"Captain Zhang out."

// SHALL I BRING THE PROBE ON BOARD // HUMAN USER 001? // LUKE MAN?

"Hell yeah, Computer. You heard the woman, it's our ticket home. Oh, and call me Remini."

35

EPILOGUE

LUKE

What's a guy like me doing in a place like this, hey? By "guy like me," I obviously mean post-atomic-bomb-piece-of-human-kebab. And "place like this," I mean... Earth. Specifically, a grimy sports bar in my old home city.

Well, they've got all the sports channels, cheap beer, and greasy burgers. Right now you're probably thinking, "How did he get to Earth, out of hospital, *and* out of jail, after rocking up in an alien ship with secret nuclear blueprints?"

All of these are valid questions, just like your feelings. Both your feelings, and your questions are valid. Skip the jail bit, add in a particularly quick-learning alien computer, plus a handy bit of back-channel diplomacy from Admiral Edwin, and bob's your uncle. I walk free.

Courtesy of one mammoth NDA, of course. Which is always a bitter pill for a journalist to swallow, let alone a loudmouth like me. The feds made it *very* clear I would get prison for life should I utter a word about exotic matter or the anomaly to anyone before the government files become declassified ten years from now. So the greatest act of bi-lateral cooperation in half a century will have to be a beautiful story for the grandkids someday. The public have no idea that there's a secret mission going on to eradicate the lethal, self-replicating exotic matter from our solar system. Not knowing probably helps them sleep a hell of a lot better than I do each night.

But, for all the paperwork, lawyers, embargoes, and threats, I *did* actually get a medal. How cool is that? It's the first medal I truly deserve. I once got a medal from a college marathon, but I only entered that thing to impress a girl, and truth be told I caught the metro after the first six miles. So it's nice to finally have something I feel is deservedly mine. Not that I can tell anyone about it. But I wear that fucker every day. What? You wouldn't? Let's see what you do if *you* ever get a secret hero award. I wear it everywhere I go, under my vest. I'm just relieved they didn't give me a trophy.

Oh, it's been three months, by the way. I should probably have made that clear. Hang on...

Three Months Later

There we go. So what have I been up to? Most of it was hospital. Though I briefly left to go and collect my *second* journalist of the year award. Well, I say "collect". Really, I watched it in absentia, via a secret video feed from Lanelle. Oh, the government agreed that the least damaging way for them to explain everything was for my disappearance to be framed as a tragic accident while investigating a mining story in the asteroid belt. Cute, right?

Chang knows I'm alive, but we seem to have found a truce, despite me owing him "shit ton money." I think he was surprised to see me appear in Tessa's parents' kitchen CCTV, deactivating their domestic robot, flipping him the bird, and cutting the feed. Particularly after he'd received my dismembered head in the mail several weeks prior. Yeah. I think it's fair to say Chang and I have reached a new, mutual level of respect.

They're lovely people, by the way, Tessa's parents. And once I'd explained the whole trashing-their-equipment thing, and relayed Tessa's messages of love and sorrow to them, and got them to sign a few government NDAs, we had some *really* top notch lemon drizzle cake.

Hmm, what else... My ex-wife and kids know I'm alive. That was obviously a condition. In hindsight, I could've broken the news of my miraculous resurrection plan a *teeny* bit better... Though it was kinda gratifying to know they were upset by my death. Not that any of them are speaking to me now I'm alive again. They're super pissed. Top tip: if you ever conspire with the government to fake your own death, and let newspapers show footage of your bloodied severed head – which Lanelle *totally* peeked at by the way – then maybe let your immediate family know you're all tickety-boo first. Apparently that's considered "good form". How was I supposed to know? It was my first time fake dying!

Oooh, speaking of, it's time for the news. Here we go, today's a big one... It's the one story the government *did* let me break from this whole escapade.

CEO of Lunar Three in Court on Charges of Treason.

Ha, Nenge looks *so* grumpy. Well, that's what you get for trying to monetize treachery. A face like a buttered blob fish.

... Dr. Nenge is charged with multiple counts of murder, including that of the International Lunar Inspector, a

Northern Lunar One engineer, dozens of Lunar Three mining staff, and, of course for the death of the man who uncovered it all: Journalist of the Year Luke Remini, who died saving the truth...

That's what I'm talking about, hell yeah!

... Remini was also able to lead police in the International Bloc to some critical evidence before his death, linking Dr. Nenge to an international arms ring.

OK, that particular link may have involved some, shall we say, "fancy footwork" on my part, but given the constraints of my NDA, this was our best shot at justice. The government wanted a credible fall-back story should word of the exotic matter ever leak prematurely - and being able to pin it on Nenge and Capaya's alleged bioweapon deal was the perfect fit. Until all this can be rewritten in ten years. Or however long it takes them to clean that stuff out of existence, and ensure no one *is* able to turn it into a bioweapon. Ooh, this next bit's kinda neat...

...Eric Capaya has also been convicted for the murder of his own father six years ago, following additional evidence uncovered by the late Luke Remini. Police from the International Bloc say their new findings fully exonerate former suspect Tessa Williams, who was one of Dr. Nenge's innocent victims on Lunar Three, along with her fiancé Sienna Constantina.

I should explain. Tessa's legacy on Earth didn't sit right with me. Not after all she sacrificed for the rest of us. So I used the information she'd given me, plus some of her personal files and call histories that I "acquired" from Lunar Five, to set the record straight. OK, maybe not "straight". There may have been an element of airbrushing in there. But sometimes you gotta decide what's more important: the absolute truth, or the relative impact? The world may not be ready to know about the anomaly, and what Tessa did to save us from it, but she deserved to have her name cleared for the one hit she *didn't* actually commit. Namely, that it was her asshole *brother-in-law* Eric Capaya who killed his own father, not her. Sure, Tessa was no angel in her former career, but she came good in the end, right? It's gotta count for something.

So what's next for good old Luke Remini? Great question. I'm thinking it's time I retire. You know, move to that farm in the country, or condo by the beach, or whatever it is retired people do. Play golf and complain about immigrants? Sorry, I shouldn't stereotype old people like that. Some of them play bridge.

...To our other main story: Rainforest destruction was allegedly halted years ago, yet scientists say CO_2 and methane levels have been rising sharply across the country...

Ah, that's why I should *never* watch the news. Other people always half-bake it. That's not a news story, that's a *pitch* for a news story. Any editor worth their salt would kick your ass outta the office to go find out what's actually going on! Pff. Amateurs. They need someone to show them how it's done. They need the artist formerly known as journalist of the year. Twice. RIP.

I didn't fly to the edge of the solar system, cremate myself riding a nuclear shock wave, and lose a dear assassin-friend, only for some assholes to go fuck with the very planet I was trying to save. Especially not its rain forests. No way. No sirrreee. Not on my watch. Grab the mosquito spray folks. We're going to the jungle.

DEAR READER,

It's Marcus here. Thanks so much for reading this copy of *People of Dust*, I truly hope it resonated with you. I'm an independent author, which means I publish all my work myself, and bear all the associated costs. The traditional publishing industry is incredibly tough for new authors to break into. After my first series *Convulsive* was rejected by fifty different agents, I realized that to achieve my dream of becoming a writer, I would have to strike out by myself. So I did.

It's terrifying, but I know I can do it; I have wonderful readers like you, who send me encouraging emails out of the blue which always brighten my day. It's my sincere hope that you may be kind enough to sponsor my next book by donating at marcusmartinauthor.com/support. On the next page you'll find out why, and what a massive impact your support will have.

It took five years to write and self-publish the *Convulsive* series alongside stressful day jobs, often working seven days a week. But within six months of completion, the series hit number one in the international Amazon bestseller charts for its genre. That was the single greatest moment of affirmation I could've wished for. I quite literally danced around the room with joy. It didn't come with a windfall of cash like you might think - book margins aren't big - but it was enough for me to finish recouping the editing costs and fund an audiobook version. In fact, since starting out, I've reinvested every cent I've ever earned from my books straight back into my writing - because I know it's the only way I'll grow.

It's still early days for me as a writer, which makes each new book a white knuckle ride. In 2020 I took a leap of faith and left my job to become a full-time author, knowing I would be living off savings and reinvesting any profits to make it work. In that year I gave it my all, and wrote four new books, one of which you've just finished.

I want to continue. My aim is to write four books a year, and keep bringing bold sci-fi ideas to readers like you. I know I can do it, but I'll be honest: there's still no guarantee it'll work out. Mainly because I don't get advances on book deals like conventional authors do.

I love creating new worlds, and I'm a damned hard worker. If you believe my writing deserves a future, and would like to see more books from me each year, I would be so hugely grateful if you would support me with a donation of your choosing. It only takes a moment, just visit **marcusmartinauthor.com/support**

With the support of readers like you, I can produce more groundbreaking sci-fi. I would be humbled to offer you an acknowledgement in one of my future books, and you will have my heartfelt thanks forever.

In gratitude - Marcus.

Cambridge, England, 2021

Convulsive

International #1 bestselling series

A pandemic like no other

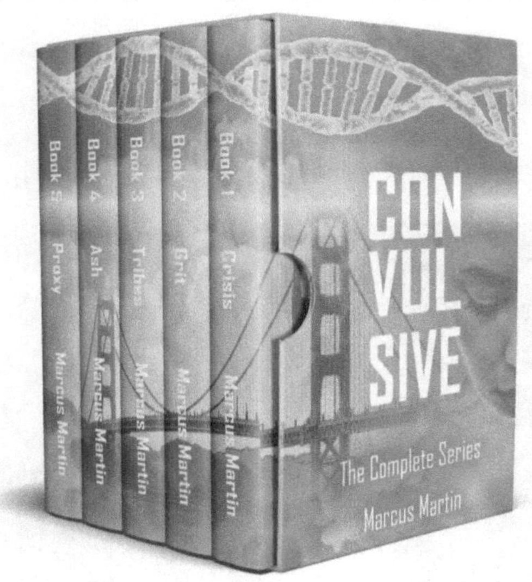

Completed five-part epic.

Binge your way through the apocalypse.

Don't miss Marcus Martin's next book.

Join the email list:

marcusmartinauthor.com/email
subscribers also get free advanced copies
and exclusive content.

ACKNOWLEDGMENTS

Boom. It's shout out o'clock. My sincere thanks go to these fine legends for their insights and feedback, and in helping me whip this novel into shape.

John Kerr, Martin White, Marie Thorpe, Carol Keen, Rick Hannegan, Matthew Clark, Chris Hutchings, Heather Binder-Pollard, Hinda Rochel Anolick, and Craig Dyson. Thank you all!

To my family, you're the best and I love you. Thanks for always having my back.

To all the brave souls committed to reversing climate change. To those on the front line through no fault of their own. To those taking a stand, to demand the change we need. Together, we can do this.

Oh, and to anyone who actually cracks commercially-viable nuclear fusion in the next few decades, do us a favor and donate the patent to all of mankind, will you? Sharing is caring. Cheers.

ABOUT THE AUTHOR

Marcus Martin is a British author based in Cambridge, UK. He originally trained as a composer and classical pianist at King's College London & the Royal Academy of Music, before taking a meandering route into a Master's degree in the psychology of music at the University of Cambridge, followed by a postgraduate diploma in religion and politics.

Marcus has performed at the Edinburgh Fringe Festival a number of times as both a stand-up comedian and actor. After living and working in the US and Germany for six months he returned to Cambridge where he wrote and staged his first three plays, before embarking on a career in authorship.

He's worked as a barista, a decorator, a builder's assistant, a teaching assistant, a data entry clerk, a marketing executive, a compliance officer, a pianist, a choral assistant, a musical director, a script editor for BBC Radio 4, a voice actor, and a jingle writer, to name but a few.

Alongside books and voice acting, he's host of the cult sci-fi podcast *Make It Soon*, which brings scientists and comedians together to discuss iconic sci-fi inventions that are becoming a reality. Listen for free at makeitsoon.com

Marcus is currently working on a new book series, as well as several standalone novels. He loves receiving emails from readers, and replies to each one. You can reach him at: marcus@marcusmartinauthor.com

For a sneak peak of Marcus's upcoming releases, join the email list at: marcusmartinauthor.com/email

You can also follow him on social:
facebook.com/MarcusMartinAuthor
goodreads.com/author/show/17601586
bookbub.com/authors/marcus-martin